The Mill-Race

Pamela Street was born in Wilton, Wiltshire, the only daughter of the late A. G. Street. She was educated at the Godolphin School, Salisbury. Her first book, a biography entitled *My Father, A. G. Street*, was published in 1969 and has been reprinted several times. This was followed in 1971 by *Portrait of Wiltshire* which she completely updated in 1980, after the publication of another of her books: *Arthur Bryant – Portrait of a Historian.* This is her fourth novel. Her first novel, *Light of Evening*, is available in the Pavanne imprint published by Pan Books

Also by Pamela Street
in Pan Books
under the Pavanne imprint

Light of Evening

Pamela Street

The Mill-Race

Pan Books London and Sydney

First published 1983 by Robert Hale Ltd
This edition published 1984 by Pan Books Ltd,
Cavaye Place, London SW10 9PG
9 8 7 6 5 4 3 2 1

ISBN 0 330 28332 4
Scanned and phototypeset by
Comprehensive Text Processing, London
Printed and bound in Great Britain by
Richard Clay (The Chaucer Press) Ltd, Bungay, Suffolk

In affectionate memory
of my parents
Vera Florence (née Foyle)
and
Arthur George Street

1

She could hear the water, slapping, gurgling and rising beneath the downstair floorboards, as she lay but a few feet overhead in the small back bedroom. It was a far more urgent and ominous sound than the one to which she had become so accustomed during her married life. For thirty-two years the mill-race had simply been an echo in the background, albeit a relentless, insistent one, yet as much a part of her existence as the mill hooter which marked the passing of the hours on weekdays, and the bells of St Mark's, which helped her to chivvy the various members of her family to church on Sundays.

Tonight, a little earlier on, those bells had been ringing out for well over an hour, for the rector was a firm believer in practice making perfect and Christmas 1918 was only two days away. Sadly, she realised that there would be no question of her going to any of the services, unless the man beside her in the bed took a turn for the better and she felt able to slip away to midnight mass. But she doubted that would be the case. Propped up by bolster and pillows, her husband, Sidney Lodge, lay awake restlessly, the cough which she had come to dread as the winter months closed in each year, now seeming a greater threat than the floods which so often accompanied it.

Above them, in the attic which stretched out, mercifully, not only over the tiny cramped house, but also for at least twenty feet along the top of one of the adjacent mill buildings, the girls—as she always thought of them—lay sleeping: Florence, thirty next birthday; May, twenty-seven; and little Katy, not yet seventeen. In the front bedroom, leading—as did the attic steps—straight from her own, she was aware, as she had been aware for nearly twenty-one years, of Neil, her youngest son, who, because he was a simpleton, would never really come of age. When Henry, her middle boy, came home from France, they would have to share the same bed. Of Frank, her first-born, who had been killed on the Somme, she tried not to think.

"Sid," she said, after the latest bout of coughing had left her husband exhausted. "Sid, please go and stay with Edith tomorrow. She's asked again." Edith was their only married daughter.

"No, Sarah." In spite of his lack of breath, a fierce, almost frenzied tone had crept into his voice. "You know I shall never set foot in Edith's home, however much she goes on about it."

"But it's so much higher and drier, Sid, on downside. You'd get better quicker. It's no good staying here. The Willon's getting up every minute. I reckon we shall have a foot of water in the house by Christmas Day, maybe two. You know how it was the first winter of the war. And it took five weeks to go down. Five weeks, Sid."

The man beside her became even more agitated. His hands plucked at the coarse sheet. He was not, normally, an irascible character, but any mention of visiting Edith, his once favourite daughter, always seemed to make him so. For the girl, as far as he was concerned, had defied him. She had wilfully become the wife of Herbert Lench, a mill-hand. He, Sidney Lodge, was the mill manager, despite the near-slum in which the mill owners—a brother and sister called

Fielding—appeared to think it fitting that he and his family should dwell.

Yet, as he had pointed out to Sarah when he had first been offered the job and immediately proposed to her on the strength of it, there were definite compensations. They might not have a tap indoors but, because it was a felt mill, there were huge vats of hot soapy water where she would be allowed to do her washing. There was a large garden where he could grow all the vegetables she might require. And even the earth closet at the bottom of it, with its adjoining wood and concrete shed, was prettily covered with honeysuckle. Besides, they would be the occupants of what had always been known as the Mill House. She would be able to put that at the top of her letters when she wrote home. It was this last advantage which had finally won Sarah's hand. Her parents—well-to-do West of England clothiers—had been just as much against her marrying Sidney—the seventh son of an impoverished farmer's widow—as he himself had been against Edith marrying Herbert; although she had had the good sense never to remind him about this.

Sarah could recall many a conversation they had had about Edith and Herbert during the summer of 1914, just before war broke out, particularly one evening in June when they had taken a walk together along the river path through the water-meadows. "Sid," she had said, "Herbie's not a bad lad. He's a good time-keeper. Never been in any trouble." And she could remember clearly her husband's reply: "Oh, I know, Sarah. But he's a station below. I have to pay him each week, don't I? He stands in line wi' all the others in Main Building. He'll never get anywhere. Too meek and mild. It's not as if he could ever take over from me one of these days. There's no initiative there, unless . . .", and here, Sidney had hesitated a little before going on, "unless you count courting Edith. But I daresay she made most of the running."

Sarah had sighed, knowing only too well how she had been constantly having to chide her headstrong, nineteen-year-old daughter for standing about outside the house when the mill hooter went for the men to clock on or off. She was a beauty all right, their Edith, with her mass of auburn hair and bright blue eyes, always laughing and singing and keeping the two younger children, poor Neil and little Katy, amused. She made no bones about the fact that she wanted to get married and have children of her own as soon as she could. Sarah and Sidney had already managed, albeit not without difficulty, to put a stop to more than one unsuitable youthful romance. But although she, too, would have preferred a better match for the girl, "We can't keep thwarting her, Sid," Sarah had said after his last remark. "She needs a husband. If we tell her she can't marry Herbie, goodness knows what might happen." And then, for ever afterwards, in her mind's eye, she had retained a picture of her husband standing stockstill under the Black Arch, where the South Western Railway line crossed the valley, and thundering, "What do you mean, Sarah? If Edith, or any child of mine for that matter, brings disgrace on our home, they shall never set foot in it again."

Yet she knew that her words must have had some effect. After that, Sidney no longer showed quite such open opposition. He simply got up and left the room at any mention of Herbert's name. Plans for the wedding were undertaken, conspiratorially, by the distaff side of the family. Edith's wedding-dress, made by her two elder sisters, was kept hidden in one of the attic cupboards. There then came a Friday when Sidney Lodge paid his future son-in-law in the evening and, barely audibly, gave his daughter away to him in St Mark's church on East Street the following afternoon.

Soon after that war was declared and the army medical authorities discovered that Herbert Lench was unfit for service owing to a weak heart; although not weak enough, Sidney was sometimes apt to remark uncharitably, to beget a son nine months after the wedding and twin girls after a further eleven. Funny-looking children, he'd always thought them. Ugly. Not a bit like their mother. Only yesterday, when Edith had brought them down to the mill and asked if he would like to take a quick look at them, he'd said no—he only wanted to see Edith by herself for a while. He was always glad to have her visit him in his own home, just as long as Herbert was never brought into it. But he supposed that after sitting by his bed and hearing him cough, she must have gone straight downstairs and said something to her mother again about wanting to nurse him up on downside. Silly girl. She ought to have known better. So ought Sarah. If they thought that he was going to accept Herbert Lench's charity because he happened to be ill, then they must want their heads seeing to. He, Sidney Lodge, had lived at the Felt Mills for thirty-two years and a foot or two of water in his living-room wasn't going to drive him out now, bronchitis or no bronchitis. Besides, Sarah could be wrong about the floods. He'd known them go down quite quickly sometimes. True, both they and his cough had started early this year. Usually February was the worst month. February filldike.

"Sarah," he now said, suddenly, "tomorrow morning, first thing, I want you to get our Katy to take a note up to Ted Shergold. I reckon he hasn't got them hatches working properly near Bulbarrow sluice. There's probably not enough water getting away through Lower Croft. Silly young fool. He'll never make the drowner his father was. Maybe he didn't do that repair job on 'em that I warned him about back in the summer when the Willon was low."

"All right, Sid." Wearily, Sarah leant over and blew out the candle on her side of the bed, making a mental note that she must warn Katy to go up to the Shergolds' cottage through East Street and not take the river path. Anyone who slipped on the planks that had recently been put there could be carried away in no time. It was curious, she reflected, considering all the water which had surrounded them these many years, that none of her children had learnt to swim, not that that would be much help with the currents as swift as they were now.

She wished that she could send silly, simple Neil on this sort of errand instead of Katy. She was such a fragile little thing. Sometimes Sarah wondered how she had ever managed to rear her. All those broken nights, nursing her through one childish illness after another, that terrible year when she had caught diphtheria and then developed meningitis almost straight away afterwards; although by that time Flo and May had been old enough to help her, just as they were doing their best to help her now over their father's illness. They were good girls. All of them were good girls. Still, it wasn't quite the same as having a stalwart man about the place. It would be nice when Henry was demobilised and came home. She was more worried about her husband than she cared to admit, even to Flo. His chest was far worse this winter than she'd ever known it. He'd had much more time off sick; and only yesterday, when Miss Fielding had called with some lemons and honey, Sarah had sensed that she and her brother were none too happy about the frequency with which things had had to be handled by Tom Henstridge—the conscientious but far less experienced under-manager—in his absence. It crossed her mind that Sidney might have fallen victim to the terrible epidemic that was sweeping the country—Spanish 'flu they called it, although she couldn't, for the life of her, see what Spain had to do with it—but, so far as she knew, no cases had as yet been reported in Wilhampton, for which, along with all her other prayers, she thanked God on her knees each night, before climbing into bed.

The man beside her was seized by another paroxysm of coughing. If only it would slacken. She'd put the chamber-pot on top of the commode by his side, so that it would be within easy reach if he wanted to spit; but she doubted that he would need it for this purpose tonight. His breathing was too quick, too harsh, his body far too hot beside her own.

2

Katy Lodge was pleased at being sent up to the Shergold cottage soon after it became light on the morning of Christmas Eve. It gave her a sense of importance. As the youngest and frailest of the family, who had always been treated as somewhat of an invalid, it irked her never to have been considered capable of undertaking anything but the most modest of tasks, such as whitening the front step with hearthstone after it had been scrubbed each morning, and then helping Flo and May in their workroom at the bottom of the garden, where all three plied their trade as seamstresses; although, so far, Katy had usually only been entrusted with tacking, hemming or oversewing and was not yet allowed to make button-holes for the clothes which Lady Fairfax, up at the Hall—and others of her ilk—were constantly ordering.

Happily for Sarah and Sidney Lodge, their two eldest daughters had, over the years, established quite a name for themselves in the dress-making line, not only in the small town where the family lived, but also in its surrounding neighbourhood. The Misses F & M Lodge of *The Mill House, Wilhampton*—as they wrote in firm, immaculate script at the top of their bills—were much in demand, young ladies to be treated with respect and, at times it had to be admitted, a certain amount of judicious flattery—even coaxing—according to the urgency of their customers' desires.

They were never at a loss for work, invariably taking on more than they could accomplish—that is, reasonably accomplish—without having to burn the one oil-lamp in the living-room of their home well into the night. Kind-hearted, proud, but eager to do their best for all and sundry, they found it as hard to refuse a commission from her ladyship at the Hall as they did from Mrs Perrick, who kept the sweet-shop at the top of the lane, charging the former only a fractional amount more for their services than the latter. When both ladies required their respective outfits by a certain date, Katy was sometimes apt to feel used, indignant at being bribed to take out the tacking on Lady Fairfax's two-piece of an evening, with the promise of a little bit of lace left over from their distinguished client's latest ball-gown. On such occasions she bitterly resented the short apprenticeship with a certain Miss Maidment in Wilhampton which, at varying times, her mother had forced all her daughters to undergo, wisely deeming it a most prudent measure should they never marry. With Flo and May her foresight had been more than justified. For, despite the fact that both had above average good looks, impeccable dress sense and had never lacked for beaux—particularly of the officer class during the war—they had as yet remained spinsters.

But as far as Katy was concerned, she saw everything rather differently. Like Edith, she reckoned on finding a husband as soon as she could, although there the similarity in their reasons for desiring matrimony ended. The youngest Lodge daughter harboured ideas, ideas altogether too far-fetched and romantic her mother might have said, had she been fully aware of what went on in the child's mind. Katy wanted someone very much better than a mill-hand and privately considered that both Flo and May had been silly in letting several most debonair suitors slip through their fingers during the war. But whereas, in this respect, the same view was held by Sarah, the latter completely failed to understand the vividness of a youthful imagination which so much illness, coupled with a great deal of reading, had only served to foster.

Moreover, having always been the delicate 'baby' of the family, Katy did not particularly yearn after children herself, and could not see what Edith found attractive about looking after them. She thought it would be far better to find a man who would look after *her*, but preferably someone handsome, rich and dashing. (It was a little beyond her at this stage to appreciate that such an individual would be unlikely to possess the attribute of father-figure as well.) She felt a tall dark foreigner might do, or possibly an actor, or even, with luck, a potential lord, someone like Lady Fairfax's son and heir who had just married the most ugly duckling, the eldest daughter of Sir Roger Broadbent from Westonbury House. Katy had stood in the crowd outside the church watching the bride both before and after the ceremony, and a plainer young woman all decked out in white velvet it would have been harder to find. But rumour had it, according to Flo and May, that the Broadbents had recently come into money, and everyone knew that the Fairfaxes were short. That was why Lady Fairfax was always getting the Misses Lodge to copy—in different colours and materials—some specimen dress which she had bought in London. Katy thought it was a mean trick. Her sisters' outfits were infinitely better finished. But when she told them how she felt about it she got severely reprimanded and was reminded of how good her ladyship had been in sending down delicacies from the Hall when she had been ill as a little girl. It was flying in the face of Providence, they said, to say things like that about the hand that had fed her.

Katy kept thinking about all this as she dutifully picked her way through the puddles and potholes of East Street that Christmas Eve morning. She wished she could have seen things the way her elder sisters seemed to see them, but somehow she couldn't, not that she hadn't always been most respectful to her ladyship's face whenever the latter had called at the Mill House; although that had been a rare occurrence. Usually, Flo and May were summoned to the Hall at a given time, returning with vivid descriptions of carpets so deep and soft that their feet had sunk into them; of red and gold walls covered with priceless pictures and portraits and tapestries; of ceilings high, white and carved "like heavenly ivory", May had said—although even Katy's imagination could not quite envisage that. Then there were doors which were opened and shut by noiseless butlers and parlourmaids, and huge windows from which, in summer, they could see lawns, according to May, "like emerald velvet", ancient spreading cypresses, a fountain—"and a pergoda", Flo had added.

Katy had had to go and look up the word in the

minuscule dictionary which old Dr Fitzherbert had given her when she was recovering from meningitis. She was upset at not being able to find it. It was not until many years later that she came to learn that Flo had made a mistake and it was a 'pergola' she had been on about.

But it was her elder sisters' most recent visit which had intrigued Katy most. Only a month or so ago, just after the armistice, she had had the vicarious pleasure of hearing how they had gone to the Hall to fit Lady Fairfax's beautiful daughter, the Honourable Alicia, for her wedding-dress, and the girl was still in her bath when they had been shown up to her bedroom. Then, quite unexpectedly, Alicia's fiancé, an A.D.C. and a baronet's son, had arrived from London on leave and she had quickly struggled into a rest-gown and rushed downstairs to greet him, much to her mother's anger and agitation. "She was so excited, dear thing," said May. "She hardly stopped to dry herself. Of course, we couldn't have expected her to stand still for a fitting after that. It's obviously a love-match."

A love-match. That was what Katy was after, even if she only knew these things dimly, as through coloured glass. But it would have to be a love-match with someone a little more exciting than Herbie, someone who would sweep her up and away from her present environment, take her to London perhaps, in the same way as the heroine had been transported by the hero in the Elinor Glyn novel she was reading clandestinely each evening when Flo and May spared her the time. She had just got to the place where the girl had 'all but succumbed' to his advances. She wasn't quite sure what the author meant, but she sensed that it must be wildly exciting and she wished someone would enlighten her a little more. But she knew it was no use asking her mother or Flo or May.

Sometimes it seemed to Katy as if there was almost a conspiracy on the part of the distaff side of the family to keep her in the dark about certain things. She knew that her elder sisters strongly disapproved of her reading so much. Quite often she had to smuggle her current book upstairs when she went to bed, and then quickly blow out her candle when she heard Flo or May climbing the narrow wooden steps to the attic. Of course, the trouble was that a rapidly diminished candle always gave one away. Flo, in particular, was adept at gauging by this means just how long she had been reading. "You'll ruin your eyes, Katy," she was wont to say. "Besides, it's wasting candle-grease." Yet she never said anything about eyesight or burning oil when she wanted Katy to go on working downstairs by lamplight, when the Misses F & M Lodge were up against a deadline for delivery.

Katy couldn't understand why her elder sisters objected to what seemed such an innocent pleasure. Considering all the time she had missed at the National School through illness, she felt that they ought to have been glad that she had acquired such a liking for books. It sometimes seemed as if they were fearful of her growing up, as if they wanted her to remain a child. She still hadn't started her periods, and although she knew roughly what to expect and was eagerly awaiting the first 'show'—even if it was accompanied by pain—she sensed that all the women in the family were glad that she was 'on the late side'. "'T'will be time enough," Flo had said one day. "You ought to be thankful. Think of all that extra washing every four weeks. You surely don't want that do you?" And Katy, suddenly reminded of the big slop-pails of water kept in the attic at certain times of the month—in which the soiled towels of her elder sisters were put to soak, until they could be taken to wash in the mill of a

Saturday afternoon when no men were about—tried to become more resigned.

Yet Flo's and May's obvious relief at her immaturity still puzzled her. In some strange way she believed that it had something to do with Neil. She could recall snippets of conversation, hastily broken off whenever she entered the room: "Mother should have had him put away." "'Tisn't fair, with Katy growing up." "I don't like the way he keeps looking at her." "She's never to be left alone with him." What, in heaven's name, did they imagine poor simple Neil was going to do to her? She couldn't make it out. Nevertheless, she had begun to watch him covertly, aware now herself of how much he stared at her. She became uneasy in his presence, yet it was an unease she was at a loss to explain.

It was not exactly the same unease which Katy experienced on the morning of Christmas Eve when she at last reached the Shergolds' cottage, but as she tapped the door she definitely felt a certain sense of timidity. She knew that Mrs Shergold, albeit not much older than Flo, had a reputation for being loud-mouthed and somewhat of a termagant. It was said that she gave poor Ted a bad time of it, that she was always grumbling about him being down in 'thic medders', despite Sidney Lodge's pronouncement that he wasn't half the man at his job as his father had been. Nancy Shergold now came to her front door, a slatternly figure, wearing on her head an old cloth cap belonging to her husband and clad in a dirty overall, to which two equally dirty-looking children clung at either side.

"Yes?" She scrutinised her young caller with small, black, boot-button eyes.

Silently, Katy handed her the letter. The woman tore it open, although it had been carefully addressed to her husband. She took so long in studying it that Katy began to wonder whether possibly she was unable to read. Presently, when the silence between them became embarrassing, she volunteered, shyly, "It's from Father. About the hatches near Bulbarrow sluice, I think."

Nancy Shergold redirected her gaze once more towards Katy. "I can see that, little Miss Know-All. What do you think my Ted's doing now? He went down to thic medders wi' a lantern at cockcrow, risking life an' limb. If it wasn't for him all you upstart mill folk would have been washed away in your beds many a time. You can go home and tell Mr Manager Lodge that if he knows a better way to stop his house getting flooded, then he'd better come up here himself, instead of sending a little flibbertigibbet like you with fancy orders."

"But Father's sick, Mrs Shergold." She could feel tears of grief and mortification beginning to well up, uncontrollably.

"Sick, is he? My Ted hasn't time to be sick. If it wasn't for him the water'd be all over Wilhampton by now. Good-day, young lady."

Mrs Shergold closed the door. Katy was not even certain whether she would give her husband the note.

She turned and stumbled home, defeated, the troubled grey eyes overlarge in the small white face, the skinny body on its spindly legs slipping from time to time on the planks over the pavements, which had been placed there by the council workers even since she had started out on her errand.

3

Three days after Christmas, Sidney Lodge died.

The end came quite suddenly, soon after midnight. Dr Fitzherbert had come to the mill the previous evening after Flo had gone up to his surgery and said, "Father's no better, Doctor. He's worse. Can't get his breath." And the good man had left his other patients and come straight back with her down River Lane. He had wanted to get him into Westonbury Infirmary there and then, but here he came up against a fierce opposition.

Sidney Lodge's refusal to be moved came out between short, sharp gasps. "I'll not go, Doctor. If I'm . . . to die . . . t'will be in my . . . own bed. Sarah's the best nurse . . . There's nothing the Infirmary . . . can do for me better."

And Dr Fitzherbert knew, despite the foot of water downstairs in his patient's living-room, that it was probably best to let Sidney Lodge go to his Maker in the way he wanted. His condition was too advanced, now, to remedy. One lung was completely collapsed. The Infirmary could not do much more than prolong life a day or so. Moreover, the move, in itself, might even hasten the end.

Sarah took to widowhood hardly. Many was the day she lay in bed grieving, the small paraffin heater failing to take the all-pervading dankness out of the atmosphere, just as it had failed so lamentably during Sidney Lodge's last illness. The girls did their best, taking it in turns to see that she was never left alone, constantly reminding her that she had done everything she possibly could for her late husband. Edith, leaving her children in the care of a neighbour, visited her mother daily, bringing meals which could be heated up on a small Primus stove, begging her, as she had so recently begged her father, to come and stay for a while in her own home. But she was met with the same stubborn resistance.

"Here is where I shall stay, Edith. Your father wouldn't have wished it otherwise."

And Edith would pick her way over the raised duck-boards from the bottom of the narrow winding staircase to the front door, taking a short walk up through the mill buildings to where Herbert was man-handling wool into one of the huge, deafening machines, and report that she had failed in her mission once again.

In their workroom at the end of the garden, which, mercifully, had escaped flooding, Flo and May continued, whenever possible, to execute their orders, while Neil sat, cretinous yet cheerful, in a corner by the small coal fire. Their conversation almost always took the same line.

"D'you think the Fieldings will let Mother stay on?"

"They ought to. When you think of what Father's done all these years. The mill would never be the place it is today but for him."

"Who d'you think they'll put in his place?"

"The Lord only knows. But I can tell you one thing. They're not going to get another manager to go into the Mill House, not like it is, anyway."

"That's what makes me think they'll let her stay. They couldn't turn her out. Not now."

Their fears and conjectures were eventually silenced one afternoon some six weeks later by the sudden arrival of Ernest Fielding on the Mill House doorstep. He wore a stiff wing-collar and a long, heavy, tweed overcoat draped over his tall ungainly figure. Fortunately, his visit happened to coincide with one of Sarah's better days and, as the floods had subsided, she had been able to get busy early after breakfast with all her customary cleaning. Now, having changed out of her working clothes into a black serge mourning dress, with a little tucker of lace at the neck, she ushered him into her living-room, gravely and with composure.

Sarah had never liked Ernest Fielding any more than she had liked Edwina, his sister, but she was well aware that the man before her held the fate of herself and her family in his thin, bony hands.

"May I get you some tea, Mr Fielding, sir? The kettle's all but boiled."

"Thank you, no, Mrs Lodge." He spoke authoritatively, yet tinged with a certain unctuousness. It was nothing she could define, but she did not altogether trust him. They now sat, one on either side of the range, and there seemed to be something insensate, even bird-like, about his small head perched on the too-long neck.

"You must have been wondering about the future, Mrs Lodge," he continued, in a curiously high, nasal voice. "About this house, for instance."

"Well, yes, sir. I . . . we . . . couldn't help but want to know."

He inclined his head and paused, almost as if he was savouring keeping her in suspense. "Edwina and I," he went on, at length, "have been giving a lot of thought to the future management of the mill. Rather than promote Henstridge to your late husband's post, we have engaged an outsider, a young man called Fuller."

She could feel the colour come to her cheeks, a dampness in the palms of her hands which were now clenched. If Henstridge had been given the job he would probably have still remained in Number Ten, River Lane. It was a nice house with a good garden, close enough to keep an eye on things all the time. A new man, this outsider, would want the Mill House, wouldn't he?

"Yes," she heard her visitor continue, in the same unattractive intonation, "we felt it best to make a clean break. A new broom, as it were, always sweeps clean . . . Not, I may hasten to add, that we have ever had any reason to find fault with your husband's management. On the contrary. We realise only too well that Henstridge would not be able to step into his shoes satisfactorily. The man isn't up to it. That is why we have got Mr Fuller coming from Westonbury."

"*Westonbury*?" Fear now crept into her voice. Her initial composure vanished. Still the man before her procrastinated.

"Yes. But there are slight problems. Mr Fuller would prefer to stay in the house in which he is now living and in the town where his children are already at school. I understand his wife . . . is delicate. He is a little concerned about the water . . ." Ernest Fielding broke off suddenly, conscious that he had made a gaffe. It was not his intention to denigrate in any way the magnanimity—or what he felt to be the magnanimity—of the offer he was about to make.

"So the long and short of it is, Mrs Lodge," he continued, "that Edwina and I felt that in return for your late husband's services over so many years you should be given six shillings weekly, and allowed to remain at the Mill House for your own lifetime on the understanding that you would still perform certain little duties for us. For example, locking the main gates each night, taking Mr Fuller tea every afternoon in the office we shall be making for him and also . . ."

and here he coughed slightly, "watering the plants which, as you know, I like to cultivate in the greenhouse at the back of the main building, which I believe one of your daughters has kindly attended to during these last few weeks. You would, Mrs Lodge, still be the mistress here, as it were. I trust that you find my . . . er . . . our offer completely to your liking." He smiled, sanctimoniously, showing stained, yellow teeth. He did not say that Dr Fitzherbert had warned him, at the cemetery after Sidney Lodge's funeral, that the Mill House was little more than a death-trap and ought to be pulled down, and that it would be criminal to put another family there, let alone one with young children.

"Thank you, sir. It's very kind of you, I'm sure." Although relief had flooded over her, Sarah's hand had instinctively gone to her throat, where she nervously fingered the cameo brooch at its centre. She wondered why her visitor did not now rise and depart. She could hardly wait to go down the garden and tell the girls. But the man in front of her still appeared to have something else to say. As he recrossed his legs and coughed again, he went on, "There is just one small point, Mrs Lodge, which I feel I should mention at this stage. About Mr Fuller's office."

"Office?" Sarah frowned uncomprehendingly, unable, for the life of her, to see what the manager's office had to do with her.

"You are well acquainted, I am sure, Mrs Lodge," Ernest Fielding continued, "with the lay-out of the mill," and here he gave another of what Sarah felt to be his small, false smiles. "You must know it better than I. You will appreciate that as Mr Fuller will not be resident here he will need a bigger office. I fear we shall have no alternative but to install him in the . . . er . . . workroom which your daughters are at present using."

"The *workroom*, Mr Fielding? But where would the girls do their sewing?" Anger now had begun to displace fear.

This time it was her visitor who showed unease. "There must be other premises, Mrs Lodge," he said, vaguely. "Or maybe . . ." he looked round the small cramped living-room, and she was quick to sense what was going on in his mind.

"They could not possibly do their dress-making here, sir. All the cutting-out . . . the treadle sewing-machine. Lady Fairfax could not be expected to . . . to be fitted *here*." Unconsciously, Sarah had made a diabolically clever reply. Looking back, she wondered how it had come into her head, considering how rare it was for her ladyship to be fitted anywhere other than the Hall.

Ernest Fielding shuffled his feet again. At the mention of Lady Fairfax his attitude seemed to change. His voice became conciliatory. He had not reckoned on her ladyship being brought into this particular little tête-à-tête. He and Edwina were hoping to be invited to a kind of joint reception which he had heard she would be giving for her newly married son and daughter, for all those whom it had been impossible to invite to their respective weddings. He had not appreciated that the Misses Lodge were favoured by her custom. It would not do at all for Lady Fairfax to hear that he had been anything other than immensely generous to the family of the late Sidney Lodge. He seemed to remember Edwina having said that her ladyship had shown especial interest and benignity towards one of the daughters—the youngest one, he believed—when she had been ill as a child. He must be careful. Perhaps, after all, there was some corner in the mill buildings which could be made into a larger office for Mr Fuller without too much cost, possibly partitioning off the long storage room where the bales of wool were kept.

He took a quick look at the handsome, serious-eyed widow opposite him and then back to the fire in the range. He had noticed, reluctantly, the water marks above the wainscoting left by the recent floods. She was no fool, the late manager's wife. He remembered Edwina having once told him that. Seven children in this small, hopelessly inconvenient house. What must it have been like? Trying to rear them in a single downstair living-room, where a piece of worn tapestry served as the only door, and a table with a green chenille tasselled overlay took up most of the available space. Yet the general impression of care and cleanliness was unmistakable. It seemed to him that the net curtains at the windows were as white as the lace tucker on Sarah's dress. The walnut grandfather clock in the corner was far more highly polished than his own. The brass candlesticks on either side of the mantelshelf positively gleamed. There was not a speck of dust on the rest of the furniture: the mahogany whatnot with its countless knick-knacks, including a mounted emu's egg and a pewter jug filled with a mass of honesty pods; the upright piano, on which rested a number of family photographs in wooden frames; the glass-fronted cabinet displaying some blue, willow-pattern, Staffordshire china.

Ernest Fielding was not a family man, his imagination was sadly limited, but there was something about the woman before him which commanded respect. "Naturally," he said slowly, choosing his words with care, "we do not want to cause unnecessary hardship after your recent loss. I will have another talk with my sister tonight. I can see that it might be difficult for your daughters to work here. I understand they are most industrious, clever with their needle."

"Yes, sir. They are all good girls," Sarah answered simply and, to her relief, her reply now seemed to bring his visit to an end.

As Ernest Fielding got up to take his leave, he had an uneasy feeling that the mistress of the Mill House had quietly got the better of him.

4

The eagerly awaited news of Corporal Henry Lodge's home-coming came one blustery day in the middle of March. Sarah was taking down some washing from the clothes-line in the garden when she saw the telegraph boy cycling through the front gates of the mill. Quickly, she dropped a bolster-case into the basket at her feet and went towards him.

"For me, Percy?"

"Yes, Mrs Lodge, ma'am."

It wasn't so bad nowadays, Percy Hooper thought, being a delivery boy for the Post Office. Not so long ago he had always seemed to be the harbinger of bad news. But he happened to know what was in this particular message, even though he reckoned that there was a bit more to it than Mrs Lodge was expecting. All the same, it wasn't like the one from the War Office which he had had to deliver that autumn morning about two and half years ago, informing the family that their eldest son had been killed in action. He hadn't quite known what to do when Mrs Lodge fainted. He had somehow managed to ease her fall and then he had run up through the mill to find Mr Lodge. The first person he had come across was Edith's husband and he remembered how Herbie Lench had been quite efficient. He had found the manager almost at once and together they had all three come running back to the house. He and Sidney Lodge had arrived first because poor Herbie got breathless on account of his heart. But by then Flo and May were somehow on the scene and, reluctantly, Percy had had to cycle off. He hadn't seen any of the family for some time after that. They'd kept themselves to themselves. And now Mrs Lodge was a widow, poor thing. Still, she had her daughters to keep her company and soon she'd have a *daughter-in-law.* Percy went off whistling, wondering what she would say to that.

Sarah didn't say anything at all when she first read the telegram. She did not faint, like last time, but she certainly suffered a sense of shock. She went into the house and sat for a while, holding the message in her hand, frowning and looking at it again from time to time. Then, slowly, she got up and walked down the garden path to the workroom.

Flo was bending over the big deal table cutting out a chemise when she entered and remained, at first, concentrated on her task. Neil, sitting on his usual stool by the fireplace, gave her a cheerful vacant smile. Katy was nowhere to be seen. Only May, who had just come to the end of sewing some lace on a collar, looked up and said, "What is it, Mother?"

Silently, Sarah handed her the piece of paper and sat down in the small arm-chair, too wrapped in thought to admire the finishing touches which her second daughter had been putting on the stiff, navy-blue moiré dress for Mrs Betts, the new mayoress of Wilhampton, in which she had previously—despite her grieving—shown a certain interest. Had Sidney Lodge lived, Sarah herself would have become the next mayoress.

"Oh, chippatoo! Oh chippatoo!" May, always the

most excitable member of the family, made the curious exclamation which she invariably used whenever she was particularly aroused. No one knew from whence she had coined it. It was something she had started saying when she was quite a small girl. Petite and dainty, she now began drumming her little heels on the floor, rocking herself backwards and forwards, her pink and white complexion more flushed than usual, half in surprise, half in pleasure. "See this, Flo. Our Henry's got himself a wife. French by the sound of her." She held the telegram out to her elder sister.

Flo put down her scissors and scanned the missive incredulously. Her reactions were always slower than those of her other sisters. She was altogether less spontaneous and, since Sidney Lodge's death, she had assumed an even more sober manner, the weight of responsibility for her mother and the rest of the family hanging heavily on her shoulders. Having read the message once, she now read it again out loud: "Married last Saturday. Arriving with Marianne Wednesday. Henry."

Flo took off the steel-framed spectacles she had lately taken to wearing for close work and stared at the three other occupants of the room. Then, with swift practicality, May said, "Where will they sleep, Mother? At Edith's?"

"I suppose so." Sarah fingered her cameo brooch, as she so often did in times of stress, well aware that because she and Sidney had hitherto always refused Edith's offers of help, it now made it all the harder to ask for it—not that her married daughter would refuse it. The girl was generous to a fault, even if she and her brother, Henry, had had many a fight as siblings. "We'd best get a message to her," she said, at length. "Where's Katy?"

There was an awkward silence and a certain embarrassment in Flo's voice when she finally spoke. "She's gone to the fair, Mother . . . The Perrick girl came down after dinner and asked if she could go with her. It was difficult to say no. She'd worked hard all the morning and we thought a bit of fresh air might do her good. She's been looking so peaky ever since . . ." Flo broke off uncertainly, not liking to put into words the simple fact that Katy's periods had started profusely soon after the shock of her father's death.

Sarah Lodge stood, or rather drew herself up. Although, lately, her striking-looking face, with its huge grey eyes and high cheek-bones, still framed by brown hair without a touch of grey, had often seemed worn and haggard and her neat well-corseted figure somewhat bowed, yet, when she wanted, she was still able to take command of a situation, a little as she had done at the end of Ernest Fielding's visit.

"You mean you girls saw fit to give Katy leave to go without asking me?"

"Well, yes Mother. And we thought you were maybe resting . . ." Flo broke off, once again, uneasily.

This time Sarah rounded on her, the fire and passion in her voice making it easy to see how she had managed to weather so many long years of trial and tribulation. The way she now spoke made her eldest daughter feel about ten again.

"You know perfectly well, my girl, that I have not rested during the daytime these many weeks past. You also know that I expressly asked that you should all honour your late father's memory by behaving in a decent, quiet and seemly fashion. He has not yet been dead three months. Apart from going to church and the cemetery, I have not set foot in the town, nor kept company at home. And now I find that behind my back you have allowed Katy to go to the *fair*. It will be all over Wilhampton by tomorrow. How do you think I shall look, not yet out of mourning?"

Save for a slight crackling in the grate, there was silence in the workroom now. Even Neil appeared to have registered his mother's displeasure, his weak blue eyes, beneath a thatch of fair hair, cast downwards towards his large black boots.

Then, with one hand on the latch, Sarah made her final salvo: "As Katy is unable to take a message up to Edith, one of you two girls had best go—at once." She let herself out and went back up the garden, collecting the remainder of her washing on the way. She could not have staged her departure with more effect. Quickly, Flo put on her coat, tied a scarf over her head and set out for downside.

Edith took the news of her brother's marriage and home-coming calmly and good-naturedly. He had always been a happy-go-lucky type, like herself. She would be delighted, she said, to accommodate Henry and Marianne on the brass-railed bedstead in the little back bedroom for as long as they wanted to stay. "French, you say, Flo? Oh la la. Well, I never. Reckon she'll teach us a thing or two, even if some of our own ancestors did once come from over the water. How's Mother taking it?"

"So, so. I don't suppose she likes it much. I expect she naturally thought that Henry would still be fancy-free and live at home. But right now she's more upset because we let Katy go to the fair."

"*Did* you, now? Poor kid. She doesn't have much fun on the whole, does she? All that illness. Sometimes I don't think our Katy's quite like the rest of us. Takes after Mother's grandmother, shouldn't wonder."

"What? The one who ran away and went on the stage?"

"Yes only we're not meant to know, are we?

Anyway, tell Mother I'll start airing the spare mattress straight away. Incidentally, what do you think Henry's going to do now?"

"The Lord only knows. I suppose he must have some plan. He wouldn't have married, else." Flo stood up. "I must be going, Edie."

"You'll not stay for a cup of tea?"

"No thanks. There's so much to do. It's as if half Wilhampton wants new clothes this month. Don't bother to come to the door," she added, as one of Edith's twins let out a piercing yell, "it looks as if you've got enough on your hands, too."

The wind cut across downside as Flo hurried off. High in the tossing elm trees by the allotments, a colony of rooks was noisily going to bed. Below her, the lights of Wilhampton were beginning to appear, one by one. She could still just discern two tall familiar landmarks: the tower of St Mark's and the mill hooter pointing upwards to the darkening sky. It would be good to get home. Although it was downhill all the way, the journey somehow seemed longer this evening. She shivered slightly, the cold, clear air reminding her that she must move the buttons on her new black worsted coat. As it was, they were letting in too much draught, especially since she had lost weight lately. But it had never been a perfect fit, even at the beginning, although that was hardly surprising, she reflected, considering the speed at which all the mourning had had to be made. Some day, if ever she had a moment to spare, she would get down to a whole lot of alterations.

Now, as she turned into River Lane, she wondered whether May would have finished Mrs Betts's dress during her absence. She hoped so. She knew that the mayoress was anxious to have it, even though the reception for which it was wanted was not for another couple of days. It would be nice, if possible, to get it to her tonight. She was apt to be pernickety, fussy about the smallest detail, not that there ever seemed anything to fuss about. Quite often she asked for some minute alteration and then came back next day with a silly affected smile on her face to say, "You were *quite* right, Miss Lodge. I should *never* have asked you to take that extra tuck. You *always* know best. I do want to wear it at once. Do you think you could possibly . . .?" And stifling annoyance and resentment, either Flo or May would set to work to do her bidding. A proper old 'tab', the latter was apt to call her on such occasions, although where she got the word from, no one quite knew, just as the family had always been mystified by 'chippatoo'. But proper old tab or no, if her latest dress was now ready and Katy was back, Flo resolved to send her straight up to The Chantry with it just as soon as the child had had her tea.

Katy was indeed back when Flo came into the house; but she was sitting on the old horsehair sofa in tears. Around the table, all set with cups and saucers and plates, Sarah, May and Neil were seated in their customary places. Spread out at one corner on the spotless white cloth there appeared to be a necklace of large, cheap-looking pink pearls, shining—almost defiantly—in the glow of the oil-lamp. Flo looked questioningly from one to the other, their faces all turned expectantly towards hers, as if they were waiting for her to act as some kind of referee.

"I am not saying," Sarah began, slowly, after Flo had taken off her coat and was seated at the table herself, "that it was entirely Katy's fault. Others older than she should have known better than to let her go to the fair in the first place. But what I cannot allow to go unpunished is Katy's own, unthinking, disgraceful behaviour once she got there." Sarah picked up the bauble by her side, held it disdainfully for a while between finger and thumb and then let it fall, heavily, back on the table. Her action suddenly made Flo think of Edith's remarks about their great-grandmother which had been made but a short while ago. Almost, she felt, Sarah could have been an actress, too. Certainly, in that one small moment of time in the spring of 1919, the living-room of The Mill House, Wilhampton, with the lamplight flickering over the faces of the five members of the Lodge family within it, seemed vaguely reminiscent of a stage set.

Flo looked from Sarah towards the smallest, most shadowy figure, still huddled on the sofa. The face alone seemed to stand out, the enormous grey eyes still brimming with tears, the usually chalk-white skin blotched and swollen. If her mother thought that Katy had been unthinking, how much more had she been herself in her initial responsibility for the whole sorry situation. Suddenly, she felt strangely tired, the burden of being eldest of the family altogether too much for her thin square shoulders. She ought to have had more imagination, she should have foreseen what might happen. Although, for the life of her, she couldn't quite see what Katy could have done at the fair to engender quite such wrath on her mother's part. She was sure that she could not have acquired the necklace through any illicit means. She must have won it, although, for all its vulgarity, it was a cut above the usual prizes waiting to be netted or ringed or shot for on the garish tawdry stalls.

"What happened, Katy?" Flo asked, quietly.

But the question only brought a fresh bout of weeping. Sarah had put the fear of the Lord into the girl, all right. She had always been able to do that with all her children, that is, apart from poor Neil, to whom she showed an uncustomary and touching compassion. Now, she simply answered Flo's query herself.

"It seems she won it for acting. There was some extra show this year. Ena and Katy decided to go to it. The stage-manager asked for volunteers."

"Volunteers?" It was May who now spoke.

"Yes. He offered a prize for the best turn."

The corner of May's mouth twitched a little. She had always been able to see the funny side of things.

"And what turn did you do, Katy?" Flo spoke gravely but kindly, aware that the sobbing had subsided a little.

"I sang," came a small muffled voice from the sofa.

"And what did you sing?"

But now Katy was not even given a chance to reply.

"She sang," Sarah intervened, in a sepulchral voice, *Our Lodger's Such A Nice Young Man*, with her father not dead three months."

5

Ever afterwards, Katy always thought of the first day of the Wilhampton spring fair, in 1919, as the day she grew up—or, strictly speaking, perhaps the night she grew up.

She had been sent straight to bed after tea, with the admonishment that there would be no more sustenance forthcoming until morning and on no account was she to read. As for any ablutions, they appeared to have been waived. In any case, the important ones were mostly done of a morning, when members of the family—other than Sarah, for whom a dipper of soapy water was brought up to the washstand in her bedroom—would creep downstairs and into the mill to perform whatever was necessary before the six-thirty hooter sounded and the men arrived for work. Baths, either in a tub by the coal range in the living-room, or sometimes in one of the vats in the mill itself, were invariably reserved for weekends.

Katy had not really minded this particular form of punishment. In many ways it was a relief. She had been feeling too sick to manage anything other than a cup of tea; and she was glad to escape from the tense unhappy atmosphere downstairs. As for reading, however much she had been looking forward to getting on with her current book, *A Peep Behind the Scenes*—hopefully hidden beneath her mattress—she was far enough into the tragic story of an ill-treated consumptive wife of a fairground manager, to realise that just at the moment the subject was a little too close to real life for her to find altogether enjoyable.

So, having undressed, slipped into a flannelette nightgown and undone her thick brown hair which she had lately taken to pinning up in the fashion adopted by Flo and May, she simply lay in bed, savouring, in retrospect, the extraordinary reception which had followed her début on the small raised platform in the largest tent in the fairground.

Not even Sarah's accusations and anger could take away the exquisite pleasure of seeing and hearing once again, with total recall, the manager coming onto the stage after she had already given three encores, how he had lain one hand on her shoulder and held the other up to the audience, while he had said, "Ladies and Gentlemen, I think you will agree. We have here a second Marie Lloyd." And there had been so much thumping and clapping and cheering that Katy had been obliged to do yet another encore, this time with everyone else joining in.

Ena Perrick hadn't said much about it on the way home. It was obvious she was pretty jealous. The poem she had recited—*Lord Ullin's Daughter*—hadn't gone down nearly so well. There had only been a few, perfunctory, half-hearted claps. But so great had been Katy's own triumph that the manager had asked her if she would come back and do an evening performance. She had refused, having the sense to know full well that she would never be able to get away with that. Yet, flushed with temporary euphoria, she had murmured something about possibly returning the following afternoon.

Now, of course, after Sarah's violent reaction there would be nothing like that—nor would there ever be. Her mother had pounced on her as soon as she had entered the door, her eyes immediately spotting a little bit of the necklace showing above the collar of her coat, and then breaking into a merciless castigation. By the time May and Neil had appeared on the scene, she had begun to feel not only wicked but unclean. "Fair people are dirty folk, Katy. Actors and actresses are worse. How you could *expose* yourself in such a way at a time like this, I simply do not understand."

In spite of her remorse and wretchedness, Katy had taken special note of the word 'expose'. She couldn't see that she had actually done anything like that. It wasn't as if she'd undressed in public or even made a spectacle of herself. She'd been a success. A great success. Besides, she was vaguely aware that Flo and May used that particular word in relation to something naughty which only men did. She seemed to remember overhearing them whispering in bed one night during the war when they thought she was asleep, and May had referred to having been seen home by a rather elderly colonel who—and here her sister's voice had become more muffled and indistinct—had "exposed himself in River Lane". Katy couldn't imagine what poor Colonel Whittingham had done, especially as Sarah or Sidney might easily have been waiting, keys in hand, on the inside of the high heavy mill gates. For, unless it was a very special occasion when, reluctantly, they allowed the small trapdoor to remain open a little longer—on the strict understanding that the latecomer would lock it up carefully with the key hidden inside—nine thirty p.m. was the time they insisted each member of the family should be home. Indeed, Sidney Lodge went even further. Rather like a shepherd, he was not really happy unless his flock was safely indoors by sundown, deeming it somehow unseemly and wrong for anyone—especially women—to be seen after that hour "howling about at night", as he was apt to put it.

Katy had had no idea exactly when Colonel Whittingham had brought May back to the mill, but she had pondered over the incident a long time, particularly as she became aware that May's association with this seemingly most respectable officer had ceased abruptly from then on; and when, a little later, Sarah had enquired, quite kindly, what had happened to that "nice Colonel Whittingham", May had all at once appeared to close up, her manner becoming uncharacteristically terse and defensive as she had replied, "I really don't know, Mother. He's probably been posted." Katy knew very well that nothing of the sort had happened because she had seen the Colonel coming out of the Victoria Arms only the day before, but naturally she hadn't said anything. One always stood by one's sisters, even if one did think they might be telling tiny white lies.

Katy wished very much that her mother hadn't used

this mysterious word of obviously double-meaning in relation to herself; but presently she forgot about it and started drifting off to sleep. The excitement of the afternoon and the emotional upset after it had worn her out. She was therefore quite oblivious to the sound of someone climbing the attic steps until there was a noise right beside her. She sat bolt upright in sudden terror. This was no Flo or May, coming to bed gently and quietly in slippered feet, shading their candles for fear of disturbing her. In the moonlight filtering through the chinks in the curtains, she became aware of a different figure, a large, ungainly man's figure. Neil.

Panic-stricken by she knew not what, Katy opened her mouth to scream, but no scream came. She pushed at him blindly, only to have him come closer. He was kneeling now by her low little bed—not much more than a camp one—and she watched in a kind of fascinated horror as, grunting and gasping, he began fumbling with the lower part of his person.

It was May who found them thus. In later life, with possibly one exception, Katy could never remember being more overcome with relief. Still unable to shout or speak, she watched the light from her sister's candle gradually getting brighter as she mounted the attic steps, the bobbing shadow of her neat, reassuring little figure, looming larger every second against the opposite wall.

For a moment May appeared to be unaware of what was happening. Neil also was too engrossed in his clandestine, unwholesome activity to heed her presence. Only when she stooped to place her candle on the floor, did May hear the unaccustomed sounds and notice the two figures in the far corner of the attic, the one on the bed, rigid and silent, the other beside it, panting and swaying.

"Oh my God!" May was across the room, pulling her brother away from Katy with all the force of her two tiny arms. Suddenly, the boy seemed to crumple, lying on the floor in an awkward heap.

May turned to her younger sister. "Lie down, lovey. Keep quiet. I want to get him back to his room before Mother comes up to bed."

Then, kicking at her brother with her little foot, she hissed, "Get up, Neil. Get up this instant." Sheepishly, the boy did as he was told. Putting a finger to her lips—one of the signs she knew he was quite capable of understanding—she more or less manhandled him across the room and led him down the attic steps.

When she returned five minutes later, Katy was trembling uncontrollably. "Did he," May said, and this time, in her agitation, she spoke almost harshly, "Did he . . .?" To her relief, before she could quite bring herself to finish the difficult question, Katy shook her head, even though she was only half cognizant of the exact intricacies of the function to which May was alluding. All she did know was that her sister's eyes seemed to be searching and probing, travelling all over her hunched, skinny body, willing it not to have been violated.

"But he exposed himself!" her elder sister said, at length.

"Yes." Katy now understood only too well the coarser meaning of the word.

"For how long?"

"I don't know. A minute. Maybe two."

"He didn't come?"

"Come?" This time Katy was really puzzled again. How could May say Neil hadn't come, when he had very definitely come up to the attic? Was she trying to make her pretend that the incident hadn't happened? "Come?" she said, again, wonderingly.

"Oh, Katy dear. I'm sorry. How should you know?" May sat on the bed and put her arms round the still-shaking body. "It won't happen again, I promise you, although I don't think we'll let Mother know about it just yet. You've had enough trouble for the time being. Suppose you come and sleep in my bed tonight?" And when Flo came upstairs, some half an hour later, she remained unaware till morning of the two forms huddled up together, the younger one fast asleep in her elder sister's arms.

But though Katy had soon dropped off in May's comforting embrace, the latter, her body cramped and her mind racing, had stayed awake most of the night. She knew something would have to be done about Katy. If her mother wouldn't have Neil taken away, then she and Flo would have to see whether they could find a job for their youngest sister which would enable her to live away from home. They had probably already made a mistake in trying to shield the girl for so long from the facts of life; but she had seemed such a fey, capricious, innocent little thing, albeit now fast becoming prettier every day. No wonder she had brought the house down with—of all songs—*Our Lodger's Such a Nice Young Man.* Poor child. She'd had a rude awakening tonight. May still wasn't quite sure how much she understood. Tomorrow, she would try to have a serious talk with her. But then she remembered that Henry would be arriving with Marianne, and there might not be much opportunity.

During that long, uncomfortable night, May thought back to her own initiation into the mysteries of sex. Sarah had never said a word of enlightenment. It was Lilian Perrick, oddly enough, who had lent her a book called *The Cradle Ship*, which had given her a lot to think about, although it had been altogether too vague and allusory for her liking: all about a young wife and mother-to-be thinking beautiful thoughts every day for nine months in order that she should grow a beautiful baby inside her tummy. It never went into any details about how the baby got into it in the first place. There were a great many pictures of the woman wearing lovely, long, loose-fitting garments and, in each one, her husband seemed to be hovering somewhere in the background. Because of this and constant references to his presence in the text, May—who had been thirteen at the time—gathered that a man was somehow necessary for producing a child; but she had sent Lilian Perrick into fits of laughter when, on returning the book, she had asked whether, if Lady Fairfax had not married Lord Fairfax, she could nevertheless still have had all her babies because she always had a butler around.

May had certainly become much more enlightened about such things during her teens, but it was really the war which had opened both her and Flo's eyes a great deal further. Wilhampton lay in one of the valleys south of Salisbury Plain where, it seemed, most of the British Army was stationed at one time or another. There was never any shortage of men anxious to have and—up to a point—willing to give a good time. May especially, had learnt how to flirt and use her big blue eyes. She was reputed to have the smallest waist in Wilhampton and was well aware that she was attractive to the opposite sex; but neither she nor Flo would ever have dreamt of letting any man go further than a kiss or a cuddle. There were too many veiled—and not so veiled—parental threats of 'never darkening my door again' if they misbehaved, even though the misbehaviour might not have been spelled out in so many words.

All the same, there had been that one terrible occurrence which Sarah and Sidney, thanks be, had never known about and which, to this day, May had done her best to forget. But somehow, the recent events had unhappily brought it all back as if it were yesterday. She recalled how Major Walter Perkins—by far the most handsome and amusing of her beaux—had asked her to lunch with him one Sunday in April at the White Lion in Westonbury. In her new beige outfit and white and beige beribboned hat, she had walked the three miles into the town in high anticipation. She knew him to be fancy-free and that many a local girl was after him, for he was a real charmer and it was quite a feather in her cap to have had this particular invitation.

As she had hurried along that morning after church—her new, narrow, pointed shoes pinching her small feet on the uneven, dusty, white road—she began to wonder whether, if he *asked*, she might say yes. It wouldn't have been her first proposal by any means, but possibly because she had already been a little spoilt by the sheer number of suitors dancing attendance on her, she had been apt to play one off against the other, feeling that there was still plenty of time and she could afford to be choosy. One day 'Mr Right' was sure to come along. But what had taken place in the spring of 1916 had certainly altered her ideas about men. Although, afterwards, she had still gone out with them and enjoyed having compliments paid her, she managed to keep them at a distance. She was not at all sure that she wished to marry. She did not think she could face up to the physical side of such a relationship; and Flo, sharing vicariously her sister's experience and subsequently undergoing a rather different kind of disillusionment with a member of the opposite sex, had begun to think likewise.

For when May had arrived at the White Lion that day, Major Perkins was not waiting to greet her in the lounge, as she had been given to understand. When she enquired for him at the desk, she was told that he was indisposed and had asked if she would go up to his suite. It did not occur to her to think that there was anything dubious about such a request, despite the rather sour, disapproving look on the face of the porter who showed her the way. For all her twenty-four years, there was then still a charming naïveté about her. Because Walter was an officer, she took it for granted that he was a gentleman. As far as she was concerned, the poor man was ill. She could, perhaps, do something for him before going home.

She found him to be not exactly ill, but certainly strangely flushed and over-animated. He opened the door in answer to her light tap, wearing a silk dressing-gown over what appeared to be a pair of fawn mufti trousers. Behind him, in the sitting-room, there was a table laid for luncheon, on which resided a bucket with two bottles of champagne, one of which had already been opened.

Walter Perkins had tried to gather her in his arms at once, but she had held back, fear and suspicion quickly dispelling any previous feelings of trust and hope. There was something wrong. She should never have agreed to come upstairs. Whereas his words, "May-darling-you-look-good-enough-to-eat—I-adore-you", would, in any other circumstances, have sent her spirits soaring, now, in this silent, second-floor, private suite of the White Lion, they had the reverse effect.

"I only came up because I thought you were ill, Walter," she remembered saying, primly, once she had got her breath. His own smelled of alcohol. She had tried to leave, but he had forestalled her. She could recall, clearly, how his manner had suddenly changed, that it became petulant and he had more or less dragged her across the room, thrusting a glass of champagne into her unwilling hand, telling her that it would help to chase away "that ridiculous, Victorian conventionality imposed on you by your misguided mother".

It was the contemptuous reference to Sarah which had made May fighting mad. Had she been more experienced, more a woman of the world and aware that he had been drinking quite heavily, she might have been able, with a certain amount of tact, to have extricated herself forthwith from the whole unfortunate situation. As it was, she now found herself not only in a mental but also a bitter physical struggle with Major Walter Perkins. It was hardly surprising who had won. He had carried her from the sitting-room into his bedroom and there, as she afterwards told Flo, he "had had his way with her". Too ashamed and too terrified to make a sound, she had then quickly left his suite, praying that the porter at the White Lion would not notice a certain disarray in her previously immaculate attire.

For eighteen days afterwards, she and Flo had agonised as to whether May would have a period. When, on the nineteenth day, no such occurrence had taken place, she remembered having stood by the mill-race for a long while, watching the water cascading into the boiling inferno below, wondering whether to throw herself into it. But something—God, her parents, fear of dying, even basic love of life—had made her desist. When, that night, she felt the warm welcome wetness between her thighs, she had sent up a little prayer of thanksgiving for deliverance from a fate which had, until those sobering moments by the mill-race, seemed worse than death.

For the remainder of the war, May had known how to take care of herself. She had learnt her lesson. Later on, it had even been reinforced by a second not quite so traumatic one—the whispered account of which, Katy had partially overheard—on an evening when she was being escorted back to the mill by someone whom she had considered eminently safe. After this, she felt that no man, not even Colonel Whittingham, M.C., who came of good family and had hitherto appeared to have such impeccable manners, could be trusted. For when she had held out her hand to say good-night to him, he had suddenly proffered something very different than his own in return. Disgusted, she began to despair of finding a man who did not want 'one thing' and who, on possibly obtaining it, would probably leave a girl with a life sentence: either in the undisguisable form of an illegitimate child or the more nebulous, but sometimes almost as damaging, acquisition of a bad reputation. Though she still could not help harbouring romantic notions of matrimony—a vision of a cream satin wedding-dress and a train of Brussels lace floated often into her mind—that, sadly, seemed about as far as she could get.

Neither did Flo fare any better in reaching the altar. The following year, just before Henry was sent to the front, she had been very much in love with a Captain Guy Armitage. He had courted her so assiduously that the Lodges had begun to take it for granted that she would become his wife. Then, for no apparent reason that Flo could see, his attentions had suddenly ceased. No more little notes, flowers or chocolates arrived at the Mill House. Puzzled, she had still gone about her daily duties as conscientiously as ever, but with a heavy heart. One Friday morning, she had happened to glance at the back page of the *Westonbury Journal* before going down to the workroom and was hardly able to believe her eyes when she read:

ARMITAGE—SINCA. On July 7th, in London, CAPTAIN GUY LEONARD ARMITAGE, elder son of Mr and Mrs John Armitage of St. Vincent Place, Edinburgh, to GRACE MARY, only daughter of Mr Thomas Sinca and the late Mrs Sinca, of The Warren, Wilhampton.

Flo had rushed out of the house and shut herself in the closet until May, having hastily picked up the discarded paper and seen the news, hurried after her. Here, on the broad, well-scrubbed, wooden seat, she had sat down beside her and, putting her arms around her eldest sister, had done her best to comfort her. When she was at last able to coax Flo out, she insisted that they leave their sewing for a while and take a walk.

May had already heard rumours about Guy and Grace, but she had kept them to herself, hoping the affair would blow over. She was aware that there was always gossip about the Sincas, for their presence on the outskirts of Wilhampton was something of a mystery. They had arrived at the beginning of the war: an ageing invalid father and his bold-eyed, blonde-haired daughter. Possibly because of their foreign-sounding name and Grace's off-hand manner and looks, they had never been accepted in the little town. They seemed aliens in every sense of the word. Soon, it was being put about that they were enemy agents and that Grace's entertaining of army personnel was done for a specific reason on her part, even if it was enjoyed for an altogether different reason by the countless uniformed officers who could be seen walking the half mile to and from The Warren at all hours of the day and night.

Aided by shocked but eager denigrators, Grace's reputation became more and more lurid. It was rumoured she made flashing signals from the house after dark, although whether this was for the purpose of attracting lurking German spies or the much more ready and waiting British troops stationed nearby was left to the listener's individual interpretation.

"She'll never make Guy happy, that's for sure," May had said on their return journey, as Flo strode on unseeingly through the meadows on a day when she would normally have welcomed being out and about, with the lush green countryside lazily enjoying that traditional lull between haymaking and harvest: honeymoon time, as the farming fraternity called it. "If Guy could fall for a woman like that," May continued, trying to be as helpful as she could, "you're well out of it. He's got what's coming to him. She's a . . . Well, *you* know what she is. All Wilhampton does. Percy Hooper's brother said he once went to The Warren to mend the front gate and she was standing at an upstairs window just as God made her. Although . . ." and here May had paused for rather longer, remembering her own misfortune and colouring slightly before going on with a rush, "well, I mean, she can't have been exactly like that in a long while, can she?"

When, three months later, Guy Armitage had come back from Passchendaele with both his legs blown off, May could not help regretting her harsh words. Nevertheless, she consoled herself by thinking that they had been said in good faith. And if they had helped a sister in distress, it was all that really mattered. That was what families were for.

As time went by, and May and Flo were both in their late twenties, the inhabitants of Wilhampton were invariably surprised that such pleasant, good-looking girls remained spinsters. Little did they guess that, for reasons best known to themselves, the Misses F and M Lodge, though never lacking in admirers—

especially while the war had still been on—nevertheless preferred to ply their trade, sitting in their little workroom: cutting, tacking, machining and stitching, having decided, by a mutual, almost unspoken agreement, that for them a husband was a doubtful asset.

6

The first thing that Flo noticed when Henry and Marianne alighted from the London train at Wilhampton station was that her new sister-in-law appeared to be most unsuitably dressed. She supposed she was pretty in a dark-eyed, flashy kind of way. She was very obviously foreign, although there seemed to be more of an Italian look about her than a French one—not that Flo knew much about either. It was just that Marianne's olive skin and jet-black hair, done up in tight curls, reminded her of some of the paintings of the Fairfaxes' ancestors up at the Hall, who had reputedly come from Venice.

But it was Marianne's clothes which distressed her more than anything. Flo hardly liked to think the word, let alone use it, but they were *common*. The Lodge family might live in what many people would consider privation, their home one of the most humble and inconvenient in the whole of Wilhampton, yet there was something about them, a *je ne sais quoi*—not that Flo understood about that either—which made them out of the ordinary. Way back, on both sides, there had been *breeding*, even if Sarah's grandmother had run off to go on the stage. For want of a better word, they had style, an unconscious knowledge of what was what, which most plainly revealed itself in the way they dressed. Like the county families they served, they never went in for bright colours. They wore browns, greys, navy or beige and, on occasion, white in summer and, of course, black for mourning.

The young woman now confronting Flo on the wind-swept platform was wearing a scarlet coat trimmed with some cheap, coarse fur, under which she appeared to have on a dress of shiny blue sateen. Perched on the black curls at a rakish angle there was a tam-o'-shanter of an even brighter blue; on her feet she wore black ankle-strap shoes with at least four-inch heels. To make matters worse, there was about her a smell of cheap scent and round her neck she sported a necklace, not unlike the one which Katy, poor child, had been forced by Sarah to return to the stage-manager at the fair that very morning. After they set off for the Mill House—Henry having arranged to collect their luggage a little later on by means of a hand-truck borrowed from the mill—Flo wondered how her sister-in-law was going to be able to manage a good mile's walk. And during it, unfortunately, it seemed as if they were destined to meet half Wilhampton.

Henry, with his cheerful, hail-fellow-well-met disposition, had been a popular boy and everyone was glad to think, especially after Sarah's recent widowhood, that he had come home. More than once the little trio was obliged to stop and pass the time of day and the introduction of Marianne naturally caused surprise and sometimes friendly banter; although Flo herself, at these moments, simply stood aside in acute embarrassment, something which gradually increased, with the awareness of many a lace curtain twitching behind a window as they proceeded towards their destination. She dreaded the time when mother-in-law and daughter-in-law met.

Sarah, as Flo had rightly envisaged, was at the door to greet them. Wearing her best black dress, her coiffure immaculate, her work-worn hands clasped a little nervously in front of her, at first it seemed as if her whole countenance lit up on seeing them coming through the mill gates, and then, just as quickly, changed to frowning bewilderment as they drew closer and Henry said, "Mother, this is Marianne."

The latter—'to give her her due', as May, who was standing behind Sarah, remarked afterwards—said, "Bonjour, Madame," pleasantly enough, and then kissed her mother-in-law on both cheeks. But, on entering the house, any initial goodwill such gestures might have engendered was quickly dispelled by her looking round, also in obvious astonishment, and saying, "Plis, la toilette?" She was not the first visitor to discover that the Lodges' actual home by no means came up to the standard automatically presumed by its somewhat grand-sounding name.

It was a rather wan-looking Katy who was detailed to take Marianne down the garden. Here, she shyly pushed open the door of the closet and stood back for this strange, unaccountable sister-in-law to enter, only to be confronted a moment later with a vehement shaking of the tight black curls and a torrent of "*non, merci*!"

Still suffering from the events of the previous twenty-four hours, Katy looked at Marianne dumbly. She knew not one word of French, but it was fairly obvious that some alternative to an earth closet was required. Yet she was painfully aware that this could only be the commode in her mother's bedroom or a chamber pot in the attic. Neither solution seemed exactly expedient. Why couldn't this silly hoity-toity French-woman do what she needed to do and stop making a fuss. After all, judging by the way she was clad, she did not exactly appear to have come from a palace.

"I'm afraid," said Katy, at length, doing her best to mime her reply, after a further unintelligible spate of French had abated a little, "we only have this." Even in her frail, rather shocked state, there was a certain dignity about the child, as she finally spread out her hands in a gesture of despair.

She watched Marianne frown. She had no means of knowing whether she had made herself understood; but she felt that this new wife of Henry's must surely have picked up some English from him by now. To her relief, possibly because of the simple, direct way she had spoken, Katy now saw the newcomer give a little shrug of resignation and disappear into the closet on her ridiculous high heels which she noted, not without satisfaction, had become coated with mud.

Yet the situation was only temporarily alleviated. Once Henry's wife reappeared, she began muttering something which sounded like "lafay". In frustration, when this produced no response, she, too, began to mime, making it quite clear that she wished to wash her hands. Miserably, Katy escorted her back to the house, wondering whether her mother would fetch a dipper of hot water from the mill and put it on the table already laid for dinner. But, luckily, this requirement appeared to have been carefully anticipated. May took Marianne up the winding staircase to Sarah's bedroom, where a jug of warm water was standing in the blue and white china basin on the washstand, together with some soap and a clean towel.

At last, at two p.m., the family sat down to their midday meal, which, owing to the various delays, was not at all as Sarah would have wished. She had asked Mr Pritchett, the butcher, for a special joint in honour of Henry's return, and the good man had delivered what she had told Flo and May was a 'pretty piece of meat', a sirloin of beef which, because of its expense, she would normally never have thought of buying. Now, as she took her first mouthful, having anxiously watched Henry carve none too carefully, she regretted that she had not made an ordinary stew. All the food was overcooked and she noticed that Marianne, Katy, Flo and even May—who, considering her small waist was nevertheless usually possessed of a hearty appetite—seemed only to make a pretence at eating. Sarah herself also felt totally unable to do justice to the meal. Only the boys, Henry and Neil, tucked in, the former announcing cheerfully—but tactlessly, from his wife's point of view—that there was nothing like a bit of his mother's home cooking.

At last, when the dirty plates had been stacked away behind a curtain in the tiny so-called hall of the house, Sarah broached the question which had been uppermost in her mind since her son had arrived home. She had hoped that he might have brought the subject up himself. As he hadn't, she decided to wait no longer.

"And what, Henry, do you intend to do now?"

There was a momentary silence in the living-room. All eyes turned expectantly—with the exception of Neil's vacant ones—towards Henry, those of his wife semi-knowing and supercilious. Suddenly, her husband's breezy self-confidence deserted him. He had forgotten just how forthright and direct his mother could be on occasions. He had known that his future plans would displease her but, with his customary insouciant optimism, had gone ahead, hoped for the best and trusted that he would be able to find a suitably propitious time for imparting his news.

Now, with obvious reluctance, he said, slowly, "I've signed on, Mother. I'm a regular."

"You never!" At moments like these, Sarah's

grammar was apt to slip. She looked at her son, incredulously. Being a regular soldier would mean he might go anywhere. There would be no chance now of a man about the place. She had neither expected nor wanted him to work in the mill, for, with the advent of Mr Fuller, she knew it was unlikely that Henry would be able to follow in his father's footsteps. Besides, he was such an outdoor type. She had reckoned on him obtaining some other sort of job in the district of an individual nature, possibly on the Fairfax estate. After all, head-keepering was quite a good position. Everyone in Wilhampton seemed both to fear and revere the present, ageing Fred Ashford, and although Henry's nature was rather different from that of the stern tight-lipped Fred, nevertheless he was good with a gun, having been instructed how to use one when still a young lad by none other than Fred himself. Moreover, it was possible, if Henry worked hard, he might do even better. He knew a lot about the countryside, thanks to Fred; indeed, much more than Lilian Perrick's brother had ever done when he had started on the estate, and look where he was now: managing the Fairfaxes' Home Farm. All these things went through Sarah's mind as, in order to gain time and hide her emotion, she bent to make up the fire with hands which shook, partly in anger, partly in grief.

"Where," asked Flo, trying to ease the tension, "will they be sending you first, Henry?"

"York," he replied, quickly. "I have to report next Wednesday."

Still with her back towards the others Sarah said, "Perhaps you'd best be getting off to the station now, Henry, for your luggage. Katy here will take Marianne straight up to Edith's."

With relief, the little party broke up. While Marianne and Katy were putting on their coats, Flo went into the mill with her brother to look for a suitable hand-truck he could borrow.

"It's only natural," she said quietly, as they went along the narrow passage leading to the main building in search of the foreman, "for Mother to take on a bit. I mean, after Frank going and then Father and . . . well, Neil being like he is. We hoped you'd be around somehow."

Henry's usual carefree countenance had now completely changed. He wore the look of a chastened, crestfallen bloodhound. Suddenly, before they reached the heavy sliding door, he caught hold of Flo's arm and pulled her back.

"Mother would be even more upset if I did stick around," he said. "That's why I signed on. You can tell this to May but no one else, mind. Marianne's expecting. She's almost three months gone. I want her to be right out of the district when her time comes. Then we might just be able to get away with saying the baby was premature. Mother would never be able to hold up her head in Wilhampton again, if the truth came out."

7

It was a chance remark made by Lady Fairfax's daughter one evening in early April which gave Katy Lodge her deliverance from the mill, although not, by any means, in the romantic way she was apt to dream about. No knight in shining armour—or, at least, some eminently desirable personage driving one of the new motor-cars which were increasingly to be seen on the Wilhampton streets—arrived to claim and carry her off into the wider world. Her escape was destined to be far more mundane.

It came about because Flo and May had been summoned to the Hall by the now pregnant Honourable Alicia Moreton, who happened to be staying with her mother and wanted some maternity clothes. "They will be so much better, dear Miss Lodge, than anything I could buy or have made in London," the charming young mother-to-be said to Flo, as the latter knelt at her feet taking measurements. "I swear there is no one like you two in the whole of the West End. If you could only set up in Bond Street, you would make a fortune." And Flo and May had made appropriately appreciative sounds, storing up the conversation to be retailed later on when they got back to the Mill House. In her delight, May had even scrawled Bond Street at the bottom corner of the page in her notebook, where she was writing down such items as Length and Shoulders and Bust, well aware naturally, that ample allowance must be made for an increase in the latter. Dear Miss Alicia had quite a few months to go yet.

How pretty she was, May thought, as she sat in the chintz-covered window-seat, with pencil poised, while a discussion took place concerning how many inches a certain day-dress should be off the ground. At these moments, May was always quite happy to leave the decision to Flo and their client. After all, her sister was the senior in the partnership and it was only right that she should advise on such matters. Fortunately, there had never been any sibling rivalry between them. They worked well in double harness, performing their individual, self-appointed tasks with no other thought than the production of a first-rate garment when these had been completed. In their separate ways, both were perfectionists. May supposed that that was what the Honourable Alicia had been getting at when she had made the flattering remark about setting up in Bond Street. Idly, she wondered what it was like. She had never been to London. She had seen pictures of the capital, of course, sometimes with fashionable ladies and gentlemen strolling about the streets and parks or riding in hansom cabs, but it wasn't the same thing as going there and taking stock with one's own eyes. How wonderful it would have been if she and Flo could have become West End couturiers.

And then, 'as luck would have it'—another of May's pet phrases which she had used to describe the scene afterwards—just as they were leaving, Lady Fairfax had come into the room and her daughter had started reiterating some of her previous remarks about Flo's and May's expertise, but this time adding an even more thought-provoking one: "So sad, Mummy. Nanny's niece who was coming as nursery-maid has been quite ill with rheumatic fever, and her parents don't want her to leave home now. It's going to be difficult to find someone else whom Nanny Barlow approves of."

It was then that May's brain, always quicker than Flo's, suddenly got to work. The Fairfaxes' old nanny, who was now safely ensconced in the Moreton household busily preparing for the happy event, knew Katy quite well, didn't she? Katy had to be got away from the mill. From Neil. Katy, being the youngest of the Lodge family, mightn't know quite so much about babies, but she had often been sent up to look after Edith's little ones in emergencies. Besides, she was quick and well-mannered. Katy, under the auspices of Nanny Barlow and this kind, gentle, knowledgeable young matron, could come to no harm, could she? Even in the big city. May did not want to speak out of turn but . . . She looked across at Flo, wondering whether she, too, had grasped the implications, the timeliness of the whole situation. But her elder sister was putting away her tape-measure and patterns and samples of material. To May, so much the more impulsive, it seemed now or never. She looked at the Honourable Alicia very directly.

"Then the vacancy for a nursery-maid is still open, madam?" she enquired.

"Why, yes," Lady Fairfax's daughter replied, somewhat in surprise. "Had you anyone in mind?"

"It's just," said May, simply, "I feel that my youngest sister . . ." and here she turned towards Lady Fairfax herself, "you remember, your ladyship, Katy, the one you have always been so kind to, might possibly be suitable for the position. She has passed her seventeenth birthday now and is quite capable and good with her needle. Her health has much improved. She is altogether fitter these days thanks, largely I am sure, to your ladyship's kindness when she was young."

"Why, what a perfectly splendid idea." Lady Fairfax and her daughter spoke almost with one voice. "Katy is such a sweet, unusual and conscientious young girl."

"It would, of course," May added hastily, gaining confidence, albeit trusting she had not gone too far, especially as she had been unable, firstly, to test her elder sister's reactions, "be for our mother to decide."

"But naturally, Miss Lodge. Naturally. It would be entirely up to Mrs Lodge. But from our point of view, I cannot think of a happier solution."

After they had been shown out by a parlourmaid through one of the side entrances, Flo and May elected to take the longer route home through the surrounding parkland. Such licence was one of the little perks connected with their somewhat unusual position, just as long as they were careful—which, of course, went without saying—never to abuse it and meticulously to eschew any of the more formal gardens adjacent to the Hall itself. Now, they took the winding path along by the river, while the evening sunlight came slanting through the willows and a yellow carpet of daffodils tossed hither and thither in a gentle westerly breeze.

"D'you think Mother will let her go?" It was Flo who began the conversation, as she rested for a moment by one of the bridges, her face lined and anxious. May was relieved that her elder sister appeared to have accepted her own spur-of-the-moment proposition, although not for the first time did she notice how much Flo seemed to have aged since their father's death, almost as if the burden of trying to take his place was too much for her.

"She mightn't like it, but I think she'll be bound to agree, once she hears what Neil tried to do. We've got to tell her now. If it hadn't been for her getting so worked up over Henry, we'd have done so before." More or less unconsciously, May found herself continuing to assume the lead over this particular problem.

"But it's service. *Personal indoor* service, May. Mother always vowed she'd never let any of us do that. Her hopes of Henry one day becoming head gamekeeper on the estate was something quite different."

"Oh, I know. But it's not as if Katy would be working for just anyone. It's the Fairfax family. They've seen her grow up. Look what Lady Fairfax did when she was little. It's my belief she's got a soft spot for the child."

"Maybe." Flo gave a little shrug of resignation. "But sometimes I wonder . . ." she went on, and then broke off.

Quickly, May took her up. "What do you wonder?"

"Oh, I don't know. About life . . ." Flo, her mouth

set, her little tapestry bag with the tools of her trade dangling over one arm, strode on, purposefully. "Families," she continued, tossing her head and throwing the word, as it were, over her shoulder at her sister. "Mother, in particular. D'you think she's ever been happy? Really happy? I mean, she's always had such a hard time of it. Bringing us all up. I can't imagine how we survived. When you think of all that water round the house. None of us able to swim, yet we had that boat. She can't have known a moment's peace. And then Neil being simple. It's pathetic the way she dotes on him."

"It often happens, doesn't it? With children who aren't quite right. I suppose a mother feels extra responsible for having brought that kind of baby into the world." May hurried along, finding it hard to keep up with Flo's longer strides. She was surprised at the weary cynicism that had crept into her elder sister's observations; although she knew, for all Flo's usually sweet and gentle manner, she had never really got over her unhappy love affair in the war. By a kind of silent understanding, they did not talk of Guy Armitage. Nor did they ever walk past The Warren.

"Yes, I realise that," she now replied. "But I think Father ought to have left her alone afterwards. It must have been ghastly for her when Katy was on the way, wondering whether she'd be the same."

May was silent. She remembered how quiet Sarah had been during her final pregnancy and how badly she had gone down after the birth. May had only been eleven at the time. She hadn't understood it. Her mother had seemed so tired and listless. Katy, thank God, had been quite normal—even if she had turned out to be rather delicate to rear—but Sarah had taken so little interest in her, leaving Flo and herself to take care of the baby and the other young ones as best as they could. It had never occurred to May to query her mother's malaise too deeply. She had been too young. She had simply accepted it as she had accepted Sarah's eventual return to health. Now, when Flo came out with her next statement, it was as if a whole host of half-forgotten memories came flooding back in sharp relief.

"I always reckoned Lilian Perrick had a lot to do with Mother getting better in the end," her eldest sister suddenly vouchsafed.

"*Lilian Perrick*?"

"Yes. Or rather Lilian Firman, as she was then, keeping house for her brother up on downside, just before she married. I mean, Mother was in such a bad way, always lying on her bed and leaving you and me to do for Katy and the others, that quite often there just wasn't a meal for Father when he needed it, so he started going up to the Firman house for a bit of comfort. Of course, Lilian always was a bit of a one for the men. Anyway, when Mother got to hear about it, she pulled herself together pretty quick."

"I see." The light was fading now and May fastened the collar of her grey flannel coat. She had begun to feel chilly. Her mind had gone back seventeen years. She recalled how she had sometimes wondered where her father was of an evening, why her mother's apathy had all at once turned into something more positive, manifesting itself in overt weeping, red eyes and occasionally a raised voice in the bedroom, and how astonished she had been one night when her father, usually so equable and kind, had become taciturn and short-tempered, so that she had crept into Flo's bed in order to seek comfort, just as Katy, albeit for different reasons, had crept into hers not so very long ago. Was there no peace or respite for a respectable woman, ever? She supposed that money and position helped.

Yet had there not been more than one ugly rumour going around the district lately connected with Sir Roger Broadbent and Grace Armitage. Was it possible that both Lady Broadbent and her own mother had, at some time or other in their lives, been sisters in distress?

"Anyway," Flo continued, "we'll just have to see what Mother says. I expect you were right to seize the opportunity. We'll all of us miss Katy. For one thing she's become more and more useful, but I know she ought to get out and I can't, for the life of me, think of a better place she could go at the moment."

They were nearing the head keeper's cottage now and became aware of Fred Ashford, gun under arm and retriever by his side, walking towards them. Usually he would only nod or, at best, give a curt greeting; but on this occasion he actually stopped and passed the time of day.

"I hear young Henry was home a little while back," he remarked laconically, as an opening gambit, his keen blue eyes looking first at one sister and then the other.

"Yes, Mr Ashford. Just for a week. He's signed on," Flo answered.

"So I heard. Married, by all accounts."

"Yes."

There was an uncertain pause in the conversation. Fred Ashford made a derisory sound, somewhere between a snort and a grunt. Then, beginning to move off again, he said, "Ah well, 'tis none of my business. Good-evening."

The sisters walked on, for the most part in silence. As they passed the west lodge and went out through the gates, Flo said quietly, "Now he's lost his only son, I reckon Fred would have liked to have had our Henry under him and trained him on. They say he's disappointed in Percy Hooper's brother. Best not mention our meeting him to Mother. I don't think she'll ever forgive Henry for becoming a regular, and we've got quite enough to tackle her with at the moment."

It was getting quite dark by the time they walked down River Lane and through the mill gates. The oil-lamp had been lit in the house and, at the still uncurtained window, Katy's slim figure could plainly be seen bending over the table, ironing.

"Poor kid," said May, softly, suddenly realising she had gone ahead without making any allowance for the person whom her proposition would most affect. Of all the family, she had always felt that her youngest sister had something about her which set her apart, that she was possibly destined for better things than sewing or ironing, or indeed, becoming nursery-maid to Alicia Moreton's first child.

Yet an inherent common sense told her that, although by no means beggars, the Lodges could certainly not afford to be choosers.

8

For the second time in less than three months, Flo stood on Wilhampton station, only now, instead of awaiting two arrivals from the London train, she was saying goodbye to two people who were setting out for the capital: Katy with a third-class, six-and-elevenpence-halfpenny single ticket; May, who was escorting her, with a twelve-shilling day return.

It was the first week in June and, although it was not yet nine o'clock, the sun had broken through the haze and the three sisters—especially the travellers, wearing straw hats and white gloves and carrying coats over their arms—were feeling the heat.

Katy's trunk—having been trundled up to the station earlier that morning by Herbie with a hand-truck—was now safely in the guard's van, packed, as perhaps only the Lodge family could pack, with a neatness which, had the Honourable Alicia Moreton or Nanny Barlow been able to take a look inside, would have more than reassured them—should they have needed reassurance—of the wisdom of taking on such a youthful and untried employee. Indeed, had Katy been older, it might well have made her new employer wonder whether she might have been rather better engaged as a lady's-maid.

For, instructed by Flo and May, Katy had meticulously placed all her bulkier accoutrements at the bottom: her winter boots, for instance, her new black indoor shoes, her bedroom slippers, all encased in appropriate bags, speedily run up on Flo's machine from the countless remnants of material stored away in old ottomans in the Mill House attic; then, stacked at each little corner, came such items as bible and prayer-book, writing-case containing note-pad, envelopes and two dozen penny-halfpenny stamps, a tin of acid drops (purchased by May from the Perricks' sweet-shop), a photograph of the family in a wooden frame, another bag—made from a scrap of the mayoress's latest cream tussore over-blouse—containing brush and comb, and yet another one—this time of jaconet—which held toilet requisites. Somewhat as a *pièce de résistance* was a white wicker sewing-basket—a present from Sarah—most beautifully appointed, together with an erstwhile tea-caddy full of assorted buttons. Along the whole length of one side of the trunk lay Flo's smart, new, black umbrella.

"After all," she had said, magnanimously, "we've got another one between us here." And making a flat even cover for this miscellany, Katy had spread two dozen, home-made, linen sanitary towels.

Next, swathed in copious sheets of tissue paper, there was a navy-blue winter coat made of West of England cloth and a carefully-folded velour hat, cardigan and mittens of the same colour. Above these lay two pairs of woollen combinations, knickers and knicker linings, a couple of liberty bodices, two flannelette night-dresses, a thick plaid dressing-gown and two blue serge uniform dresses. Dotted about to fill up convenient spaces were six pairs of neatly rolled-up black woollen stockings.

Further up in the hierarchy came lighter wear for summer: a second uniform dress of navy-blue tobralco—Katy was already wearing the other—a second sea-island cotton vest, cotton knickers and linings and two silk camisoles trimmed with lace. In the tray of the trunk lay four, pristine, white, starched aprons, two strange little white caps of a design particularly favoured by the Fairfax family, a dozen fine lawn hemstitched handkerchiefs embroidered 'K' which were tucked into a pink sateen sachet, together with a larger night-dress case of the same material, two nainsook nightdresses and petticoats, a hair-net and an assortment of ribbons. All this was topped by a white, picot-edged, muslin rectangle exactly the size of the trunk which "you could use," May had said, hopefully, "to throw over anything that you might want to keep specially clean. London's a terribly dusty place, by the sound of it."

The Lodge family might have been forcing its youngest member into personal service, but it was certainly doing so in style. It was doubtful whether any prospective nursery-maid had started off better equipped.

The train, belonging to the South-Western Railway Company, had drawn in dead on time. Mr Cutler, the station-master, was out on the platform to welcome its arrival and then, having allowed it the statutory four minutes' halt and seen all its passengers, together with their respective luggage, disembark and embark, he waited while the guard lifted his green flag by the last carriage and promptly blew his whistle. Flo stood waving while May, for the fraction of a moment, leaned out of the window, before hastily drawing it up and sitting down in the opposite corner to a somewhat tearful Katy, as the Brunel Belle steamed round the bend and pressed on towards the next stop at Westonbury.

"We'd best both have one of these," she said, taking a tin of Mothersill's Sea-sick Remedy out of her handbag. "It's a long journey and we don't quite know how we shall feel by and by. We'll probably be quite all right, but it's better to be safe than sorry. Nanny Barlow always told me she swore by Mothersill's whenever she and the family went travelling."

Still half bemused by all that had recently taken place, Katy did as she was bidden and then sat staring out of the window. She had not known what to think when she had first heard about the prospect of becoming a nursery-maid in the Moreton household. A little like Sarah, half of her immediately rejected the idea; the other half saw it as opportune. She was not particularly enamoured of babies, but the thing which, as far as she was concerned, tipped the scales was the fact that she would be going to *London*. Here, she differed from her mother, who looked on the capital as, at best, a place of artificiality and temptation—at worst, certain ruination. Sarah Lodge had heard for instance, about the white-slave traffic, in which young girls were lured by procurers and procuresses into seedy hotels and never seen or heard of again. There was also, she believed, a great deal of vice and gambling which went on in the West End; although exactly where or how Katy might come into this, she had no idea. Then there was the question of what she might do on her half day off each week. Sarah had a remote cousin living in Tooting Bec, but it might be far too long and hazardous a journey for her daughter to undertake.

When the letter had arrived, formally offering Katy the post at an initial salary of seven shillings and sixpence a week, although Sarah knew that in the name of good manners, it must be answered as soon as possible, she had nevertheless procrastinated. For several days and nights she had gone about in a state of such mixed feelings, that she was to be found, as she often was in times of stress, shaking her head and muttering: "I don't know. I don't know, I'm sure," as she bent over her washing or walked down the garden, or climbed the stairs to bed, spending an inordinate length of time on her knees to the Almighty before she actually got into it.

Flo's and May's disclosure about Neil's conduct had, of course, put an entirely different bearing on the situation. Had it not been for that, Sarah knew that she would never have entertained for a moment the idea of her youngest and most delicate daughter going off to London to become a nursery-maid in the Moretons' household. It might just have been acceptable, she felt—albeit chiding herself for the unworthy thought—if the Honourable Alicia's father-in-law, old Sir Harry Moreton, had died, and the family was in possession of Bishopsdown, his country seat in Suffolk. But she believed he was quite a sprightly septuagenarian and there was no knowing when his estate would pass to the young people and they would spend more time in safer, healthier surroundings, rather than, as at present, the other way about.

It was on the fourth day of Sarah's tribulation that May had suddenly come back into the living-room during the afternoon to fetch a pattern she had forgotten and found her mother sitting at the table, her head resting on her folded arms. Beside her lay pen and ink and writing-pad, on which she had written in immaculate copper-plate hand-writing: *The Mill House, Wilhampton, Nr. Westonbury. April 14th, 1919.* She looked up now and stared at her daughter. Almost, there was a defeated look in her eyes. "She'd best go," was all she had said. "How do I start the letter? Dear Mrs Moreton? Dear Madam? Madam?"

May had not been sure and she had gone to fetch Flo. Together, all three had agonised over what they trusted was a satisfactorily grateful, but not ingratiating, reply, and asking what date Katy would be required to take up her position. At the instigation of Flo, a small rider was added that if they could be sent details of the uniform which would be needed, this would be attended to forthwith.

It was not until long afterwards that Flo and May heard the reason for Sarah's final capitulation: that, by a curious coincidence, she had happened to meet Lilian Perrick by the mill gates earlier that day and the latter, although she had not exactly named names, had hinted that these days she felt it necessary to keep Ena under stricter supervision, not knowing who might be about. A twenty-year-old retarded youth had even more to do with Katy going off to the metropolis than she herself ever knew.

Now, as she sat in a third-class compartment of the Brunel Belle, all the traumas of the last-minute farewells over, she felt both scared and relieved: relieved that, whatever the outcome, there was now no turning back. She was glad of May's company, even though she knew that they were both equally ignorant of the capital. But with this particular sister Katy shared a special kind of empathy, which the episode over Neil had only served to foster. She felt secure in the knowledge that May—who she sensed had had, in some mysterious way, more experience of life than Flo—would invariably understand, that she would make light of Katy's fears, whereas Flo would be apt to ponder over them; and although she knew that both sisters had her ultimate good at heart and that by taking her responsibilities so seriously, Flo's judgment might be the more soundly reasoned, yet she sometimes felt that May's straight-from-the-heart spontaneity caused her often to arrive at equally satisfactory conclusions by happier and less laboured means. Had Flo been with her today, Katy felt sure that she would already have been worrying over the problems of porters and taxi-cabs at Waterloo, whereas May was now obviously viewing the whole business as a great adventure.

Having been lucky in securing window-seats opposite each other, more than once her elder sister leant across and caught Katy's arm, pointing out some item of interest; and the latter, however apprehensive she might have been feeling at entering such a strange new world, had had her mind taken off it by being forced to admire some unusual scenery or, as they neared the capital itself, a whole host of enormous buildings, the like of which neither of them had ever seen.

Once on Westminster Bridge—their arrival at the station and the securing of both a porter and a cab having gone surprisingly smoothly—May, whose remarks had been made *sotto voce* in the railway carriage in deference to the other occupants, now burst forth in unrestrained pleasure. "Oh, chippatoo! Oh, chippatoo! Look, Katy. Just fancy. That'll be the Houses of Parliament and Big Ben. You'll be able to come down here on your half-day, maybe, and look for as long as you like." Little did either sister know then that Katy would actually be able to see both edifices from her tiny bedroom at 89 Upper Brook Street.

When the cabby was forced to draw up for a while in the centre of the bridge, and the River Thames, sporting innumerable little tugs and barges, lay sparkling in the sun for as far as the eye could see on either side of them, May could hardly contain herself. "Oh, Katy, it reminds me of a poem we learnt at school. I wish I could remember it. By Wordsworth, I think. Something about 'Earth has not anything to show more fair.' Isn't London just beautiful? I'm sure you're going to be very happy here."

Despite her now increasing nervousness, it was hard for Katy not to share, just for a little while, some of her elder sister's enthusiasm, although the grave, forbidding appearance of Mr Walker, the Moreton's butler, as he came—as if by magic—down the steps of Number 89 exactly as the cab drew up at the door, and quickly instructed the driver to go round the corner to a side entrance, soon sent her spirits sinking again. It made her more painfully aware than ever that she was, after all, going into *domestic* service, something to which she knew that her mother, for all her curiously sudden acquiescence, was still most strongly opposed.

Moreover, although she was relieved to find that her trunk, with all its precious possessions, was being efficiently dealt with by a young man in a baize apron and that a plump, pleasant-looking parlourmaid had arrived on the scene to show her and May up to the nursery quarters on the fourth floor, by the time she found herself in the presence of Nanny Barlow, Katy became practically tongue-tied. She had forgotten just how large the woman was and how well-known her reputation for sizing people up in a disconcerting fashion, her eyes missing nothing as they travelled up and down, back and forth, all over one, while they seemed to search for an undone button or a stray wisp of hair. Yet, possibly having secretly approved of the slender, immaculately turned-out little figure before her, Nanny Barlow now held out her hand agreeably enough and said, "My, Katy, and how grown up you are. I'm very glad you've come to help me well before the bairn is due. I hear that you sew and knit well, and there is still much you can be doing. Besides, it will give you good time to get used to the ways of the household." And then, turning quickly to May, almost as if she felt that she had paid more than enough attention to her new trainee, she added, "I'm sure we shall get along fine, Miss Lodge, just as long as your sister is conscientious and willing to learn and always remembers who she is working for. There is no better household, other than Lady Fairfax's own, of course, into which she could have come, I'm sure."

May did not seem to take such words amiss. Katy, in her innermost heart, did. Somewhere, beneath the pale, polite demeanour, lurked the Katy of spirit, the Katy of her great-grandmother, the Katy of the fairground who had sung *Our Lodger's Such a Nice Young Man.* She did not feel quite right in the nursery of 89 Upper Brook Street and hoped that she would not always be a nursery-maid or, at best, a children's nanny.

As the trio sat down to a simple stew and rice pudding, brought up by yet another minion in the Moreton establishment, such feelings were unfortunately only reinforced when Nanny Barlow suddenly said, "Tomorrow, Katy, you will be able to fetch our meals from the kitchen yourself. But with your young legs that should not be too much for you." Sadly, what Katy was finding too much for her now was trying to finish the rice pudding which had been heaped on to her plate.

Although she was dreading her sister's departure after the meal was over, it was a relief when Nanny Barlow offered to accompany May "just for a few steps", as she put it, in order to point out the way to the place she was set on seeing: Bond Street, and how from thence she could easily walk down to Piccadilly and catch a bus to Waterloo. Katy was glad that neither of them could see the tears which fell fast as, miserably, she then began to unpack her trunk in a room which, for all its fine views over London, seemed little more than a cupboard.

9

Alicia Moreton and Marianne Lodge both gave birth to sons within a few weeks of each other, Alicia's child, John William Harry, arriving at the end of August, Marianne's Frank François (the two names bestowed on the infant in an effort at some kind of *rapprochement* with Sarah) being born in the middle of September.

The latter made no comment as to the alleged premature arrival of her new grandchild. The fact that there would now be another Frank in the family was merely acknowledged by a carefully-worded letter to

Henry, saying that she trusted the little boy would live up to his deceased uncle's good name. She did not write to her daughter-in-law, nor send any kind of token to the child. Neither did she make any reference to wishing to see Frank François, even though Henry was now much nearer home, having recently been posted to Aldershot. Sarah Lodge had, in fact, with a ruthlessness which often confounded her family, cut Henry off, not with the proverbial shilling—which, in any case, she did not have to give—but with the affection which she might otherwise have accorded him, had he not acquired a foreign wife of dubious status, who had produced a child within less than seven months of marriage. "There were," as May and Flo remarked to each other after hearing the news, "no flies on Mother," apart, they agreed, from the extraordinary tenderness which she showed towards Neil, invariably turning a blind eye to his unfortunate behaviour, as if by pretending he was not as he was, she could almost bring herself—and, hopefully, others—to think of him as normal.

But that autumn and winter May had many more things on her mind than making conjectures about Sarah's character. What was bothering her was the obvious deterioration in Neil's state of mind, and, though not so obvious but strangely insidious, the deterioration in Flo's state of health. She could not help noticing her elder sister's pallor, the deep shadows under her eyes—especially at certain times of the month—and a lassitude totally alien to her usual hard-working nature. Once or twice on such occasions, May was surprised at being asked to take over the machining for a day or two. Flo was 'flooding', as she put it, and the constant movement of her legs on the treadle made it worse.

"You ought to see Dr Fitzherbert," May said, one

afternoon in early November, when she felt sure that Flo was in more discomfort than she cared to admit. "He'd give you a tonic."

"Maybe. I'll see." The older woman bent to pick up the flat-iron that was heating on a tripod over the grate. "I don't much care for the thought of him examining me," she added.

"But I'd be there." It went without saying that a female member or friend of the Lodge family always accompanied another female patient on a visit to the doctor.

"Oh, I know. But let's just wait a while. Could be, I'm a bit like Katy. Remember how bad her periods were when they first came on after Father died."

May was silent. That was different, she felt. Young girls often flooded at the start of menstruation. Many women flooded at the change of life. But Flo was only thirty. That event might well not overtake her until she was fifty or more. Why, Sarah herself, though irregular, hadn't finished yet, although she was always trying to disguise the fact from her children, as if there was something indecent in such a state of affairs in a sober, middle-aged widow. May went on stitching buckram into a collar, listening to the hissing sound of the iron as it made contact with the damp cloth laid over a partially completed broadcloth coat.

Presently Flo said, "Shall we give over now when I've finished this? We can take the other stuff up to the house to do after tea. There's a lot of hemming and oversewing to get through. I must say I miss our Katy in more ways than one, don't you? She was a better little helpmate than we realised."

"Yes." May started gathering up the various bits and pieces around her. It was unlike Flo to want to leave the workroom so early. Usually they kept on until the light had all but faded, but she guessed that today, just standing over the ironing, had probably fatigued her sister enough.

Now, as May came towards the door of the Mill House, it irked her to find Mr Fuller returning the tea-tray which Sarah had taken up to his office earlier that afternoon. There was no need for him to do so. She felt it was slightly *infra dig* for a manager to perform so menial a task. Yet she knew perfectly well why he did. For although George Fuller was a married man with two children, she was aware that he fancied her and would make any excuse to visit the house on the off-chance of seeing her. She disliked him intensely and, whenever his motor-bike could be heard chugging in or out of the mill gates, she was apt to make disparaging remarks. With his scrawny neck and weak blue eyes, he reminded her a little of Ernest Fielding. "Here comes Duck and Collar," she would sometimes say, much to her mother's disapproval, or, "I don't know why his lordship has to make quite such a din, unless it's to make sure we all catch sight of him on his chariot riding by."

Once, when Sarah had had a bad cold and she herself had felt obliged to take Mr Fuller's tea-tray up to his office at the appointed time of three o'clock, he had tried to get her to sit down and share some of the food with him. "Your mother makes such delicious cakes, Miss Lodge. I fear I'm fast putting on weight, but I just can't resist them. I am not used to such luxury at home." And May had inwardly fumed because, although his wife was reputed to be careless and lazy, she felt that it did not absolve him from making veiled references to such failings in the worst possible taste. She had been almost rude as she made a hurried departure, saying that she had too much to do to waste time eating in the middle of the afternoon. But, even so, it had not put the wretched man off. He had said that this must be the reason why she kept so slim a waist and, as she went down the steep wooden steps, she had still heard him muttering obsequiously in the background, "So good . . . so industrious . . ."

On this particular afternoon she nodded curtly and would have gone into the house without a word, had he not purposely waylaid her. "Miss Lodge, I was wondering . . . could I speak to you for a moment about your brother?"

"My *brother?"* May stared at him, incredulously, her tiny figure temporarily coming to a halt, while curiosity, even fear, for the moment overcame the desire to shake the man off. Behind her, she could hear Flo locking up the workroom and then, unfortunately, going into the closet before coming up the garden path. "What about him?" she asked, guardedly.

From the window of the living-room in which a lamp had just been lit, she could see the figures of her mother and Neil moving about. It had seemed a relief that afternoon when Sarah had suggested that she should look after her son because he would be able to undertake the small job in which he delighted: that of scooping up into a wheel-barrow the horse's dung left after the carrier's cart had made a delivery to the mill, which it had done just before dinner-time. Surely, Mr Fuller wasn't going to make some objection to that, was he? After all, it was good to have the main pathway cleared of manure and sometimes Ernest Fielding asked for a little of it to put in the rain-water-butt by his green-house, so that his precious orchids might reap the benefit when they were watered.

At length, George Fuller replied in the kind of Uriah Heep manner with which she had come to associate him, "I hate to say this Miss Lodge, but I thought it best to warn you rather than distress your poor mother further."

"Yes?" Impatiently, her tone demanded that he got on with whatever it was he had to say. He looked so silly, she felt, standing there with the tea-tray in his hands, but she made no attempt to take it from him.

Still the man parried. Bitterly, she resented the way his eyes appraised her, as he at last continued, "I'm afraid your brother seems not altogether to have stuck to his little task this afternoon. He was found in one of the mill buildings, the one where the women and girls work. That could be dangerous . . ." He coloured slightly. "The machinery," he added, with a small embarrassed cough.

"Yes. Yes, of course. I'm sorry. My mother usually keeps a good eye out for him." May was finding it increasingly hard to remain civil.

"Oh, I know she does, Miss Lodge. She is a wonderful woman, altogether admirable. You all are. But I believe, lately . . your brother has been a little more difficult to manage?"

May bit her lip. What a long time Flo was being in the closet. After all, she was the eldest, wasn't she? Duck and Collar should have addressed his complaint to her. Then, quickly, May's innate sense of fairness reasserted itself. Flo wasn't well, not that Mr Fuller could have been expected to know that. Yet even so, there was no reason for him not to have approached May herself. She was hardly a child and, besides, she had happened to be around. She could just as well deal with the matter.

"I'll see it doesn't occur again, Mr Fuller," she replied, coldly, this time taking the tea-tray and disappearing indoors.

She could tell immediately that Sarah was in one of her states or, rather, silent humours. May wondered how Mr Fuller had heard of the incident so quickly. His office window did not look out on the main pathway where Neil had been 'working'. She wondered whether one of the older women had brought Neil back to the house and then, relishing her role of informer in the drama, gone to find Tom Henstridge. Please God it wouldn't have been Cissy Lawes. Cissy had always been the main target for her mother's contempt. Loud-mouthed, forward and 'no better than she should be' was how Sarah invariably referred to her. In the light of hindsight, May realised that such hostility towards the woman and, indeed, all the female members of the staff who had been taken on during the war, probably sprang from her mother's deep feelings of jealousy and resentment due to their close proximity to her late husband—not that she could remember her father being anything other than beyond reproach, in so far as the management of the mill was concerned.

Sarah did not say anything about the afternoon's occurrence when May came in. For one thing, although she would die rather than admit it, she felt she might have been somewhat to blame. Yet she kept telling herself that she had watched Neil just as carefully as usual, firstly from out of the window and then, when he had got up as far as the furthermost building, she had kept popping out of the front door to see how he was getting on. When she thought he was almost finished she had gone inside to take a cake out of the oven, expecting any minute to hear him trundling his wheel-barrow past the house and down the garden path. When he did not, she had gone out to take a further look, surprised to find the barrow still where it was and Neil nowhere to be seen. She had begun to run then, picking up her long black skirt and stumbling in her lace-up boots on the uneven ground.

Her fright had not lasted long. Instinct told her to look in the women's building first and, sure enough, there was Neil with Cissy Lawes and one or two others laughing at him and throwing the loose wool, which they should have been feeding into one of the noisy giant machines, all over Neil so that he was beginning to look like a snowman. They had stopped at once at the sight of Sarah and, shamefacedly, gone back to their work while, stony-eyed and without a word, she had caught hold of her son's arm and hurried him away.

Now, as the damp, raw, November evening began closing in on the Mill House and its occupants, there was a deep sense of unease in the living-room, each member of the family strangely quiet and subdued. After tea, Flo, unsure of exactly what had taken place, but sensing that she would be unlikely to hear until she and May were in bed, picked up her sewing, listlessly. In any case, at the moment she felt almost too drained and tired to bother. Sarah simply knitted in silence, a long grey woollen sock for either Herbie or Neil gradually taking shape as the clicking of her steel needles mingled with the ticking of the grandfather clock in the corner: May worked some buttonholes on the nigger-brown herringbone tweed suit they were making for Mrs Donaldson, the Rector's wife. Neil, still with a few flecks of wool in his hair and on his jacket, sat hunched by the fire opposite his mother, occasionally, under her watchful gaze, prodding it with a poker through the iron bars of the grate.

All of them went to bed early. Sarah had even taken the lantern and locked the mill gates soon after the six o'clock hooter had sounded for the men to stop work. George Fuller's motor-bike had been heard chugging by some time before that. His hours were naturally not those of the mill-hands. Nowadays, since Flo and May had ceased to lead the kind of social life they had been used to during the war, Sarah was apt to 'shut up shop' earlier than ever, for although Tom Henstridge had duplicate keys with which he opened the gates each morning, the nightly ritual of locking-up was completely in her hands. It seemed to her daughters that she derived a definite sense of satisfaction, security and even power for this to be so, to know that her flock, albeit diminished in size, was, as her late husband would also have wished, safely indoors, if not actually in bed.

Tonight, after drinking a little soup made from the stock-pot she invariably kept on the range during winter, everyone was upstairs before nine. Sarah had seen to Neil's undressing and then, with candle-stick and matches—carefully never left with him for a moment—had retired to her own room. Overhead, she could hear the girls murmuring, but only for a little while. Presently, all was quiet save for Neil's snores, but she herself was unable to sleep. The clock above the town-hall in the market-square struck the hours and still she tossed and turned. A kind of nameless panic took hold of her. For all her outward appearance of hardness, adopted for self-preservation's sake, she was much more vulnerable than even any member of her family knew. The previous day's events had upset her stomach and, at five that morning, after only a couple of hours' sleep, she was obliged to take the lantern and go outside to the closet. Nothing, save extreme urgency, would have made her use the commode on such an occasion.

She must have been gone, she supposed afterwards, less than ten minutes. She had returned and climbed back into bed, praying that she might just drop off again for a few moments before the girls' shrill alarum rang out and they came down from the attic and through her own room on their way to wash in the mill.

But sleep still eluded her. Flo and May appeared at

six o'clock and then reappeared not long afterwards with the customary dipper of soapy water which they placed by the basin on her washstand. Wearily, Sarah performed her morning ablutions, put in her false teeth and began to dress, lacing up her stays with fingers which she had noticed lately were becoming increasingly stiff. She had just put on her working-dress and was pinning up her hair, when the six-thirty hooter sounded, and the men who had been patiently waiting outside the gates now streamed through them and jostled noisily past the house. Sarah sighed, remembering the days when Sidney would have been out to start them all off. With resignation, she picked up her candlestick and went into Neil's bedroom to shake him awake, knowing that no extraneous sounds were usually of any assistance at such times.

His bed was empty. For a moment, open-mouthed, she simply stared at it, the only movement in the room being the flickering of her shadow on the opposite wall. Then, with a small stifled scream, she let the candlestick crash to the ground and heard Flo and May hurrying up the stairs in the dark.

Groping, May managed to find the matches, strike one and bring some light back on the scene, after which she, too, saw the empty bed.

"Oh, my God!" The blasphemous ejaculation, coming instinctively from her lips, very different from her usual, happy-go-lucky 'Oh, chippatoo!' would, at any other time, have elicited a rebuke from her mother. Now, all three women simply looked at each other in horror and bewilderment.

Then, her brain suddenly getting to work again, Sarah said, quickly, "Find Herbie. Neil can't have gone long. I went to the closet about five, but I was back in ten minutes."

Yet, even as she spoke, all of them were aware that a lot could have happened since then.

Flo ran up through the now lighted mill, already thrumming with life at the start of a new day. May, clutching a torch, sped towards the mill-race. Sarah took her lantern and hurried, almost involuntarily, towards the Perrick house. Although she realised that Neil had not taken her keys and that it would have been virtually impossible for him to climb over the gates, yet she knew—as she supposed her simpleton son, in his slow, confused mind, probably also knew—that there were other means of exit and entrance to the mill: small, secret and dangerous, a labyrinth of little passages, narrow planks without hand-rails, spanning swift, sinister streams and mostly known only to those who lived and worked there. The gas-lamps were still on in River Lane shining over the deep, murky, silent water which flowed beside it. Anxiously, Sarah held her lantern on high, the better to light it up, but it picked out little save the grey-green undulating weeds and the Perrick boy's boat, moored on the opposite bank.

No one found Neil until daylight. His body, clad only in night-shirt and jacket, was spotted by Tom Henstridge, lying against the hatch of one of the tributaries which branched out close to the mill-race. Herbie and Tom brought it back to the house and Dr Fitzherbert was sent for, not, as they all knew, that there was anything he could do—at least, not for Neil. The boy had been in the water some time. But it was imperative that the doctor should come, at once, just as the Reverend Donaldson would be needed a little later on.

It was May who hurried up to the surgery, knowing that she would find Abie Grant, the dispenser, in his starched white coat, already busy amongst his large glass jars of Mist. Pot. Brom., Mist. Gent. Alk., or 'Grey' powder. In his tiny box-like room, Abie could be relied upon to be almost permanently at the ready, checking his supplies and waiting to produce whatever bottle of medicine that Dr Fitzherbert prescribed, meticulously doing up each item in stiff white wrapping-paper securely fastened by a blob of red sealing-wax, its label proclaiming in his immaculate script the name and dosage for whomsoever it was required.

Today, the place was already filling up as May came through the entrance, hurried over to Abie's small hideout and rapped on the panelled 'window'. It shot up at once and Abie's face, behind its steel spectacles, peered at her cautiously. In many ways, he was not only the doctor's dispenser but also his protector; for Abie was possessed of an uncanny ability to know whether a certain person was crying wolf, or trying to be seen by the doctor ahead of others without due cause. There was not an inhabitant in the whole of Wilhampton or, indeed, most of the surrounding district, whom he did not know and whose character he could not size up to a nicety. Now, his mind immediately went back to the day, just after last Christmas, when it had been Flo Lodge rapping on the panel of his little dispensary when her father was dying. Could it be, he wondered, that this time it was Sarah . . .? He remembered that she had gone down badly after Sidney's death. He had scarcely seen her in the town all the year.

"Mr Grant." Conscious that her abrupt and purposeful entry had aroused more than a little interest and that several pairs of eyes and ears were waiting on her with curiosity, May leaned well forward across the prescription shelf and whispered her message.

Abie, registering both shock and concern, gave a quick, "Wait here, my dear," and drew down his little shutter. Almost immediately, he reappeared through another door at the end of the waiting-room and summoned May into Dr Fitzherbert's inner sanctum. The good man, who fortunately had not started to see his first patient, was already putting on his coat. "Your poor mother," he said, and then, as they hurried back to the Mill House together, "Your poor, poor mother," he said again. For so short a distance, he had deemed it quicker to go on foot, much as he was beginning to rely—especially in emergencies—on the 12-horse-power Doctor's Standard Coupé which he had recently acquired in favour of his old pony and trap; although, even in this, he seldom drove at more than fifteen miles per hour, and still proceeded to lean slightly forward on going up hill and backwards on coming down, just as he had done to help along his one-horse-power former mode of transport.

Herbie and Tom Henstridge were at the door when they arrived, the under-manager keeping a sharp look-out for any would-be ghoulish inquisitors and chivvying on any of the hands who gave the slightest appearance of dawdling past the house as they went about their duties. Inside, upstairs in Neil's room, Sarah was kneeling by the body which, still muddied, soaking wet and reeking of river, had been laid on the bed. Tears were streaming down her face. Beside her, chalk-white and shaking, stood Flo, trying, without success, to get her mother to take a little brandy kept by the family strictly for medicinal purposes only.

Yet, even in her grief, Sarah remembered her manners. She stood up on the doctor's arrival and he, gently hinting that he would like to make his examination in private, suggested to Flo and May that they should take their mother downstairs to lie on the living-room couch. Unwillingly, Sarah allowed herself to be led away and Dr Fitzherbert closed the door.

Presently, he, too, came down to join them, doing his best to comfort Sarah and asking that someone should come back to the surgery in half an hour's time to fetch a sedative which he would get Abie to make up. Then, at the front door of the house, while Flo was seeing him out, he said, quietly, "No need to say anything to your mother now, my dear, but I'm afraid that there will have to be an inquest."

"An *inquest?*" Flo's eyes opened wide with fear, her nostrils flared. "Oh, *no!*" She put out a hand and steadied herself at the threshold. She could feel a sudden discharge of blood between her legs. Her forehead broke out in a sweat. Dr Fitzherbert laid one of his own hands on her shoulder.

"You must be brave, my dear." His keen blue eyes under the bushy eyebrows searched hers. It was hard for him to tell whether her present appearance was all to do with the tragedy which had just taken place. He hoped so, but he did not like the feel of her thin, bony shoulder, the way she seemed to have lost so much weight since he had last seen her. "It will only be a formality," he said. "I'll try to see that Dr Machin makes it as short and painless for you all as possible."

"But you mean Mother will have to attend?"

"Well, yes. She was the last to see your brother alive. But try not to worry. I will get in touch with the authorities and someone will come to take Neil's body away to the mortuary as soon as possible. And I know that the Rector will be down at once when I send word to tell him what has happened."

Flo nodded. "Thank you, Doctor."

It seemed to her like only yesterday that death had come to the Mill House, that the surrounding waters had, in some mysterious way, claimed another victim; except that in Sidney Lodge's case there had been no question of an inquest.

10

Katy was putting some of John William's nappies through the mangle in the basement of Number 89, when Nanny Barlow came to find her. She was surprised. It was unlike such an august personage to make many sorties below stairs. Katy was fast learning what a tight, enclosed, little world it was on the nursery floor of the household to which she now, so unexpectedly, belonged.

"How are you getting on, my dear?" The use of the endearment made Katy even more surprised. Though basically a kind, good woman, Nanny Barlow was quite a hard taskmaster. It was usually 'Katy this' and 'Katy that', and 'Mind you rinse those nappies well, especially the Harringtons. If any soap stays in them, a baby can get nappy rash. None of mine has ever had that.' So far, Katy had hardly been allowed to touch John William herself.

"I've nearly done, Nanny," she replied, quickly. "Was there something else you wanted me to do?"

"Presently, my child. But as soon as you've done down here, come straight upstairs. I've something to say to you."

Katy completed her task, wonderingly. The woman hadn't sounded exactly cross, but the "something to say to you" seemed ominous. She tried to think of what she might have done wrong. Gathering up the pile of damp nappies, she took them into the drying-room, let down the wooden rack from the ceiling, hung them over it and hoisted it back into position again. It was a shame, she thought, that they couldn't go out into the garden and have what her mother would have considered essential: 'a good blow'. But even if Number 89 had a garden into which they could go, it wouldn't have been any good. As May had rightly said, she was finding London, for all the beauty of its parks and splendour of its fashionable West End residences, an incredibly dusty, dirty—and often very lonely—place.

Back upstairs, she found Nanny Barlow sitting beside the heavily-guarded fire, giving John William his bottle. Although the older woman was far too loyal a servant ever to have voiced such an opinion, Katy sensed that it was a source of regret to her that the baby had been weaned from birth and never offered the breast. But she discovered that this was quite usual in such circumstances, for she had written to May about it, who had explained in her next letter that Mrs Moreton probably had so many engagements to fulfil which would make breast-feeding impossible, "and besides", she had added, "the dear thing would want to get her lovely figure back quickly." Katy had pondered over this for a while, wondering about the importance of both Mrs Moreton's figure and the social round in which she and her husband took such an active part: the almost nightly dinners, dances or theatres which seemed to take place in London's West End. Often, she had lain awake, wishing she might be part of them, vicariously savouring a sudden burst of laughter, the sound of a cab stopping outside the house, the light-hearted exchange of goodnights, footsteps on the stairs. Sometimes, she even caught a faint whiff of cigar smoke.

But today, she simply stood enquiringly at the door of the nursery, a small, upright, fetching little figure in her cap and apron. She had filled out since her arrival and, contrary to what might have been expected, London had put some colour into her cheeks. Even in the few months she had been away from home, Katy Lodge, always a fast learner, had definitely acquired a certain poise.

"You wanted me, Nanny?"

"Yes, Katy. Sit down."

She walked across the room and took the wicker chair opposite the fireplace.

For a few moments there was silence, except for the sound of the baby sucking and an occasional spluttering noise as a live coal fell from the grate. Then, when John William had finished his bottle Nanny Barlow sat him up gently to be winded and said, "I had a letter from your eldest sister this morning, Katy."

"From Flo?" Terror seized her. Imagination ran riot. Could something have happened? To Mother? To May?

"Don't take on, child. It's probably all for the best. God's will, I daresay."

"But what . . .?"

"Your brother, Neil. He was found drowned yesterday morning."

"Drowned? Oh *no."* Immediately, her youthful, generous heart went out to Sarah. Hard though she often appeared, and seemingly unfair in her strange, obsessive love for her youngest son, Katy could not bear to think of her mother's suffering. As for herself, she simply found it difficult to take in, to realise that this unfortunate brother of hers, so limited and inarticulate, yet whose presence had been such a constant, positive factor in all their lives, day in and day out, for twenty-one years, was no longer living. What would it be like at home without him?

"The funeral . . .?" she enquired, tentatively.

"It will not be until a week today. Next Saturday. But it seems . . . your family think it best you should not go. The travelling . . ." Nanny Barlow added, quietly. Both knew that, expense apart, Katy was considered to be on the young side for undertaking such a journey alone. What neither knew was that Flo and May had managed to overrule their mother in the decision not to drag her youngest daughter home; for, even in the midst of her shock and sorrow, Sarah had nevertheless said that it was only right and proper that all the other members of the family should attend—even Henry.

"I see." Katy still felt numbed. She could not cry for, since the night when Neil had made his hideous and frightening foray up to her bed in the attic, she had shunned him. Though he was her own kith and kin, he now filled her with revulsion. Whereas, at one time, his cheerful idiot's smile had simply been seen as inoffensive and acceptable—even, at times, a cause for compassion and tenderness—she no longer experienced any such emotion. She looked on him as an alien: an ugly, loose-limbed, ill-co-ordinated predator, demanding and soaking up, like some huge sponge, all the love which Sarah should, by rights, have been giving to the rest of her brood.

Suddenly, she heard Nanny Barlow start to speak again. "I'll get Clara to take you along to the Grosvenor Chapel in South Audley Street on Saturday afternoon. Maybe you would like to go inside and say a prayer or two while the funeral's taking place. You could be with them in spirit, like?"

Katy looked at her, dumbfounded. Is that what others did? She did not care for the idea at all. She and Nanny Barlow had often passed the chapel on their walks. It was such a grand place. She wouldn't dare to go inside alone. She wondered if Clara, the head parlourmaid, would come in with her. In any case, what could she pray? She could say the Lord's prayer, she supposed, and ask Him to take care of her mother. When people died, the bereaved sometimes prayed for their souls, didn't they? Would Neil go to heaven? If one was mentally deficient, how much soul did one have? She began to feel guilty at not being able to feel sad at Neil's passing. But wasn't it better for him not to go on living? She sat staring at the fire, lost in thought, thoughts somewhat unusual and mature for one of such tender years and scanty education.

"There now. You'd best be washing John William's bottle, Katy," Nanny Barlow broke in on her reverie. "Then put it in the bowl of water on the gas-ring and I'll do the boiling-up later. Mind and clean the teat with salt, and rinse it well." She got up and took the infant back to his crib. She was glad the girl had taken the news so sensibly. She was a good little thing. Well brought up. Came from a reliable family, apart from the poor boy who had just died. She wondered how that had happened. Flo hadn't said much. She'd probably get a letter from Mrs Harwood, the Fairfaxes' housekeeper, in a day or two, telling her more about it. She wondered what John William's mother would say when she returned from the charity bazaar she'd been attending all day. She would be sure to be concerned for, like her own mother, she was a good mistress, always taking an interest in the personal lives of her employees.

Alicia Moreton was, indeed, extremely distressed when she came up to the nursery after tea and heard of the tragedy. Fortunately, Nanny Barlow had been able to have a word with her in private, for Katy had been in her little bedroom busy writing home.

"I'll come back and see her when I've dressed for dinner, Nanny. Best to let her finish her letter now, so that she can run out with it to catch the seven-thirty post. Otherwise I think someone else will have to take it to the special eight o'clock box, as there's a fog coming down fast. I'm sure she's hoping it will be in the Wilhampton Sunday delivery tomorrow. Perhaps you would see she puts an extra halfpenny stamp on, in case it has to go into the later collection."

Charles Moreton was none too pleased when his wife failed to join him in the drawing-room before dinner that night. Aperitifs were just coming into fashion and, although at the homes of their respective parents these were never served unless there were guests, Charles had acquired a liking for them each evening, even if Alicia, who was practically teetotal, only sipped a little fruit-juice in order to keep him company.

He had scarcely seen her since she had come in. He himself had been at his club all the afternoon, and they had simply exchanged a few remarks in the hall about the pea-souper outside and the time that it had taken Rutherford, their chauffeur, to drive her from Belgravia. He recalled her having murmured something about having to go to see the new nursery-maid later on who had suffered a bereavement. Sometimes he felt that she overdid her involvement with their servants, especially on the personal side. *Noblesse oblige* was such a motivating force in the Fairfax family, not that his own mother, when she had been alive, hadn't done her bit in that direction. But Lady Fairfax was a kind of queen in the art. He hoped Alicia wasn't going to turn out just like her. She had seemed so happy and carefree when they had been engaged. He supposed that John William coming along so soon after their marriage had somehow sobered her. It would have been nice to get right away now, just the two of them, especially as the nursery arrangements appeared to be working so well, even though he himself found Nanny Barlow a tiresome old battle-axe. She seemed to think she was still as much in charge of his wife as John William. He really must try to put a stop to these long sessions they had together, which he felt sure were having an adverse effect on Alicia. He had a good mind to take her abroad for their first wedding anniversary that was just coming up. His job in the city was not arduous and there was no reason why they should not take advantage of the new commercial airline service which had just opened. They could easily flip over to Paris for a few days. He would mention it when she came down.

Alicia did not arrive until the gong sounded and during the meal it was difficult to say much while Walker, the butler, waited on them. But once back in the drawing-room, he brought the subject up.

"Fly to Paris?" She frowned. "You must be mad."

"Why?"

"I'm a mother now. You have a son and heir."

"So?"

"I wouldn't trust myself to one of those machines."

He was silent in the face of her all too logical objection.

"Besides," she continued, "we'll all be going away soon. Christmas isn't far off and Mummy wants us to stay at Wilhampton for at least a month."

"A *month?*"

"Yes. I mean, you could always come up to town in the week if you've got to, but it'll be nice to get some country air. I think John William could do with it. And Nanny can't wait. Neither, I expect, can Katy."

"Katy?"

She wished he wouldn't keep repeating her last words in such a stupid, parrot-fashion way. She supposed he had forgotten where their nursery-maid had come from.

"Yes, Katy," she repeated. "Don't you remember?

The girl from the Felt Mills. Her youngest brother was drowned there yesterday. That's why I was up in the nursery talking to her before dinner."

"Oh, I see. I'm sorry."

He was standing with his arm on the mantelshelf, one foot on the fender, half turned towards the fire. She was conscious of how strikingly handsome he was, even though his figure did not cut quite the same dash as it had in the uniform which he had worn a year ago. Her mind went back to that time. She had only known him three months before they were married. It had been such a whirlwind romance. The war had still been on; there had been no knowing that he might be killed. Sometimes she had felt unable to wait. She suspected that John William had been conceived on their wedding-night.

Presently, he turned, came across to where she was sitting and knelt by her chair.

"Alicia, darling." He took hold of both her hands and looked at her intently. "A penny for them."

She flushed. "Not for sale, I'm afraid."

He lowered his head into her lap. They were both the same age but she felt altogether older, as if he needed not only a wife, but someone else: a mother perhaps, even more than John William who, in any case, had an experienced nanny to take care of him.

Suddenly, he looked up. His smile was totally disarming. "We don't," he said, "often have an evening to ourselves. Shall we make it an early one?"

11

"So the long and the short of it is Ada," wrote Emily Harwood to Nanny Barlow, "that there's to be an inquest. I expect," the letter went on,

that's why they didn't want Katy back for the funeral. There have been some ugly rumers going around. By all accounts, the boy has been making a proper nuisance of himself lately. Well, I mean, what can you expect? His *age*, you see. And he's very strong. I always said Mrs Lodge ought to have had him committed. It wasn't fair on the others, specally the little young one up with you. It seems as how he's been trying to give the family the slip more than once since she left. Been found in the place where the women work and also (here the word 'loitering' had been misspelt twice and firmly crossed out) hanging about up River Lane. At least, that's what Lilian Perrick says, although you can't always be sure, with her. She's been hinting he was after Ena. The trouble is that Ena's brother Archie, you know the one who never seems to be able to stay in a job longer than you can say Jack Robinson, is said to have been out and about early the morning Neil got drowned. If you ask me, Archie's a bit of a pocher. I know Fred Ashford thinks he's up to all the tricks. Anyway, with his mother always saying such bad things about Neil, you can't help wondering, can you? I mean, if the two boys met there could have been a bit of funny business. One of the mill men, Bob Harrison, says when he was on his way to work he saw Archie coming out of the little allyway over the footbridge into River Lane just after half past six, Bob being late as usual . . .

Nanny Barlow put down the letter and sighed. She knew all about gossip. She wasn't above wanting to hear a little herself from time to time; but Emmie's letter really had gone a bit far. She could just imagine the talk in Wilhampton. Now that the war, with all its constant excitements and tragedies, was over, any occurrence such as this would be bound to arouse more than usual public interest. The local inhabitants would revel in it. Poor Sarah Lodge. How it would distress her.

Sarah was, indeed, not just distressed. She was anguished. Her family had never known her in quite such a state. True, she had grieved bitterly over her eldest son's death, even more over her husband's. But, however poignant and deeply-felt her grief had been, it was within the bounds of normality.

Now, to her daughters, there seemed something altogether alien, even frightening, in her conduct. She withdrew into some private world where it was impossible to reach her. She stared at Flo and May as if they were strangers; and many was the night when, after the men had gone home, they would find her, lantern in hand, going through the mill towards the place where Neil's body had been found, often with the wind cutting across the meadows, loosening her hair and tearing at her skirts, while the sound of the mill-race echoed unceasingly in the background. On one such occasion, May had led her home gently, ahnost as if she were a child, saying, "There, there, Mother. 'Tis no good. Father wouldn't want you to take on so. No more would Neil, if he knew."

And Sarah had looked at her mutely, allowing herself to be taken indoors and sat by the fire, where she suddenly covered her face in her hands and broke into almost silent, yet uncontrollable weeping.

"I don't," said May to Flo, one evening when they were in bed, "see how she's going to be well enough to get to Westonbury for the inquest if she carries on like this." It had been one thing for Sarah, supported by Henry and Herbie on either side of her, to manage the funeral, but the ordeal ahead, so unimaginable, so public, which neither of the men, owing to their respective occupations, would be free to attend, was something dreaded by them all.

"We could ask Dr Fitzherbert about her," said Flo, suddenly. "Perhaps I'll go up to the surgery and have a word with him tomorrow."

"Yes, and then you could ask him about your own trouble."

"That's better. Besides, we've got enough to be seeing to just now." The reply was short and definite. May knew better than to persist.

But thanks to Flo's visit, Dr Fitzherbert himself arranged to drive Sarah to Westonbury the following Monday, while Flo, May and Edith took the train. It was against his principles to give lifts to patients, for he well knew the problems, jealousies and accusations which might arise from such involvement. But ever since he had finished his training and decided to take on the Wilhampton practice thirty years ago, he had always been interested in the Lodge family. Its members did not appear to fit into any particular category. They were unusual, especially the mother and the littlest one: Katy. He knew Sarah Lodge to be hard, self-willed and often unreasonable—especially after the birth of Neil, to whom she reacted quite differently—yet he thought he—and perhaps he alone—really understood the underlying reason for this. He had never, as a student, taken a course in psychology, but he had been a lifelong student of human nature. Although he was aware that Sarah suffered from the guilt many a conscientious mother felt on finding that she had brought a simpleton into the world, yet in her case he was fairly certain why she did so to such an unnatural extent.

He could remember a July day towards the end of the last century when, in the company of a female friend, she had come to ask him if she was pregnant. She had been a beautiful young woman, not pretty—her features were too finely chiselled, even aristocratic-looking, for that—but there was something about her that attracted, or, rather, commanded, attention. He did not think she seemed too happy when he confirmed her supposition. But she had said, "Thank you, Doctor," in a quiet, pleasant enough manner and the two of them had gone away.

It must have been only about a week later when he was summoned to the mill late one evening because the eldest boy, Frank, had fallen out of a willow tree and concussed himself. He remembered how Sidney Lodge, though naturally concerned about the child, had also seemed curiously embarrassed at being the only person present when he made his examination. He had wondered why Sarah had not been around. Then, as he came away from the bedroom, after pronouncing that he did not think that any lasting harm had overtaken Frank, who, though still shaken, was quite conscious again, he had happened to glance through the little glass panel high up on the living-room wall which, presumably, had been inserted at some time or another to give more light to the dangerous stairway he was about to descend. There, lying on the old horsehair sofa, he had caught sight of Sarah.

Puzzled, especially in view of her condition, duty

bade him tell Sidney that he would like to see her, and he had pulled back the tapestry curtain which served as the living-room door. She had attempted to stand, but failed. Anxiously, he had hurried across to her and suddenly stopped, noticing her glazed eyes, her breath which smelt of gin.

Claud Fitzherbert had been young and inexperienced, but he realised in a flash what had happened. Sarah Lodge had been trying to abort the child she was carrying. Moreover, knowing her to be usually such a careful and vigilant mother, he had little doubt that had she not been otherwise engaged in her desperate, pitiable attempt, Frank would not have had his accident.

It had been a difficult few minutes. Sidney, Sarah and he were all more or less of the same generation. Not only did Claud Fitzherbert know what had been taking place, but he was acutely aware that Sarah—despite her fuddled state—and Sidney knew that he knew. His whole training, indeed, his whole upbringing, had taught him that human life was sacred; he was passionately dedicated to the ideal of preserving it. Yet, as he looked round the cramped, poorly-furnished living-room and saw the two faces before him: the man's a mixture of shame and defiance, the woman's sad and apologetic, he found he could not condemn—only suffer for and with them.

When Neil had been born and Ida Whatley, the midwife, had confirmed his own fears that there was something wrong with the infant, his mind had immediately gone back to that summer night when he had found Sarah, for the one and only time in her life, with 'drink taken'. There was no definite proof, of course; he possessed no medical tract which asserted that what she had done might have harmed the foetus. Yet who could tell? And for all he knew, Sarah had possibly tried other accompanying diabolical tactics to achieve her ends that evening, such as skipping or running on the spot in the silent, empty mill. But as Neil grew larger and seemingly more helpless, many was the time he found himself wondering, as he felt Sarah too must have been wondering, whether her actions had been responsible for the wretched child's abnormality.

Until the boy was about three, she had refused, categorically, to acknowledge that anything was the matter with him at all. Even afterwards, she had kept up the pretence. When, worried about the load she was carrying, Claud Fitzherbert had suggested, gently, that there might be other ways in which Neil could be cared for, his remarks were brushed aside indignantly, even savagely. Over the years he had watched her, while the mask she had adopted became tougher, harder and more impregnable, save for the odd occasion when, just for a while, he had glimpsed the soft-spoken young matron who had visited him in the summer of 1898 when she was three months pregnant.

He never ceased to marvel at the job she was doing, at the standards she demanded, not only from herself but each—save Neil—member of her family. He was both alarmed and distressed when she became pregnant with her seventh child. But there had never been any outward sign of regret or resentment this time, certainly no attempt at trying to avoid her fate. She seemed to have become resigned to motherhood, although there had been a short period after Katy's birth when she had suffered from puerperal depression. But suddenly she appeared to pull out of it. He was never quite sure why. He seemed to recall there having been some gossip going around about Sidney Lodge and Lilian Firman; and Sarah, fighting mad, it was said, had gone up to the house Lilian shared with her brother and hauled her husband home. He wasn't sure, of course. It was difficult, sometimes, to sift out the truth, even if there was a grain or two of it in such a story. But he'd been a medical practitioner in Wilhampton long enough to know that there was usually never smoke without just a spark of fire. But whatever troubles had transpired after Katy's birth, Sarah had triumphed over them.

One Sunday afternoon, when the baby was about four months, he had been delighted to see, from his drawing-room window, the entire Lodge family out together for their customary walk up to Breconbury Woods. They had spread across the whole of East Street: Sidney, with the two eldest boys on either side of him; next, Flo, May and Edith, holding hands; and then Sarah, with Katy in the pram and Neil propped up at the other end. They were more beautifully dressed than ever. He couldn't help wondering whether this particular outing had been purposely 'staged', that Sarah, by presenting such a perfect, united front, was simply showing Wilhampton that there was nothing wrong, nor ever had been. He had continued to watch them, filled with admiration, until they were almost out of sight, comparing them to his own children, who mostly went about like ragamuffins. But then, Mildred, his wife, had always maintained that she had better things to do than bother about clothes.

It was only years later that he had learned from May Lodge that her mother always reckoned it was a good thing, in times of trouble, to put on what she called 'the ten-pound look'. It was a little maxim, her daughter explained, which she had apparently picked up from somewhere in her youth. He supposed it had come down through the generations since the time of the first Reform Bill in 1832, when ten-pound householders were given the vote. But on that particular Sunday afternoon at the turn of the century, he could only marvel at what he had just seen, wondering how the woman did it, for he imagined her husband's wages would have been not much more than a pound a week.

He supposed that Sarah might have had a bit of a dowry, although he doubted it. He seemed to recall Miss Fielding once having told him that there had been some trouble between Sarah and her parents when she had married Sidney Lodge. He believed she had been a Miss Dufosée, the only daughter of quite wealthy West of England clothiers, whose forbears had come over from France. That was probably where the dress sense came from and why he had always felt the family to be curiously unique, a strange mixture of determination, courage and common sense, yet coupled with charm, sensitivity and nervousness.

Sarah was certainly showing indomitable courage today, he thought, as she sat bolt upright beside him in the car on the way to the inquest: quiet, immaculately turned out as usual and immensely proud. Whatever she was suffering was, for the moment, contained within her mask, although he was aware that her gloved hands were held tightly together, that there were splashes of heightened colour on each cheekbone. But if Flo was worried about her mother's ability to stand up to what lay ahead, he felt fairly certain her fears were groundless. He did not think Sarah would falter in the witness-box. She would rise to the occasion.

His assumption proved correct.

She was the first to be called and took oath in a calm, composed manner, having walked up to face the coroner, her head held high, looking neither to right nor left. Her daughters noted, with a mixture of admiration and relief, that the way she comported herself seemed to quell the atmosphere of rising excitement, even hostility, in the packed little courtroom. It would seem that Sarah Lodge, as her grandmother had done more than half a century before, had come 'on stage', totally in command of both herself and her audience.

Dr Machin, as Dr Fitzherbert had predicted, put his questions to her gravely and courteously, his usual somewhat acerbic manner laid aside. He even opened the proceedings by extending his sympathy to her and her family for their sad loss, which she acknowledged with a dignified little bow.

"You were the last to see your son alive, I believe, Mrs Lodge?" he began.

"Yes, sir." She looked at him very directly, still refraining from glancing for one moment at the sea of faces around her.

"I understand, Mrs Lodge, that because your son suffered certain ... disabilities, you were obliged to give him special care?"

"Yes, sir. That is correct."

"Perhaps," continued Dr Machin, still in the same pleasant manner, "you could describe exactly what happened on the morning of ..." he glanced at his notes, "November the 7th?"

For a fraction, the woman in the box paused. Then, levelly, she replied, "I did not know anything was amiss, sir, until I went in to wake my son when the half-past-six hooter blew. We had all gone to bed early the night before ... I'd seen to his undressing ... he sleeps in a room which leads through from mine ... I never left my own until I went to ..." she hesitated again, and then continued, "the closet, at about five."

"And how long were you gone, Mrs Lodge?" Dr Machin queried.

"Not more than ten minutes, sir."

"And then?" her interrogator prompted.

"Well, then, sir, I tried to snatch a little more sleep,

but it wasn't to be. I just dressed and went in to Neil, like I always do." This time there was a slightly longer pause during which there was complete silence, so that her next four words, though quietly spoken, fell with startling impact on the courtroom. "His bed was empty," Sarah said.

"And what did you do?" Step by step, albeit kindly, she was being made to relive those hours. Dr Fitzherbert wondered what it was costing her.

"We all went looking, sir. Me and my two daughters," he heard her reply, at once.

"Which way did you go, Mrs Lodge?"

Sarah frowned a little, but still she answered unwaveringly.

"I went up River Lane, sir."

There was the faintest murmur in the courtroom, which the coroner silenced with a glance. May caught sight of Lilian Perrick and her family, leaning forward, their gaze fastened intently on the witness-box.

"You had no idea where your son might have gone, Mrs Lodge?"

"No, sir."

"Nor why?"

"No, sir," repeated Sarah, in the same positive manner.

There was louder murmuring at the back of the courtroom now, which elicited from Dr Machin a definite call for silence.

"Has your son ever done this sort of thing before, Mrs Lodge?" he continued.

"Not at night, I mean, not at that hour, sir."

"But he has sometimes wandered off in the daytime?"

For the first time, Sarah's composure seemed momentarily to elude her. She put up a hand to her face and then dropped it on to the brass rail at her side. She supposed that Dr Machin must have known that Neil had been on the prowl the day before he drowned. "Once or twice, sir," she answered, and this time her voice sank almost to a whisper. "Being as he was," she mumbled, "'twasn't always easy to . . . keep an eye on him every minute of the day."

"Quite, Mrs Lodge. I fully appreciate that. I think that will be all, thank you."

Flo and May were called next. Each corroborated their mother's statements and how they had all gone off in different directions to look for Neil on finding he had disappeared.

Tom Henstridge then went into the witness-box. He confirmed that he had found Neil's body lying against what he called 'Little Hatch' at about eight o'clock on the morning of November 7th.

"There is a small footbridge there, I believe, Mr Henstridge?" Though still framing his questions quite pleasantly, Dr Machin seemed to have reverted to his usual, more cryptic tone in his cross-questioning.

"Yes, zur." Tom Henstridge's slow, west-country voice reverberated round the courtroom in sharp contrast to the precise speech of his interrogator.

"On which the boy would have been walking?"

"Well, he *could* 'ave been, zur. Or maybe he fell into the race from the big bridge, and that's where the current carried 'im."

"Would the deceased have had much difficulty in crossing either bridge, Mr Henstridge?"

The under-manager looked at Dr Machin in some surprise. "Why, yes, zur. Specially in the dark. Stands to reason. And there was no hand-rail on the little 'un, see."

"And I believe that was a place which was not often frequented?"

"Hardly ever, zur. Except . . ."

"Except what, Mr Henstridge?" Dr Machin seemed to be chivvying now, as if he were on some scent, professional, probing, eyeing his witness keenly over the top of his pince-nez.

"Well . . ." Tom Henstridge, honest, loyal, none too bright, gripped the rail of the witness-box. "Except when 'twere used as a short cut to River Lane by them wot was in the know, like."

"Thank you, Mr Henstridge."

To the Perrick family's obvious consternation, the next person to be called was Bob Harrison. He was a short, fat, shifty-looking man, fond of beer, betting and women, who lived with his married sister on downside. Never a good time-keeper, he admitted, at the start of his evidence, that he had been hurrying down River Lane on his bicycle on the morning of the seventh, just after the six-thirty hooter had gone.

"You were, in fact, late for work, Harrison?" Dr Machin remarked, drily.

"Yes sir."

"And you have been telling people that you saw, or thought you saw, Archie Perrick coming out of the alley-way at the top?"

Bob Harrison shuffled his feet uneasily and coughed.

"Well, as I said, sir, I couldn't be sure. I was hurrying, like, and 'twere dark."

"You had a lamp on your bicycle, I presume, Harrison?"

"Well, yessir, that is . . . no sir. The battery were flat."

Again, a murmuring ripple of interest rose in the courtroom, although how much it was for or against the witness, it was impossible to fathom. This time, Dr Machin simply held up a hand and spoke slightly louder, as he framed his next question.

"What made you think the figure you saw was Archie Perrick, Harrison?"

"Well, sir, I mean . . . I knows as how Archie gets about a bit of an early morning."

"In other words, you merely guessed?"

"If you put it like that, sir."

"Are you, in fact, Harrison, quite sure you saw anyone in River Lane that morning?"

Bob Harrison coughed and shuffled his feet once more. Clearly embarrassed, he looked anywhere other than at the coroner. "Well, sir," he replied, at length, "I were goin' lickety-split, like. Fact is, I near as dammit—beg pardon, sir—ran into Mrs Lodge comin' out o' the mill gates, 'cept she 'ad her lantern wi' her."

"Thank you, Harrison."

Lilian Perrick sat back, a definite smirk of relief on her sharp little face, watching Bob Harrison step down from the box and her son take his place. Despite a certain similarity in unease which the boy seemed to share with the previous witness, he appeared to have a cast-iron alibi. He said that he had been nowhere near River Lane after five that morning, for he had left home at that time to cycle ten miles to Tom Sanger's racing stables on the old Barbury turnpike, where he had recently become an employee. This fact was corroborated by none other than Mr Sanger himself, and the smirk on Lilian's face became more pronounced with every minute that the two of them gave evidence.

It only remained for the pathologist and Dr Fitzherbert to be called as final witnesses. Both men were in agreement that it was a case of straightforward drowning, the small cut which had been discovered on Neil's right temple consistent with having knocked his head against Little Hatch in falling. Privately, Dr Fitzherbert felt that Neil, in his confused moronic mind, *had* been trying to get to the Perrick house, that sex was at the bottom of the tragedy, but he thanked God that at least, whatever had been hinted at the inquest, no definite statement to that effect had come out. He was merely annoyed that, because of Bob Harrison's loud mouth, any doubt whatsoever about Neil's death had been introduced into the proceedings, and Sarah Lodge's ordeal had been consequently unnecessarily prolonged. Before stepping down from the box, he took the opportunity, as Dr Machin had also done, of publicly extending his sympathy to the Lodge family in their bereavement and, in particular, to Mrs Lodge, who, as he put it, had been "a mother in a million".

So—the inquest was over. Dr Machin brought in a verdict of 'Death by Misadventure'. Claud Fitzherbert drove Sarah back to Wilhampton, trying, as far as he was able, to steer her thoughts on to more pleasant lines.

"I hear," he said, "from Lady Fairfax, that her grandson will be coming to the Hall for Christmas, and Nanny Barlow and Katy with him."

But from his passenger's next remark, he knew that his observation had fallen on deaf ears.

"If Bob Harrison did see someone coming out of Hatch Alley the morning Neil was drowned and it wasn't Archie Perrick, who do you think it might have been, Doctor?"

12

In the weeks that led up to Christmas, the question of who Bob Harrison might or might not have seen coming out of Hatch Alley on the morning of November 7th, became the subject of practically non-stop discussion in Wilhampton's nine public houses, especially The Punchbowl, the one most favoured by Bob himself. For many years, here was where he was most likely to be found holding court, his graphic anecdotes and vociferous opinions—aided by the help of alcoholic intake usually bought for him by others with the express purpose of being at the receiving end of them—being almost legendary, both in the town and surrounding district.

Now, he was in his element, possessed of a personal mystery story which his audience was finding far more absorbing than his views on Lloyd George and the Government, rising prices, unemployment, or matters closer to home: how Sir Roger Broadbent had managed to pepper one of Lord Fairfax's guns at a recent shooting-party and whether young Dick Swayne, up at Bulbarrow Farm on the outskirts of the town, would ever make half the farmer his elderly, now crippled, father had been.

Even Bob's constant stand-by which could always be relied upon to buy him a few more pints: speculation about Grace Sinca—or Grace Armitage as she now was—was temporarily superfluous to requirements. In any case, since the end of the war, with her father dead and an invalid husband on her hands, there were some people who considered Grace to be more of an object for compassion than anything else. Although, privately, May Lodge did not believe that leopards changed their spots and felt that, whenever Grace had the chance, she was bound to be up to her old tricks again. Indeed, Emily Harwood had often hinted as much to her—though never in Flo's hearing—and only the other day, when they had met in the street, Emily had been on about Grace's having taken to going for long walks by herself, once she had got the Captain to bed of an evening. "The Lord knows where, May," she had added, darkly, "but I suppose it's a question of anything in trousers. Fred Ashford's wife thinks she makes for the shooting-lodge on the old Barbury turnpike, and I don't reckon she's alone when she gets there."

But in the winter of 1919, whatever assignations Grace Armitage might have been keeping, the inquest on Neil Lodge's death and Bob Harrison's stories concerning it were uppermost in the majority of people's minds. "Who d'you think 'twere, then, Bob?" or "Come on, you must 'ave seen zummat" were two questions guaranteed to start him off as soon as he stepped inside The Punchbowl, to which his reply almost always began with, "Well, as I said to the Crowner, 'twere dark . . ." after which his saga would gather momentum, its dramatic qualities more than compensating for its increasing inconsistency.

Fortunately, however, as she made her way towards River Lane on the afternoon of Christmas Eve, Katy Lodge had no idea that she would soon be passing the spot which many people now considered haunted; for it was being put about in the town that Sidney Lodge's ghost had taken to springing out of Hatch Alley to accost anyone who was late for work. Katy merely hurried along, demure and dainty, acknowledging the greetings of several passers-by and ignoring, as far as possible, the curtain-twitching at front windows, which she was well aware always became more pronounced when one of the town's inhabitants returned after a period of absence.

"Katy!" May, with Flo a little way behind her, came running out of the mill gates as soon as she passed the Perricks' shop. "Oh, chippatoo! My, how good you look."

She was caught up in first one and then another pair of welcoming arms. And then, at the door of the house, Sarah held out her own, yet almost apprehensively, as if her youngest daughter had become a stranger to her, that since the child had left home, they both had travelled unknown paths.

Katy was quick to recognise the change in her mother. She seemed to have visibly shrunk. Though neat as ever—there was not a hair out of place, not a crease in the black serge dress with the lace tucker made for mourning after Sidney Lodge's death, and now worn on special occasions only—she appeared old and curiously remote. She said little and when she did speak her voice was flat and detached.

The tea had already been laid, as it was to be eaten early in order for Katy to be back at the Hall by five-thirty, the time specified by Nanny Barlow. On the side of the table, Mr Fuller's tray was waiting to be taken up to his office as soon as the kettle boiled, a duty which today Flo had volunteered to undertake. Presently, Edith and her children arrived and the family proceeded to exchange presents, Katy having brought a hand-stitched lace handkerchief for her mother, a small bottle of lavender water for each of her three sisters and sweets for her nephew and nieces. All the gifts had been carefully wrapped in tissue paper and, much as Katy longed to open those which were handed to her and which she suspected were mostly articles of clothing, she promised faithfully not to do so until Christmas morning.

"When no doubt you'll be busy," said Flo.

"Yes, but Nanny says I can come to church and maybe she could spare me for an hour or two on Boxing Day."

"Then we could go to the cemetery," Sarah broke in, unexpectedly. "You'll be wanting to see Neil's grave, and your father's, I'm sure."

Katy started. She had no wish to see either grave. Neither did she want to go to the cemetery. She hated the place, with its heavy wrought-iron gates and dreary-looking caretaker's lodge, the stench of decaying flowers which came from the dump just round the corner, the rows of neat or neglected graves. True, there were many more of the former than the latter, and that of Sidney Lodge seemed the most regularly tended, but Katy could not understand why so many people appeared to take such a ghoulish interest in them, walking up and down the grassy aisles of a Sunday afternoon, shaking their heads and sometimes reading an epitaph out loud to their companions. Even Flo and May were far from averse to going across and inspecting the resting-place of some new arrival, made manifest by its covering of wilting, floral tributes, which they then proceeded to examine carefully, reading out such words as In Loving Memory or With Deepest Sympathy, and registering approval or disapproval at the choice of phrase which had been used, especially when it came—as it almost always did—from someone whom they knew, or knew of. On these occasions, Katy would merely stand aside, looking across the valley towards Breconbury Woods, longing to run away and hide there, embarrassed and ashamed by the morbid curiosity which seemed to turn a visit to the cemetery into some form of vicarious entertainment. Now, she realised, she would have to go through it all again and, what was more, during her precious time off.

But there was no question of refusal. Katy knew what was expected of her. Already she could see two holly wreaths in one corner of the room which were obviously in the process of being made up. Besides, were they not almost at the anniversary of her father's death? Unhappily aware of dissembling, she replied, dutifully, "Yes, Mother."

"Tell us about John William," May intervened quickly, sensing the uneasiness in the atmosphere.

"Oh, he's lovely. Though I don't really do much for him. Just the ordinary jobs. Washing his nappies and such like." As soon as she had made the remark, Katy regretted it. There had been no one to do the ordinary jobs for a woman with seven children in a tiny house without even an indoor tap and she wondered whether her unthinking answer had reminded her mother of the fact. But Sarah simply inclined her head, almost approvingly, as though no such comparison had crossed her mind.

The afternoon passed all too quickly and at five o'clock it was decided that May should accompany her youngest sister back to the Hall. As they crossed the market-square, Katy said suddenly, "Mother's very thin, isn't she? So's Flo, for that matter."

"Yes, but ... Neil drowning ... you know, the shock ..." May saw no point in going into further details. And, in any case, there was nothing specific to say. There was no reason to burden the child with her own nebulous doubts and fears. Katy was still so young. She was looking so well. Yet there was a directness, a maturity about her, which was made only too clear by her next remark.

"I suppose if Neil's death had happened earlier, you'd never have sent me away."

May hesitated. "Well, no, my dear. I don't suppose so. But you're happy, aren't you?"

She was surprised at the reply.

"I don't know. It's a difficult thing to be, isn't it? I hope I don't find myself looking after other people's babies for ever."

May was silent. They had reached the west gates. Away to the left of them they could see the lights of the Hall filtering through the trees. Nearer at hand, Fred Ashford's dogs suddenly set up barking, giving May an excuse for not answering at once.

"I don't see why you should, Katy," she replied, at length, after they had passed the keeper's cottage. "You'll probably get married and have children of your own."

"D'you think so? But I wouldn't want to be like Mother. I'd sooner have someone else to care for my kids."

"Oh, Katy!" The exclamation was made half in amusement, half in gentle reproach. "We can't all be the Fairfaxes or Moretons of this world. And there's plenty worse off than we are."

"Oh, I *know*. But when I think of what it must have been like bringing us all up at the mill and then what goes on where I am now. Mrs Moreton and her husband are out almost every night, that is, when they aren't entertaining at home. Haven't you ever wanted a better life, May? Look how you felt about London and Bond Street that day you came up with me."

"Yes, but that was only ever a kind of dream, Katy," came the quiet reply.

After they had said good-night, May walked home slowly, thinking about her youngest sister's last remarks. There were no flies on Katy. Illness might have made her seem subdued and listless during childhood, but she had come on a lot since then; and being away from home had speeded up the process. There was a big difference in the child May had left in 89 Upper Brook Street six months previously and the young woman whom she had just seen disappear into the side entrance of the Hall. Katy might be only a nursery-maid but something—the family she was with, their house, the West End of London, her job—had given her a curious awareness, even a sense of importance, however much she disparaged her position. Of course, May had always known that her youngest sister had aspirations. Yet so had she herself, when she came to think about it. But perhaps Katy's stood more chance of being realised. She had youth and determination on her side. And time. There was not now—nor had there ever been, May realised—the slightest chance of the Misses F and M Lodge setting up in business anywhere other than at the mill. It had been silly of her ever to entertain the idea. They had never had the money; they knew of no one to back them. As it was, they were lucky to have a workroom for which they paid no rent. She might blame the war for initially having made them stay put, but now they had Sarah to think of. Their mother was dependent on them and would never, willingly, leave the mill. That short, sweet, tantalising vision—prompted by a little lighthearted flattery from Alicia Moreton—of seeing their name above some shop in Bond Street, had been as fanciful as it had been foolish.

Now, as she made her way home, May thought about the time her dreams had been stifled for good and all on her one and only trip to London. After leaving Katy and being shown the way to her objective by Nanny Barlow, she remembered standing in wonderment outside the windows of Asprey's and Cartier's.

She had walked up and down, pausing in front of many a clothes' shop, astonished that a simple blouse-dress of cotton crêpe with a vest of cotton georgette could cost as much as twenty-nine shillings and sixpence, that an artificial silk jumper was priced at twelve and elevenpence. And the hats: there had been one covered in pink crêpe de Chine and lace at forty-five and nine, although, on closer study, it had not seemed a patch on her own fine beige straw, the one which she had trimmed with rosettes of ribbons to wear for her ill-fated meeting with Major Walter Perkins.

In fact, although as far as May was concerned, Bond Street might almost have been in some foreign country so great was the contrast to Westonbury's High Parade, she recalled, oddly enough, having felt not altogether out of place there. As she had cast, discreetly, a knowledgeable eye over the fashionable ladies alighting from cabs or chauffeur-driven limousines, savouring every detail of their attire in order to pass on the information to Flo as soon as she returned, she was conscious of the fact that the simple tussore dress she was wearing, though not enhanced by jewellery or other costly accessories, nevertheless compared not unfavourably with the more extravagant ensembles. No one might turn to look at May Lodge twice—for one thing, she had been well aware that to be seen carrying a coat on such a hot day was a handicap—but, on the other hand, she had been pleased to feel she could go home, knowing that the dress sense, with which the distaff side of the family seemed to have been endowed, had certainly not let her down.

She recollected having been more eager to return to Wilhampton than she had been to leave it that morning, experiencing a sense of relief that she was now on her way back to a life which she knew and understood and, once in the train, it seemed as though some unseen umbilical cord grew tighter with every mile it steamed westwards. May supposed it was absurd of her, really, to think this; but more than once she had wondered whether there was not some strange magnetism about the place where she had been born. Occasionally, she had felt it had to do with the town itself; more often she connected it with Sarah; even, at times, the mill-race, as if those who lived close to it were caught up in something beyond their control.

Tonight, after saying goodbye to Katy at the Hall, as she recrossed the market-square and neared River Lane, she felt it again. She believed her youngest sister might have experienced something of the same sort. There was no doubt that the poor child had wanted to get away from it and spread her wings, to break from that cramping, even cloistered, atmosphere; although not in the way which had been forced upon her.

On reaching Hatch Alley, May was annoyed to find that she had started to hurry. Both she and Flo had heard the rumours which, as yet, had fortunately escaped Sarah's ears. There was nothing in them, of course. How could there be? May did not believe in ghosts—at least, that was what she had always maintained. Besides, good people like her father did not return to this world to scare the daylights out of those they had left behind. Yet, when she arrived at the house, she knew she was flushed and that Flo was aware of her discomposure, even more so when, on the table, she caught sight of a large, rectangular box which looked suspiciously like chocolates, on which the attached label proclaimed in thin, spidery, handwriting: 'For the three good ladies of The Mill House, George Fuller'.

"Duck and Collar brought it," said Flo, "just after you'd left with Katy. He seemed most put out you weren't here."

"That will do, Flo." Sarah's voice had almost a touch of the old acerbity in it. "Why should Mr Fuller want to see May? Are you forgetting he is a married man?"

13

"They got damaged when we had a burst pipe over Christmas. That's why they're being sold off cheap." The young man in the shop near Oxford Street had come across to where Katy was standing just inside the door, studying a trough of dilapidated books marked up at twopence each.

"I see." She coloured slightly. She had not reckoned on actually buying one, certainly not on being accosted by a salesman. She had simply wanted to look; and it had taken more than a little courage just to step over the threshold of Mason & Son. Moreover, she knew that she should really not have been there at all, but hurrying back to Number 89 with the gripe-water she had been sent out to buy at the chemist's next door. But it had seemed too good a chance to miss. She had had her eye on the bookshop for some time.

"What do you fancy?" The young man was of medium height, quite stocky, with dark hair and dark brown eyes, which were now looking at her in a courteous yet amused way. He seemed plainly eager to help.

She hesitated, her colour deepening. "I don't really know . . . I just wanted to see what there was."

"Ah, let me think, now. Have you read Emily

Brontë?" He began searching through the trough, carefully.

"I . . . no . . . I mean, what is it about?"

He turned to look at her more closely and then continued his search. "Emily Brontë is the author, or, rather, the authoress. Here." He pulled out a copy of *Wuthering Heights* and handed it to her. "I think you'd like this. It's quite a good edition. An absolute bargain at twopence."

She was blushing furiously now. She had shown her ignorance and made the most terrible mistake—and Katy Lodge did not like making mistakes. Miserably, she hunted in her small pochette and produced the necessary money. She felt that she would have given her entire week's wages to get out of the shop. She waited in agony while he went away to wrap up her purchase.

"I'd like to know what you think of it," he said, gravely, when he returned and handed it to her. "I've seen you before, looking in the window. I'm sure you must like reading."

"Yes," she mumbled, taking the package quickly and almost running out of the door.

Katy had hoped to have been able to hide it before anyone noticed when she returned to Number 89, but in this she was forestalled. Nanny Barlow was quick to observe that she was carrying two parcels.

"What have you got there, Katy?" she enquired, as she met her on the landing. "You didn't buy anything else at the chemist's, did you?"

"No. Yes . . . that is . . . I bought a book from the shop next door."

"A *book*?" Katy felt if she had said she had purchased a fur coat, the woman before her could scarcely have shown more astonishment or disapproval; and the next question not only seemed to confirm this but also to reveal a certain stupidity as well. "To read?" she added, tartly.

"Yes." What else did Nanny Barlow think she was going to do with it, for goodness sake?

"There's no good comes of stuffing your head in books, Katy. Besides, supposing if Master John had had wind and needed the gripe-water. When I send you out on an errand, I don't expect you to dilly-dally about in some fancy bookshop. You'd best make up for it by getting down straight away to that pile of sewing on the nursery table. Mrs Moreton's maid is sick and she's sent up a lot of things that want seeing to. I'm sure I don't know what your poor mother would say if she heard you'd been wasting your time and money on *books*."

"But it was cheap, Nanny. Damaged by water. I only paid twopence."

"That will do, my girl. Twopence too much. If 'twasn't for the fact that there's so much to do here, and being as how it's sales' goods I don't suppose they'd take it back, I'd send you straight up to Masons with it this very minute. As it is, you'd best look sharp and start on them petticoats. Mrs Moreton's having all her clothes shortened now, and this evening she's asked if I can spare you to go down and help her dress before she and Captain Moreton go out."

Half chastened, half resentful, Katy went into the nursery and did as she was told. She could not understand why it was that people seemed to think there was something disgraceful about her reading; that is, except for the young man in the shop. Of course, she would never go back and tell him what she thought about *Wuthering Heights*. In any case, Nanny Barlow would probably see to it that she got precious little time for reading. She must have welcomed the fact that Amy Robinson, Mrs Moreton's lady's-maid, was ill, so that there would be more work than ever to keep her nimble-fingered young nursery-maid busy. Of course, this was purely accidental, but more than once lately Katy had noticed that she had been asked to do some extra sewing for her employer, who had even complimented her on it, although not in Amy Robinson's hearing. As she started to unpick some lace from the bottom of a princess petticoat, she wondered what was wrong with the tall, thin, forbidding-looking woman with whom she had scarcely spoken. She would not altogether mind taking her place once in a while. It would be nice to be able to tell Flo and May that she had seen Mrs Moreton's bedroom and helped her to get dressed.

Later on, when she tapped on the door promptly at a quarter to seven, she was surprised, on entering, to find her employer sitting at her dressing-table, wearing a pale blue crêpe de Chine wrap and smoking a cigarette in a long holder.

"Ah, Katy. How nice. Come in."

She walked across the room, interest quickly dispelling any initial diffidence, conscious of an overall sense of softness cast by the pink-shaded lamps, the large double bed with its cream-coloured drapery, the rich pile of the pink and cream carpet. It was a room in which Katy could imagine spending hours of unmitigated bliss, yet the woman at the dressing-table seemed curiously troubled and ill at ease.

"When I've finished this," she continued, almost impatiently, waving her cigarette in the air, "perhaps you would give my hair a good brushing. It's been absolutely unmanageable the last few days since Robinson's been ill. I shall be glad when it comes off next week."

"You're having it bobbed, madam?"

"Yes, it will make life much easier."

As she began brushing the long tresses, Katy wondered what difficulties there were in a life which seemed, ostensibly, to be so free of them. She also felt a little sad at what she had just heard; for she could not imagine how Alicia Moreton would look without what the Lodge family always called 'woman's crowning glory'. She certainly had no intention of having her own hair cut. She knew her mother would have a fit if she turned into a shorn lamb, which was how most older people dubbed those who had been misguided enough to follow the latest fashion, even if they did keep their switches coiled up in cardboard boxes ready for winding round their heads on special occasions.

Deftly, she continued to help Alicia Moreton with her toilet, mentally noting every little detail so that she could write them all down in her next letter home: a new-type garment called a brassière, specially designed to flatten the bosom in order to produce the modern tube-like figure; the cobweb-thin ninon cami-knickers, trimmed with lace and threaded ribbon; the finest of flesh-coloured silk stockings. Katy was not in any way surprised or overawed by such finery. She had seen much of it—albeit in a somewhat less glamorous and extravagant form—in her sisters' workroom at the mill. Even the pale *eau de nil* satin-covered shoes which exactly matched the low-backed satin dress with its irregular hemline, the diamond brooch and earrings, the long string of pearls and the white kid gloves, did not take her breath away. She was merely glad, after putting the final touches to the coiffure she had arranged so carefully, to see Alicia Moreton finally sweep out of the door and down the circular stairway, an oriental fringed shawl draped gracefully over one arm, looking 'just lovely', as she eventually ended the description in her letter.

Yet, as one of the housemaids came in to make up

the fire and she herself started to tidy the bedroom and put away the various pots of face cream, powder, rouge—and even lipstick—on the dressing-table, part of her could not help wondering about a state of affairs whereby in order for one woman to go out for an evening's enjoyment, it took another—or many another—to help her to do so.

Although, on further thought, Katy wondered how much Alicia Moreton would enjoy herself this evening. There had been something about John William's mother which she had never encountered before. Her manner had been quick, brittle, over-bright at times. She had even smoked a second cigarette before going downstairs, while she had asked Katy a number of questions about the baby. Did she think he was hardy? Was it not strange that he had failed to gain so much weight last week? London was such an unclean place in which to bring up a child, wasn't it? Full of germs. It would be so easy for him to pick up an infection. It might be better if he were sent to his paternal grandfather's home in Suffolk, where it was bracing, or even back to Wilhampton. She spoke so rapidly, switching from one idea to another, that Katy had not known what to make of it. There was nothing wrong with the child that she could see; and Nanny Barlow seemed to be perfectly happy about him. It was not until a week later that Katy learned that Amy Robinson had left Number 89 because she was suffering from tuberculosis.

There followed a stringent examination of each member of the entire household by the family doctor, particularly John William. His mother seemed forever in and out of the nursery, gazing at the child and asking Nanny Barlow questions, which were not always well received.

"Did he ever come into contact with Robinson, Nanny?"

"Hardly ever, Madam. Once or twice on the stairs, maybe, as we were going out or coming in."

"Did she breathe over him?"

"No, madam. You know I never allow anyone to breathe over my charges, other than those who are doing for them."

"His milk has always been boiled, hasn't it, Nanny?"

"Of course, madam." Katy wondered how difficult it had been for the older woman to make the transition from Alicia to Miss Alicia to Madam.

One evening, when the interrogation seemed to have gone on for an inordinate length of time, Nanny Barlow reverted to her former role in relation to John William's mother.

"Miss Alicia. If you go on like this you'll make yourself ill, and the bairn, too, I shouldn't wonder. Dr Macleod has given him a clean bill of health. I brought you all up, remember, and we had plenty a scare. Fred Ashford's first wife had it, the one who used to do extra work at the Hall whenever we had company coming. And even the Reverend Donaldson's eldest daughter, who used to come to your birthday parties, had them glands in her neck when she was nigh on eleven. They said it was because Mrs Donaldson would insist on the Swaynes at Bulbarrow letting her have milk from one cow only, instead of doing what Dr Fitzherbert advised your mother: taking it from the best six in the Home Farm herd. But anyway, none of you caught it, thank the Lord. You mustn't fear the worst. Perhaps it would do you good to have a little holiday."

"Yes, Nanny. Maybe you're right."

Yet Alicia Moreton did not go away. Until the installation of Edna Mitchell, her new lady's-maid,

Katy found her services increasingly called upon from the floor below. She did not object, even though it meant longer hours and she was too tired to read much more than a page or two of *Wuthering Heights* each night. But in many ways the work was more interesting. From little snippets of information, she was beginning to get a slightly clearer picture of that tantalising world outside of which, so far, she knew so little. True, it was still but a blurred negative, but she was quick to retain the name of a restaurant, a theatre, a play, an actor or actress, for mostly Mrs Moreton made no secret of where she was going. Katy was never asked, as Amy Robinson had sometimes been, to wait up to all hours until her employer returned. In any case, it seemed that more often than not Alicia Moreton came home early by herself. She was curious as to what her husband did on these occasions. Sometimes his wife appeared not to accompany him at all, suddenly announcing at the last moment that she would prefer to dine quietly at home, alone. Katy wondered whether he minded such unpredictable behaviour.

Charles Moreton did, in fact, mind very much. Since Christmas, he had become increasingly exasperated with Alicia. Why could she not behave like the wives of their contemporaries, who all seemed to be enjoying themselves? They could both be having a ripping time now, if only she would stop fussing over their child and letting herself get so involved in charity work. There was so much to do, so much to see. There were the various new nightclubs being opened, where they could dance the night away to one of the Dixieland jazz orchestras to which he had become particularly addicted. He was beginning to acquire quite a collection of *His Master's Voice* gramophone records and the strains of a transmogrified *Swanee* or *Pasadena* could often be heard floating up from his study on the ground floor. Or there were the pictures and the theatre. He badly wanted to see the latest Charlie Chaplin film and he had actually bought tickets for *Brown Sugar* at the Duke of York's. He hoped Alicia would not say that she did not feel up to going to it when the time came. Sometimes, he felt her contrariness was more than he could stand. Often, he sought refuge in one of his clubs—usually the Cavalry or White's—where he could drink without feeling aware of his wife's disapproval; although, even here, the conversation was occasionally a shade too serious for his liking. He wished some of the older members would shut up about Lloyd George and his handling of the Coalition. As far as he was concerned, he didn't give a damn whether the fellow's methods were devious and disorganised, or that he was failing to live up to his promise of making post-war Britain a country fit for heroes to live in. He was the man who had won the war, wasn't he?

Moreover, he, Charles Moreton, had actually fought in it and now he simply wanted to have some fun. He was not interested in politics, nor those pillars of society who went to church on Sundays and sang Kipling's recessional: *Lest We Forget*. Personally, he wanted to forget. He'd seen a man with both his legs blown off, rescued him, in fact, for which he had been given an M. C. Why shouldn't he have a good time? If unemployment was rising and not only ex-privates but down-at-heel ex-officers were touting hardware from door to door, or sinking their gratuities in dismal little chicken farms, he just did not want to know. One day he would inherit three thousand, five hundred acres of Suffolk and he and his wife and John William—and, presumably, other children—would settle down there, that is, as long as Alicia came to her senses.

If she went on at this rate, he would have to send her to one of those blasted nerve chaps, the kind who had had to be called in on shell-shock cases during the war; although, for his own part, he had no faith in Freud and all that claptrap.

14

When spring came that year and the London parks were splashed with islands of yellow daffodils and the trees began covering themselves with lacy green veils or delicate pink and white rosettes of cherry blossom, Katy was sometimes allowed to take John William for a walk in his perambulator by herself. He was a good-looking child with a mass of fair curls and, now that he was sitting up, many an admiring glance was directed towards the pretty picture the two of them made: the slim young girl with the large, serious eyes, immaculate in her navy-blue uniform; the smiling round-cheeked baby, dressed in a powder-blue woollen jacket trimmed with white fur, occasionally waving a rattle which had been securely fastened with ribbon to the inside of the smart, shining pram.

Since Katy had stood in as lady's-maid a little earlier on, she had noticed a certain change in Nanny Barlow's attitude to her. She was less apt to treat her as a child and there had been no further disparaging remarks in connection with the undesirability of reading, although Katy was careful never to be caught doing so. It was simply obvious to her that, because she had been able to undertake her temporary role so satisfactorily and had, in consequence, gained Mrs Moreton's whole-hearted approval, this had stood her in good stead with Nanny Barlow as well. That was what made it all the more difficult to do what she was planning to do on her next afternoon off, even though she kept trying to tell herself that it was not exactly she who had made all the arrangements, but the young man in the bookshop.

They had met quite accidentally the previous week, when she had slipped out after tea to post a letter. At least, it had *seemed* accidental although, as there were two pillar-boxes both equidistant from the Moreton's house, she was vaguely aware that she invariably found herself choosing the one nearer Oxford Street. Not that she had any intention of visiting Masons again, even though she had at last finished *Wuthering Heights* and thought it quite the most wonderful book she had ever read. For this reason alone, she sometimes felt that she would like to have been able to thank the person who had brought such an opportunity about. But, while being intelligent enough to have appreciated every word, she had become greatly saddened as she reached the end: not entirely by the story itself—much as she grieved for Cathy and Heathcliff—but by the realisation of how lacking she herself was, both in experience and education. She vowed that she would do her best to remedy such matters, even if it meant finding another bookshop, or perhaps a library. Never again would she expose her ignorance in the abysmal way which she had done on the day when she had paid twopence for what was now one of her most precious possessions.

After posting her letter, she had at first taken no notice of the voice calling "Miss" behind her. When hurrying footsteps caught up with her own and she found herself looking into the same searching, dark brown eyes from which she had fled two months previously, she was conscious of the colour coming swiftly to her face, just as it had done before.

"Did you like it?" It was as if there had been no

interval of time since their last meeting, no pause in their conversation.

"Oh, *yes* . . . Thank you," she added, and then became tongue-tied.

"I hoped you'd come back. I had another book I was saving for you at the same price. I've still got it, as a matter of fact. It's Thackeray's *Vanity Fair.* Unless, of course, you've read it?"

"No." Despite her confusion, she was quick to appreciate his courteousness in not automatically assuming that he would receive a negative answer.

"We've just closed now, but perhaps you'd like to call in? Tomorrow?"

"I . . . well, no. I'm sorry."

He had looked crestfallen and she feared that she had been both ungrateful and ungracious. "I work," she continued hastily. "It wouldn't be possible."

"Are you a nurse?" She saw him looking at her uniform.

"A nursery-maid. At 89 Upper Brook Street," something had made her add.

"When d'you get off in the evening?"

"I don't. I just have an afternoon a week—from two until six-thirty."

"When's your next one?"

"Thursday," she replied, doubtfully. "I'm going to tea with some relations, in Tooting Bec."

"How d'you go?"

"By bus . . . from Hyde Park Corner."

"Right. I'll escort you. It's early-closing day."

As she had hurried back to Number 89, she realised that they did not even know each other's names. They had simply arranged to meet again with an almost frightening sense of urgency, so much so that she wasn't sure how it could possibly come about. Would he be at the bus-stop? She could never be sure which bus she would actually catch. Nanny Barlow had a nasty habit of finding extra work for her to do on Thursday mornings. He wouldn't, *couldn't*, come to the house, would he? That would be terrible. She had never met anyone with quite such forcefulness. She did not know the word 'hypnotic', but she was certainly aware of a power about him, before which she felt helpless. Suddenly, she thought how nice it would have been to be able to talk to May about it all. Dear May, with her warm, protective, sisterly love. But May was eighty miles away and her letters had been curiously short and uncommunicative lately. She hadn't even said much about Katy's detailed description of Mrs Moreton's clothes, only to vouchsafe the information that she herself was making some handkerchief-lawn nightdresses for the youngest Fitzherbert girl who was getting married in June, and if Katy happened to be passing a shop like Gorringes or Robinson & Cleavers she might just look in the window and see what ready-mades were selling at, as she was wondering whether to charge three shillings or three shillings and sixpence. "The doctor being always so good to us," she had added, "I'd like to do them as cheap as possible."

As Katy hurried along to the bus-stop on the appointed Thursday afternoon, she half hoped that the young man would not be there. For, although in a way she did not feel she was really committing any crime, for she was still doing exactly what she had said she would be doing, yet she was well aware that had Nanny Barlow known there was a possibility of her nursery-maid's being escorted by a young man, she would not only have been horrified, but would have put a stop to her afternoon off completely.

He was there, of course. As they climbed up on to the open top deck of the bus, he told her that he had been waiting since soon after one o'clock, when Masons had closed.

"What's your name?" he said, after they had taken their seats and he had insisted on paying both their fares.

"Katy."

"Katy what?"

"Katy Lodge. And yours?" she enquired, shyly.

"Philip Mason."

"*Mason*?"

"Yes. My old man owns the shop."

"Oh, I see." Now she came to think about it, he hadn't seemed exactly like an ordinary salesman. She wished she had not shown any initial surprise at his revelation, but he appeared not to mind. There was a determined kind of optimism about him.

"Look," he said, suddenly, pulling something out of his pocket. "I've brought that book. The one I was telling you about. I know you'll enjoy it."

"Oh . . ." Once more, her face grew pink. She had no idea how becoming it made her, how the impulsive young man sitting beside her, noticing the sweep of the long lashes on the blushing cheek—now somewhat carefully averted—and the soft tendrils of brown hair showing beneath the fetching little navy-blue hat, had fallen desperately in love. He was more or less thrusting the package into her hands now, willing her to take it, and she became even more flustered and embarrassed, as she tried to extricate twopence from the little pochette she always carried.

When he realised what she was about, he said, almost angrily, "But it's a *present*."

"Oh!" This time she turned towards him, her large grey eyes wide with surprise and pleasure. Katy Lodge had never been given a present by a young man before. That it happened to be a book seemed to make it doubly precious. "Thank you," she said, softly. "Thank you very much indeed. I shall start to read it on my way home tonight."

He frowned. "I don't think that's a very good idea."

"No?" She was puzzled.

"Well, I mean, I'll be with you."

She was suddenly scared. "But I can't take you where I'm going."

"I didn't expect you to. I'll get myself some tea somewhere and then be at the stop whenever you say. I could do with something to eat. I went without dinner so as I wouldn't miss you."

She began to feel really alarmed now, countless complications chasing in and out of her mind. Her mother's cousin—Aunt Bessie, as she called her—usually saw her on to the bus. Moreover, she would be sure to enquire about the parcel she was carrying. She was a most austere, censorious woman who, while always producing muffins and a freshly-baked cake on such occasions, nevertheless somehow managed to convey the impression that it was a duty which she was only doing for 'poor dear Sarah's sake'. Katy had never really enjoyed a single visit, but, unless she went shopping—or, rather, window-shopping—with Clara, she had nowhere else to go. Haltingly, she started to voice her fears to her companion, but Philip Mason merely brushed them aside.

"I'll keep the book for you in my pocket. As for the bus-stop, that's easy. You just pretend you don't know me."

She nodded. She was not used to subterfuge. Of course, there had been things at home which had had to be kept from Sarah, although she usually found out about them in the end; and then, in Katy's experience, it always made everything ten times worse.

She was beginning to think that it might be best if she did not see Philip Mason again.

15

They went to Putney Heath on the third Thursday in May. Katy had not, as she feared, altogether had to lie about it—at least, not to Aunt Bessie, because it was she herself who had put her off coming. It so happened that luck, or, rather, luck in the shape of Uncle Harold, had played into her hands. Aunt Bessie had written to say that her husband was having 'trouble'. She did not explain what kind, other than that he might have to go into Tooting Bec hospital for an operation. She spelt the last word with a capital 'O' and underlined it heavily. She added that she was very worried about him but felt sure that Katy would understand, although she hoped that she would not be too disappointed.

Katy was not in the slightest bit disappointed, although the news put her in rather a quandary. She felt that it went without saying that Philip Mason would be at the bus-stop to meet her on her next afternoon off, for he had done so regularly ever since their first assignation. But she wondered whether she ought to let him know in advance that she would not be making her usual journey. It was now Monday. Should she post him a letter? Somehow, to write seemed so forward. Besides, she did not want to do anything which might, just conceivably, prevent him from coming to meet her, even though she thought that most unlikely. All the same, might he be upset at the cancellation of their customary routine?

In the end, in an agony of indecision, she simply did nothing—relying on one of her mother's favourite maxims: 'When in doubt, don't'—hurrying to meet him on the day in question, flushed and bright-eyed and wearing, because of an unexpected heat wave, a straw boater for which she had daringly paid one and elevenpence-halfpenny in that year's January sales, and which she had trimmed exactly to match the voile dress which had been Flo's and May's present to her the previous Christmas. When Philip Mason saw her coming, his heart gave a sudden lurch. In all his twenty-one years, he felt that he had never seen anyone looking so appealing or beautiful.

When she told him what had happened he stared at her in such amazement and disbelief that, for a moment, she was afraid that perhaps he would just go away again. Then he did a most surprising thing. He threw his own straw hat up into the air, caught it with one hand, grabbed Katy with the other and hustled her away to another bus-stop. Before she had had time to know what was happening, they had boarded a bus for Putney.

"The Heath is really country, Katy. Just like where you come from, I shouldn't wonder."

"Is it?" She was excited and still breathless, for he had made her run quite fast. She felt suddenly reckless, a little as she had done on the day when she had climbed on to the stage at the Wilhampton fair and sung *Our Lodger's Such A Nice Young Man.* There was about her an unusual combination of decorum, interposed by occasional unexpected wildness. "Do you go there often?" she asked, after he had bought their tickets.

"Used to, when I was small. Dad had a shop in the

High Street in those days. When we moved into the West End, of course, what with Mother getting ill and dying, we never went so much. Come to think of it, I haven't been there for a long time."

She knew that his mother was dead and that he and his father lived by themselves above the present shop. As he had no brothers and, especially, no sisters, she wondered how they managed the domestic side of their life, but she was still diffident of enquiring.

"Sometimes, I wish we'd never moved," he continued, "but I suppose it was a good thing from Dad's point of view. He's done quite well. Still, I don't mean to spend my own life selling books."

"Don't you?" She looked at him in surprise. "But I thought . . . I mean . . . you know so much about them. You're so interested."

"Of course I'm interested, Katy. But there's something better I could do."

"What's that?" She was mystified.

"Write one, of course. One day I'm going to have my name on the cover. I'll be famous. You'll see."

"Oh *Philip*." Her eyes shone. She felt as if she were singing inside. "What will it be about?"

He looked at her very directly. "A girl called Katy, I shouldn't wonder," he replied, smiling, and thinking that no girl in the world could blush as promptly and prettily as the one beside him.

As the bus turned south and went over Putney Bridge, he said, "If I'd known where we were going today, I'd have brought a picnic. Tell you what. I'll buy some cakes in the High Street. I don't know about a cup of tea, though." He thought for a moment. "Would a bottle of lemonade do instead?"

"Lemonade would be lovely."

She realised, with nostalgia, that she had not tasted lemonade since before her father died. She remembered how, on hot summer Sundays, when they walked to Breconbury Woods, he would sometimes secrete a bottle or two in the inside pocket of his best black jacket, which he would produce when they sat down to rest before starting home. She could see him now, releasing the wire-covered top so that the round glass marble stopper went down into the neck of the bottle, and then passing it round, and how Sarah would look disapproving and say that it would spill on their clothes and, in any case, she did not like to see any of her family drinking other than from a cup or a glass, especially, as she put it, 'in public places'. Although it would have been hard to find anywhere less public than where they were sitting at the end of what May, grandly, always called the Camelia Grove—planted by an earlier generation of Fairfaxes—where they only seemed to have the birds for company and Wilhampton was lost in the heat haze far below; while even the usually white-bright chalk-pit on the distant high ridge of downs behind Westonbury appeared to have melted into a shimmering blue sky.

Today, as they reached their destination, she was both pleased and surprised to find that Philip had not been altogether wrong in assuming it would remind her of her home ground. There wasn't the view on the outskirts, of course, but it seemed much more of a wood than a heath and she took an almost childish delight in following him through the narrow pathways between the tangled undergrowth, conscious of the sweet smell of brier rose, the springy turf beneath her feet.

"How about this?" he said, at length, when they came to a small clearing, where a giant oak tree towered overhead, so that they might almost have been in some green cave, so dense was the foliage all around them.

He put down their makeshift picnic and took off his jacket, spreading it carefully at the base of the tree for her to sit on. All at once, she became acutely shy. Her previous feelings of elation gave way to overwhelming self-doubt. She knew that she should not be here at all, alone with this strange young man who said he was going to become a famous writer, but whom she had only known such a very little while. Whatever would her mother say? Or Flo and May? Aunt Bessie? Mrs Moreton and Nanny Barlow? She had been wicked and deceitful in allowing the latter to think she was going to Tooting Bec.

"Katy?" Philip, already kneeling on the ground struggling with the top of the lemonade-bottle, suddenly looked up. "Aren't you going to sit down?"

She did so, nervously, carefully arranging the skirt of her voile dress—by no means as short as most of her employer's—over her legs.

When he had at last managed to dislodge the stopper, he handed her the bottle and she took a few mouthfuls.

"Shall we have the cakes now or later?"

"I don't mind . . ." She hesitated. "Philip, have you the time on you? I . . . mustn't be late back."

"But we've only just come, Katy. I don't have a watch, but it can't be much more than half past three. Aren't you enjoying yourself?" He wore the same crestfallen look which he had done at their second meeting, when she had said that she would not be able to come back to the shop for the book he was keeping for her. She was torn between the desire to please, yet the fear of so doing.

Afterwards, she could not quite remember exactly when he had taken hold of her hand or how it came about that his arm was around her, nor how he had somehow removed her straw boater and begun to kiss her, gently at first, but then with increasing urgency. She could only recall that at one point she found herself responding to his advances with the same ardour, of a thrill, a longing, that ran right through her. But suddenly something—possibly the thought of Sarah or, even, in some confused, unaccountable way, poor Neil—made her push him aside and struggle to her feet.

There was silence between them. He picked up her hat and waited while she pinned up her hair which had become loosened. The tautness of her dress, straining over her small rounded breasts as she raised her arms, made him turn aside.

"I'm sorry, Katy," he said, as they made their way back to the bus-stop. "I meant no harm."

She nodded, still filled with conflicting emotions which she could scarcely understand or control. On the way home, in order to bring some semblance of normality back into their relationship, she asked him, diffidently, when he would start his book.

He continued to look straight ahead. "I don't know," he replied, enigmatically. "It depends on a lot of things."

She left him in Park Lane, soon after they got out of the bus, horrified to hear the clock above the Grosvenor Chapel chiming seven. As soon as she stepped inside the nursery at Number 89 and saw Nanny Barlow's grave face and heard what she had to say, she became panic-stricken.

"Mrs Moreton would like to see you, Katy. I told her I would send you down to her bedroom as soon as you came in." There was no reference to her lateness, merely a firm, subdued statement.

Her hand was shaking as she tapped on the door. Her mouth felt dry. She had been found out. Someone had seen her. It had been tempting fate to have thought that she could get away with such outrageous behaviour. In her remorse and anxiety, her imagination became completely out of control. They must have been followed. Someone from the household must have been on the bus, probably peering through the bushes, just at the moment when she had put her arms round Philip and kissed him back with an intensity of which she had no idea she was capable. Could a kiss like that make one pregnant? She would then be guilty of that sin of sins. She would bring disgrace on the family. Her mother would cast her out. Whatever happened at the moment, Mrs Moreton would most certainly send her packing from Number 89.

She was so concentrated on what she was expecting to hear that she took little notice of her employer's opening remarks, not really registering anything other than the fact that she must be on the nine o'clock train to Wilhampton in the morning—the matter presumably being so serious that there was no question of her not being able to travel alone.

She was still more or less bemused when Mrs Moreton finally stood up and she caught the words, said with both kindness and concern, "I am so very sorry, Katy. Let's hope you find things much better than you may think. After all, the telegram only referred to a *temporary* need for your presence at home."

16

It was Edith who met her. As soon as Katy saw her standing on the Wilhampton platform, she noticed a great difference in her married sister's appearance since they had met last Christmas. Her figure was somehow fatter and dumpier, her blue gingham dress clean but crumpled, her usually smiling face worn and lined, while the mass of auburn hair was flecked with more than a touch of grey. She had, moreover, obviously lost one or two teeth. Of all the family, Edith had always been the most negligent about using a toothbrush, having even said, shortly after marrying Herbie, that it might save trouble if she had the whole lot out. Though younger than both Flo and May, she seemed all at once to have become a middle-aged matron.

"Katy, my dear." She held out her arms. "I'm so glad you've come. I didn't think I could leave the children with Herbie and sit up another night at the mill this week."

"Sit up? Edie, what is it? The telegram didn't say much."

"No, well, we've been trying to keep it from you, hoping Flo would take a turn for the better, but she's been in bed six weeks now."

"*Six weeks*?" They began to hurry away from the station, Katy carrying the small suitcase which Nanny Barlow had lent her.

"Yes. It's . . . something internal. She's lost a lot of blood. But she seems to think she's getting better every day, although we can't help being worried. Dr Fitzherbert isn't very forthcoming. But that's not exactly why we sent for you yesterday."

"What do you mean?" Not for the first time during the past twenty-four hours did panic seize her. "What *is* it, Edie?" she said again. "May's all right, isn't she?" May had always come first in her affections.

"Yes, Katy. She's very tired, naturally. But you see . . . well, the long and the short of it is that two days ago Mother . . ." She broke off, uncertain of how best to impart her distressing information, and then continued, hesitantly, "Look, lovey, you must be prepared. She's not herself. She's lost her memory."

"Lost her *memory*?" In spite of her desire to get on, Katy stood stockstill in the middle of the dusty white road. "But . . . how . . . why?"

"It happened a week or so back, but only for a few hours. Herbie found her wandering about by the mill-race. Dr Fitzherbert says it's quite understandable in a way, when you come to think of it, what with Flo's illness coming on top of all she's been through. It's nature's way out, so to speak. When she came to after the first go, he said we must keep her as quiet as possible, that she ought to get away, but of course you know what she is. And she wouldn't come to me. Besides, poor May needs help. She can't nurse one invalid, let alone two, and carry on dressmaking."

"Oh, *Edie*!" They had begun to walk on now, taking the short cut across the meadows, which it was only possible to do at this time of the year. The scent of hay was in the air, the hedges on either side of them white with cow parsley, the horse-chestnut tree by the first stile covered with the pink flowering candles which Katy always loved. In the field known as Upper Croft, one of the Bulbarrow farm workers was mowing, his deep gruff voice calling out to his cart-horse to "Coom up, there, Vi'let", as they turned a corner. Further on, in Lower Croft, in a more inaccessible place near the river which Katy had always called Nomansland, Ted Shergold was cutting some longer grass with a scythe: the slow, rhythmical, swishing sound of his labours mingling with the distant call of a cuckoo and the plop of a trout rising for may-fly, as they crossed over one of the narrow, rickety, wooden bridges.

Summer was everywhere, the countryside alive with new growth. Even Edith began to refer to such things, explaining, a little shyly, the reason for her increase in weight. "The news isn't all bad, Katy," she said, "although I could have wished I hadn't fallen just now. I'm having another baby in October."

"Another?" Again, Katy was incredulous. She supposed she should say something congratulatory, rejoice with her married sister, but she could only feel dismay.

"Yes. I always wanted a big family, remember? I like to have the little ones around me. Keeps me young."

"I see." Although Katy did not really see at all. She felt that Edith's last remark hadn't made sense. Children made you *old*, surely, long before your time, unless you were fortunate enough to be in a position to have them looked after by people like Nanny Barlow or herself. She had only to think of her mother and the pregnant woman beside her to realise that. Suddenly, the morning seemed unreal. She wondered whether any of it was really happening. Only when she heard the old, familiar, relentless sound of the mill-race as they reached the outskirts of the mill itself did the stark actuality of all that she had just been told begin to sink in. As they walked down the main passageway, although the sun was still shining, it seemed as if they had stepped out of the light. She shivered slightly.

"What shall I say, Edie, about why I've come home?"

"I was going to warn you, before we went inside the house. May said she thought it might be best if you pretended to Mother—that is, if she asks, which I doubt—that you've come home early for your holiday. And to Flo too, for that matter. After all, you've been at the Moretons' nearly a year. You're due for your week next month, aren't you?"

She nodded, unhappily. One or two of the mill-hands passed by, touching their caps a little awkwardly and mumbling, "Good-morning." She caught the whiff of the same curious indefinable smell which she knew, even if she were blindfold, as well as deaf to the sound of the mill-race, would always tell her exactly where she was. It was not unpleasant, simply a 'wet-woollen-clothes-hanging-up-to-dry' smell. She had breathed it, grown up with it. It was somehow there, in her lungs, a part of her. Suddenly it seemed as if she had not been away from home at all. Mayfair, Philip Mason and Putney Heath might never have existed.

Rather to her surprise, her mother was fully dressed and lying on the couch when they entered the front door. May was attending to something on the range, but she quickly put down a saucepan and came to kiss her youngest sister. She said little, but the strength and warmth of her embrace expressed both her relief and pleasure in a way no words could have done. Then she turned to Sarah, "Look, Mother, who's come home!"

Katy went across to the couch and knelt beside it, doing her best to stifle the fear she felt on looking into the troubled, uncomprehending eyes which stared back at her, and trying not to recoil when she felt a hand come up to touch her cheek.

"Katy." The voice was curiously laboured and emotionless. "Shouldn't you be at Miss Maidment's?" Dear God, her mother must have gone back in time over three years to when she had been doing her dressmaking apprenticeship. Was this really Sarah's way of wiping out all that had happened in the intervening ones? Of letting nature, as Dr Fitzherbert had apparently suggested, help her to escape from all that she had been through during them? She turned uncertainly towards May, wondering how to reply.

"Katy's having a bit of a holiday, Mother," she heard her say, quickly.

The answer seemed to suffice. Sarah nodded and closed her eyes. Silently, May beckoned her youngest sister out of the room. "You'd best go up to Flo now. She'll have heard you come," she whispered. "She looks different, mind. Try not to show you notice."

She found Flo lying in the brass-headed double bed in Neil's old room, a thin, white-faced travesty of her old self: her long brown hair loose on the pillows, her emaciated arms resting limply on the counterpane. Yet the fine dark eyes shone with joy at seeing her and she struggled to sit up.

"Katy! What a lovely surprise. Is it really true they've given you your holiday early?"

"Yes." She bent over and kissed her.

"That must mean you've been a good girl."

A good girl? The distortion of the truth to which she knew she must adhere seemed somehow doubly distasteful and shameful. She had been anything but a good girl. She had been a wicked one. Perhaps that was why all these troubles had happened. She—or, rather, her family—was paying the price for her sins.

"Just think," Flo went on, "we'll have you with us for a whole week. Though I'm sorry you've found Mother and me so poorly. But never mind, we'll both be up and running around again before you go back to London. You mark my words." Then, as if the effort had been too much for her, Flo lay back and momentarily closed her eyes. There were beads of sweat on her forehead, her faded pink lawn nightdress, trimmed with broderie anglaise, showed signs of damp beneath the arms.

Katy sat down on the bed and held one of her hands, painfully aware of the difference between the poorly-furnished bedroom she was now in and the luxurious one where, less than twenty-four hours before, she had been told she must return home. She glanced up at the blue and gold embossed text on the wall above Flo's head which Sarah had placed there years ago when Neil had been quite small, embodying the prayer about little children, which ended: 'Suffer me to come unto Thee'. Well, poor Neil had done that, hadn't he? Or so she hoped. But what about Frank lying they knew not where, probably not even buried properly, in foreign soil? She had a sudden desire to get up and tear it down. Although it was prettier and not nearly so harsh and guilt-provoking as the ones which were pinned up each week outside the chapel at the corner of East Street, it seemed so inappropriate, even offensive, with Flo now looking like a death's head, even though she would keep on about feeling better: "All the more so," she insisted, "for seeing you, Katy."

"Look over there," she said, suddenly, pointing towards the small whatnot in the corner, on which stood a flagon of Harvest Burgundy and a glass. "Dr Fitzherbert advised it," she explained, almost apologetically, as if the presence of alcohol in her room must be excused. "He says it's excellent for anaemia. It's replacing all the blood I've lost through an early change of life. Mother's put a rusty nail inside, so as to give it more iron. It's done me a power of good already."

"I'm glad, Flo." Katy was surprised—even alarmed—at how adept she was becoming in dissembling.

"We couldn't help laughing the other day," Flo went on, with a little of her old spirit, "after Edie's eldest had been up to see me. He's such a bright little lad. He went downstairs, looked at Mother's picture of *The Last Supper* hanging over the piano, and asked if it was right for Christ Jesus and his auntie to be drinking burgundy."

Saddened, Katy left her, marvelling at Flo's implicit and almost childlike faith: presumably in God, in her youngest sister's heaven-sent homecoming and the cheap red wine which she was vaguely aware could be bought at the chemist's in Westonbury.

As soon as she re-entered the living-room, May gathered together a mass of black georgette which she had been tacking and stood up. Edith appeared to have gone home.

"Now you're here, Katy," she said, "I think I'll go down to the workroom with this. I'm so behind with everything. It's a dress for Lady Fairfax which was promised for yesterday. When she sent down for it I said that, whatever happened, she should have it to wear when they're entertaining at the Hall tomorrow night. Perhaps you'd mind the dinner, lovey, not that Mother or Flo will want very much, I expect." Then she was gone, pushing out one of her little feet to prop the front door that much further open as she went out, to allow whatever passage of air was possible to pass through the small stuffy house in which, even in the middle of a heat-wave, there had to be a fire for cooking purposes.

Katy turned towards the range, anger rising within her that Lady Fairfax's dress had to take priority over so many more grave and urgent considerations. If she—or her daughter, for that matter—really knew the conditions under which May had been struggling to make it, surely they would realise that it was neither possible, nor even necessary, for it to meet the trivial deadline of some purely social occasion? What was that compared to the needs of a seriously ill woman whose mother had lost her memory?

She knew that she was possibly being unfair, that both Lady Fairfax and her daughter were, after their fashion, exceptionally kind-hearted. She had even been sent to Waterloo that morning in her employer's chauffeur-driven Hispano-Suiza. But could they possibly understand the suffering, hardship, comfortlessness and appalling inconvenience of trying to care for the sick in the Mill House? To do that, Katy felt, they would actually have had to be there, performing the task themselves. Whatever tragedies occurred in their own lives they were, materially at least, cushioned against them. The illness of a lady's-maid, the sudden lack of Katy's own services, even the indisposition of a member of their own family, were usually but temporary inconveniences. They were not going to have to sit up with an ailing mother or sister or child. Any lack of sleep from which they might suffer during crises would only affect them mentally, never physically as well, as it was all too obvious by their worn and even dishevelled appearance had recently been the case with May and Edith. The lives of Lady Fairfax and her daughter would somehow go on without too much disruption. They might be grieved, at times even shocked, but they would at least be saved any anxiety over their inability to fulfil a dressmaking order, the problem of there being only one pair of hands—and overworked ones at that—to bring in the money, where before there had been two.

Sarah still had her eyes closed as, quietly, Katy

began seeing to their midday meal, lifting the lid of a saucepan containing a small rabbit stew, another where the potatoes were not quite at the boil. Then she squeezed round the table to the glass-fronted cabinet, extracting a cloth, knives and forks and glasses with which to set the table and lay the only tray she could find—the one she always thought of as Mr Fuller's—before picking up an enamel jug to fetch fresh drinking water from the tap in the mill. As she went towards the front door a shadow fell across the threshold and she suddenly found herself confronted by the figure of a tall, thin, fair-haired young man standing on the step, one who, at first glance, she failed to recognise.

"Miss Lodge? Miss . . . Katy?" He smiled shyly and held out his hand. "May I come in? I'm Maurice Fitzherbert. I'm living at home again, helping my father with the practice now that I'm qualified. It's been getting so large . . . a bit too much for him to handle by himself lately. He asked if I would call in today to see your mother and sister."

17

Katy took Lady Fairfax's dress to the Hall the following morning, May having worked far into the night in order to finish it. "I've put a note inside about why it's late," she explained, as she handed her the cardboard box, carefully labelled and wrapped in brown paper and string, "but you might just be able to see her ladyship yourself, if you ask for Emily Harwood when you get there."

She nodded. There had been little time for a proper

talk with May about the situation since her return, but it seemed obvious to Katy that there would be no chance of her going back to London in the foreseeable future. Flo was dying. Without having put it in so many words, May had more or less managed to confirm what Katy felt sure was the case. Even when Maurice Fitzherbert had laughed and joked while visiting her the previous day, a brief glance at the expression on his face—for a second, unmasked—after he came out of the bedroom, had left Katy in little doubt as to the seriousness of her sister's illness.

As for Sarah, it was difficult for anyone to predict what might happen. For four days she had been—according to May's brief, whispered account after they had helped her to bed the first evening—in what Claud Fitzherbert had described as another state of shock, possibly because that Tuesday she had asked him, quite directly, whether her eldest daughter had cancer and he had replied, as gently as he could, that he feared it was so; but he had apparently gone on to say that he had known remissions in certain cases and that they must none of them lose hope. One thing which was so much in the patient's favour was her own determination to get better, her firm belief in her recovery—as well, of course, as the loving care of her family. He did not add that if Flo had come to him earlier, he might have advised an operation, not that, in his experience, such a measure often gave other than a few more months' expectation of life.

After his visit, May said that Sarah had disappeared and she had become worried as to where she could have gone. For a moment the thought of the mill-race had unhappily crossed her mind. It had been late in the day, no one was about, and she had rushed straight there, but there had been no sign of her mother. Uneasily, she had returned home. She did not like to go further afield, as she did not want Flo to know of her anxiety; neither did she want to leave her alone. She decided that if Sarah had not returned within another half an hour, she would slip along River Lane to the Henstridges' cottage, much as she was loath to raise an alarm. Since Neil's death she felt that there had been more than enough talk in Wilhampton about the Lodge family. Although the stories regarding Sidney Lodge's ghost had certainly died down—especially with the advent of the long, light, summer days—she was sadly aware that Flo's illness had now taken its place. It had become a much-discussed subject of unwholesome interest, conversations often ceasing abruptly when she entered the shops or passed little groups of people in the street, the tail end of such remarks as 'poor thing', 'a bad business' or 'no age, really' seeming to hang uncertainly in the air.

Then, suddenly, May had continued, just as she was warming some milk that evening to make a junket for the invalid, Sarah had appeared at the front door in the company of the Reverend Donaldson.

"I found your mother in the church, May," he had said, "when I went to lock up. I think perhaps she is a little . . . overstrained." To her daughter's consternation and embarrassment, Sarah had simply walked straight past her without saying a word and gone to lie down on the couch, the total absence of her customary good manners making it plain to them both that, once again, something was very amiss.

Now, as Katy hurried across the market square and was nearing the rectory, she met the rector coming out of his high, wrought-iron front gates. He was a large, hatchet-faced individual, with enormous shaggy eyebrows and a very deep voice, which Katy recalled reverberating throughout St Mark's in a somewhat terrifying manner when he delivered his sermon each

Sunday. Hitherto, she had always been scared of him, although she knew that he was a good, sincere man, much respected by her mother and sisters. Once, when she had been about ten or eleven years old and had been passing the selfsame spot where she now found herself, he had happened to be taking some of the doctor's children across to the church in order to let them climb up into the belfry to see the bells. Immediately, he had invited Katy to accompany them. Halfway up the seemingly never-ending, steep, wooden steps, she had begun to feel dizzy but, sandwiched between Maurice Fitzherbert and his sister, Connie, there had been nothing for it but to go on, especially as she did not know any of the children well and stood greatly in awe of them. She had always felt everlastingly grateful to Maurice for telling her, quietly, as they started their descent, to follow him and not look down.

Today, as she began to answer the Reverend Donaldson's solicitous enquiries, she thought how little he had changed compared to the young man whom she had seen yesterday and who was now a fully-fledged doctor. As she went on her way she knew that she, too, of course, had altered. She realised that leaving home must have had a great deal to do with it, although it was strange, she reflected, that in some extraordinary way, sooner or later Wilhampton always seemed to pull its sons and daughters back to the fold again. But, be that as it may, she was very conscious that she was now being treated as an adult, whereas twelve months previously she would have been spoken to as a child. The rector had even shaken her hand as they parted, saying, gravely, "I am so very glad to know that you have come, Katy. This is your place now. You're needed at the Mill House so much."

It was good to have him say this, in spite of the fact

that she already knew, only too well, just how much she was needed. Tomorrow, if she found time, she would write Philip Mason a letter and tell him what had happened. She felt sad—albeit a little relieved—that she would probably never see him again. But it was surely right that she should resist temptation, forgo any thought of those moments of delight which had both scared and thrilled her. That was the least she could do. She still could not rid herself of the idea of some just punishment now being meted out for all her misdemeanours, for which she must try to atone.

When she arrived at one of the side entrances to the Hall, she was surprised to find that Ena Perrick answered the door. Katy had not known that Ena—a year younger than she was—had been taken on by the Fairfaxes as under-parlourmaid, although it was hardly surprising that May had forgotten to mention it. Besides, since all the unfortunate repercussions following Neil's death, she knew that there had been even more of an estrangement between their respective families, although she, personally, bore Ena no ill will and was sorry that because of this and her own departure to London, their friendship appeared to have suffered. She was distressed, now, at the cold way in which Ena greeted her, looking her up and down with a mixture of defensiveness and jealousy in her dark little eyes.

"Hello, Katy. Fancy seeing you."

"Hello, Ena. How are you?"

"All right. More than can be said for you, by the looks of it. Never seen you so washed out. London town evidently doesn't suit you."

"I . . . we've sickness at home, Ena. I was up most of last night."

"Oh." The girl in the doorway seemed slightly mollified, but not for long. "I heard something about it," she mumbled. "Your mum's wandering, isn't she?"

Katy flushed. "She's overtired, Ena. May I see Mrs Harwood, please?"

"*Mrs Harwood*?" Ena frowned. "I'm sure I don't know. She doesn't like being bothered, 'specially on a Saturday morning. She's extra busy because we've company coming. If it's just that parcel you're leaving, couldn't you give it to me?"

"I could, Ena, but I'd like to see Mrs Harwood all the same, if it's possible."

Katy stood her ground. There was silence between them. Then, resentfully, Ena turned away from the door and disappeared down the dark, flag-stoned passage.

Katy waited on the step, feeling that at least Ena might have asked her inside. Surely she would not get very far as a parlour-maid if she treated all her callers in such fashion. It was hot where she was standing, for there was no porch at this entrance and the sun was beating straight down. She wished she had not undertaken her errand without wearing a hat. In London she would automatically have put on her straw boater, however much of a hurry she was in. Could it really be less than forty-eight hours ago when Philip Mason had removed it in the bushes on Putney Heath? In spite of her sorrow and weariness and resolve not to indulge in such speculations, her flush became deeper, the memory of his kisses reawakening that strange, hitherto unknown feeling which she had so unexpectedly experienced. Still clutching her parcel, she closed her eyes and leant against the doorway, the wooden surround warm against her tired body, the scent of wallflowers in a nearby border overpowering in the heavy, noonday heat.

"Why, Katy!" She started, violently, at the sound

of Emily Harwood's voice, as she came bustling down the passage to meet her, bright-eyed and red-cheeked, wearing her black nun's veiling uniform dress, her grey hair scraped up into a neat little bun on the top of her head.

"Come into the cool, my dear. You must be fit to faint out there. I can scarce remember it being so hot at this time of the year. Tell me about your mother, and Flo."

Katy was drawn into a small pantry just inside the door and given a glass of ice-cold water, which she accepted gratefully. She knew Emily Harwood to be a gossip, yet she was also a motherly soul, in fact, more so in many ways than Nanny Barlow. She was not at all the usual forbidding type of house keeper to be found in such a large establishment. Having been left a widow at a young age with three children on her hands to support, she had been forced to leave them in the care of her own mother and, with great spirit and fortitude, gone into service at the Hall where, over the years, she had risen to her present position. Her treatment of Katy was now certainly very welcome after Ena's sourness, even if it did mean Emily was wanting to hear the latest news from the mill.

"They're neither of them too good, Mrs Harwood," she replied, slowly, as she drank the water. "That's why I've come home." She hesitated and put down the glass. "May was wondering whether I might see her ladyship. Of course, if it's inconvenient . . ." She broke off, not at all certain that she really wanted to do so, nor that it was a very good idea after all. Surely there was nothing more she could say, other than what was in the note? But she supposed May felt that by seeing Lady Fairfax, Katy would be able to testify to the seriousness of the situation, to justify the sending of a telegram—even if it had been advised by Dr Fitzherbert—which had brought her daughter's nursery-maid all the way back from London. Yet there had never been the slightest hesitation on Alicia Moreton's part about the need for Katy to return home at once and it was more than likely that she had by now written to tell her mother exactly what had happened. Katy knew that the two of them kept in very close contact. Her employer had often spoken of how she was looking forward to when a telephone could be installed at the Hall.

It was almost a relief when she heard Emily Harwood say, "I'm afraid her ladyship isn't here, Katy. She's gone to the Westonbury Show. Lord Fairfax is speaking at the luncheon."

"Oh, I see. I'd best be getting back then. Thank you for the drink, Mrs Harwood." She made for the door.

"Right you are, my dear. You run along now. May must be very glad to have your help. Tell her I'll probably look down to see you all one afternoon next week when we're not so busy here."

"Yes," she replied, trying not to sound too doubtful. She had a feeling that May might not altogether welcome a visit from Emily Harwood just at the moment, nor anyone else for that matter. It was bad enough having to keep changing the sheets in anticipation of the doctor's visit and seeing that both invalids, besides the house, looked clean and tidy. When Sarah came to again, she would not like to think that her family had not kept up appearances.

18

At first she took him for just another fisherman, when she saw the distant figure casting near the Black Arch one evening towards the middle of June. She knew that there were many people in the neighbourhood to whom the Fairfaxes gave the right to fish the River Willon and the various streams which joined it close by the mill-race. It went without saying, of course, that every tenant on the estate was given a 'day', or sometimes two, during the season, but Katy was well aware that there were many more people besides farmers who received such favours. Sometimes, they would walk home through the mill and, if they happened to know her parents and their creels were full, they would leave a trout or grayling at the Mill House, which Sarah would immediately scrape and clean and then fry in butter the following morning, so that each member of the family could be treated to a taste for breakfast.

Once, when Katy had been about ten or eleven years old, her father himself had been among the lucky ones. Old Mr Swayne up at Bulbarrow had fallen off a rick during haymaking and, as his permit was for a Saturday, he had sent word to Lord Fairfax's agent, asking whether Sidney Lodge —whom he liked and respected—might use it when the mill shut down at one p.m. To her great joy, her father had suggested taking her with him. She could remember helping Sarah to cut sandwiches and the two of them setting off, Sidney Lodge with the rod which Mr Swayne had lent him; herself, wearing a red and white spotted cotton sun-bonnet, carrying their picnic in a little wicker basket.

She had never forgotten the occasion. It had been so peaceful and trouble free. Her father had seemed altogether different, not the hardworking, often harassed manager of the Felt Mills, but a kinder, gentler, happier person, with time to explain so many things to her: that grayling were not so cunning as trout, that she must keep either close behind him or a good way away, so that she would not get caught herself when he was casting, that if he happened to hook a fish and it was under the limit, he would have to throw it back. She had wondered how he knew so much about the sport, considering she had never seen him engage in it before, other than to help the water-keepers with their annual netting of grayling or sometimes lend a hand with Ernest Fielding's eel stage; but he had told her that he had learnt a lot from his own father—a somewhat shadowy figure in Katy's life—who, until his early death caused by contracting lockjaw, had been a farmer who had come down in the world, gambling away his inheritance many miles west of Wilhampton.

Was it, she wondered, because the memory of that golden afternoon in childhood had always been so special to her that now, whenever she felt she could be spared for a while, she seemed to gravitate towards the meadows? As if mind and body were automatically seeking the place where she knew that quietude dwelled, together with the aptly-named wild heart's-ease and meadow-sweet? Certainly at this particular time of her life a few moments by the banks of the Willon helped to relieve—if only fleetingly—the thought of all the suffering which she had left but a little way behind her at the Mill House.

For although her mother's memory had returned, it

seemed but tenuous. Sarah remained both frail and fractious. As for Flo, she appeared to grow weaker daily, railing at the fact that she could no longer get out of bed unaided and that her youngest sister was having to take an extended 'holiday' on her account. This evening, before leaving for her walk, Katy had promised not to be gone long, for it was her turn to sit up during the first part of the night and she knew that May would wish to lock up and go to bed early. When she came to the first stile, she sank down on the grass gratefully and, leaning back against it, closed her eyes and lifted her face to the fast-disappearing sun, unaware that the fisherman whom she had noticed was casting downstream and gradually coming closer. Suddenly, the sound of parting rushes made her start. She turned her head and found herself looking straight into the kind, but somewhat concerned, eyes of Maurice Fitzherbert.

"Good-evening, Miss Katy. I'm sorry. I'm afraid I must have startled you."

"Oh no . . . I was just taking a rest, that's all," she replied, angry to feel the inevitable blush coming so swiftly to her cheeks.

"A much deserved one, I'm sure." Carefully, he placed his rod against the stile and then, when he saw her make a move to get up, said quickly, "Must you go? I'm sure you would have stayed a little longer if I hadn't appeared in such a singularly ungracious fashion. As a matter of fact," he went on, searching for something in the pocket of his light linen jacket, "I was intending to stop here for a smoke, before having one final flog below the mill-race. Do you have any objection to a pipe? I know my mother doesn't care for it indoors."

"Oh no." She looked at him, nervously. She still felt she should depart. On the other hand, the last thing she wanted was to appear rude. He and his father were doing so much for them all. Yet was he really meaning to linger here with her, alone, in the water-meadows, especially at this hour? Supposing they were seen? He was certainly extremely courteous and unassuming, an older, altogether different young man from Philip Mason; but, all the same, she didn't really know him at all. Besides, between his family and hers there had always been that indefinable barrier which made any kind of social intercourse seem—at least, to Katy—not only embarrassing, but somehow wrong. True, it was not such an obvious one as might have been the case had she been, say, Ena Perrick. For the Lodges had always held a rather unique position in the Wilhampton hierarchy, that is, if they held any definable position at all. For they appeared to have no particular niche, belong to no special group. They were neither working-class, nor thought of as 'trade', unless one counted Flo's and May's dressmaking business. They were simply the somewhat unusual, closely-knit family who lived at the misleadingly-named Mill House: well-mannered, exceptionally well turned out, mostly well-spoken and immensely proud.

"Do you come here often?" she heard Maurice Fitzherbert ask as, possibly sensing her uneasiness, he sat down, but on the opposite step of the stile, and began to fill his pipe.

"As often as I can." Shyness had always made her abrupt.

"It's the same with me," he replied, slowly. "I've always loved this stretch of water. I think I missed it more than anything when my training and then, of course, a spell in the army combined to keep me away from it. I suppose that's why we've hardly met for such a long time."

"Yes. Yes, I expect so," she answered, still agitated.

"And I've been away, too," she added, shyly, "in London."

He nodded and then said, unexpectedly, "Did you like it there?"

She hesitated. Did she like London? Yes and no, really. The last little bit had certainly been exciting, but she couldn't tell him that. She couldn't tell anyone, not even dear May, although she had felt obliged to explain to her that the letters she kept receiving were from a young man whose father owned a book-shop close to Upper Brook Street, whom she had got to know through the purchase of a marked-down edition of *Wuthering Heights*. Since she had written to Philip Mason soon after she came home to tell him what had happened, he had sent her many letters: strange, impassioned, originally-phrased ones, the last arriving only that morning, demanding to know why he never received any replies.

"I don't think I should want to live there always," she answered at length, almost primly.

"No. Neither would I. There was a time, when I first started training at Guy's that I thought maybe I'd try and specialize, have my name up on a plate in Harley Street one day, and then, I don't know . . . I think the war knocked that idea out of my head. I thought it would be more worthwhile to be a country doctor when I qualified. You learn more about individuals. And life. Besides, I'm needed where I am now, a bit as you are, in a way. My father . . ." This time it was he who hesitated, before continuing, "Well, it isn't common knowledge, but I think he may retire soon. He's always worked so hard. If I were in charge of his case, I'd say he ought to stop at once."

"Oh, *no*." Her response was now quite natural and spontaneous, but she hoped that she had not hurt him by it. It was simply that she could not imagine what she and her family would do without the older man. They had always depended on him so much. He had seen them through so many vicissitudes, had taken such infinite trouble over her when she was a child, even to giving her the little dictionary when she had missed almost a whole year's schooling.

"Don't worry," he laughed, not at all put out. "He's not going to go just yet. And by the time he does, I'll know a lot more. About all of you," he added, with a diffident yet almost conspiratorial grin. She started feeling uncomfortable again and rose to go.

He stood up also. "Good-night, Miss Katy."

"Good-night," she said, wishing he would not address her like that and wondering what on earth she should call him. 'Dr Maurice', as everyone else did, she supposed, as she hurried back through the mill, remembering that the only other occasions when she had actually exchanged more than a few words with him had been the time when he had helped her down from St Mark's belfry after seeing the Reverend Donaldson's bells, and another winter's morning when they had both happened to be buying sweets in the Perricks' shop. She recalled clearly how he had asked for two ounces of gobstoppers, popping one into his mouth as soon as they got outside and, because it was such an enormous sugary marble, before he had had time to suck it so that it became smaller and changed colour, it had somehow shot out of his mouth and rolled all along the gutter of River Lane. Horrified, she had watched him run and pick it up and put it back in his mouth again and, in her innocent anxiety, forgetting both manners and shyness, she had shrieked, "But it's dirty. You'll catch diphtheria." And he had replied, "Don't worry. Abie Grant will have something in his dispensary to save me from that."

How long ago it now seemed: that time when the

very sight of Abie's face, doling out the meticulously wrapped and sealing-waxed remedies from his little square 'window', was enough to make one feel that all would be well, no matter whether the actual preparations were prescribed by Dr Fitzherbert. Even when Katy had been too ill to be taken to the surgery by Sarah and had had to be visited at home, Claud Fitzherbert always magnanimously gave the credit for relief to his dispenser by such remarks as: "We'll see what Mr Grant can find, my dear, to send away the pain", or "I believe Abie has the very thing on his shelf for that throat". It had certainly made her, and most of the other children in Wilhampton, invariably feel that it was the little man in the white coat, living permanently—as they supposed—in his two-by-four, medicinal-smelling box of a room, who was the real miracle-worker.

If only Abie could now produce some cure-all for poor Flo, Katy thought, as she went into the front door, noticing May's weary face as she turned away from the range.

"I've made a pot of tea," she said. "I hope it's not stewed. I thought you'd be back sooner." Her voice was not exactly reproachful, but its usual warmth and sweetness were lacking.

"I'm sorry. I met . . . Maurice Fitzherbert. He happened to be fishing and stopped to pass the time of day." There seemed no point in concealing the fact, at least, certainly not from May.

"Did you now!" May poured out some tea and put the pot back on the hob, thoughtfully. "There's not many as come like him these days," she continued, as she started to get out the candlesticks and matches. "His parents must go down on their knees every night and thank the Lord that when he insisted on interrupting his training to join up, the war didn't take him."

19

"Earth to earth, ashes to ashes, dust to dust, in the sure and certain hope of the Resurrection to eternal life . . ." The deep resonant voice of the Reverend Donaldson, standing by Flo's grave in his long white surplice, was heard in respectful silence by the little group of mourners. Around them, on the grass, lay a profusion of floral tributes: red roses, white roses, carnations of every hue, arum lilies, love-in-the-mist, marguerites, dahlias and early pale yellow chrysanthemums, the amalgam of colour contrasting starkly, even defiantly, with the sombre setting.

It was very hot in the cemetery. Katy, her face already blotched and swollen and trying hard to fight back further tears, stared resolutely at the opposite hill, where several little ant-like figures were stooking oats. Had Flo gone to eternal life? Did this devout man really think so? But why should so good and kind a person be singled out for such pain and suffering before she got there?

Katy would like to have asked the rector about the hereafter, but she knew that even to doubt the existence of such a place was blasphemy. She was sure that May and Edith, standing one on either side of her, heads bowed and each clutching a handkerchief, would never have entertained such wicked thoughts. Facing them, flanked by Henry and Herbie on the opposite side of the grave, stood Sarah, a statuesque figure in deep mourning, her expression aloof and enigmatic, as if she were either determined not to break down or was now beyond all feeling. Katy prayed that her mother would not lose her memory again.

Half an hour earlier, St Mark's church had been packed for Flo's funeral. Indeed, Katy could scarcely remember it being so full, not even when her father had died. Wilhampton appeared to have turned out en masse, Lady Fairfax sitting, much to Katy's acute embarrassment, in the pew immediately behind her.

The former had been more than kind during Flo's last agonising weeks. Almost every other day some little delicacy would arrive from the Hall: grapes, calf's-foot jelly, sponge fingers—not that Flo could eat any of them. She had been too weak, too far gone. Towards the end, May and Katy could only get her to take a few sips of home-made barley water, bathe her parched lips in glycerine and dab her forehead with a handkerchief soaked in eau de cologne. Yet even then, incredibly, she had still talked of "When I'm better . . ."

On the morning she died, in the middle of August, she appeared to rally a little. Struggling to sit up in bed, she had gazed at her youngest sister very directly and said, "My Katy, what a beautiful girl you've grown into. You must be careful not to break too many hearts." And Katy had blushed furiously, wondering whether, by some sixth sense, Flo could possibly have known about Philip Mason. She had looked away but, even as she did so, Flo's hand seemed to become strangely limp in her own. She had turned back and stared at her, sensing at once that there was now only a lifeless body in the bed. Katy had never witnessed actual death before and for a moment she wanted to cry out. But, mercifully, May had suddenly appeared, hurried to the bedside, picked up Flo's wrist, nodded and then said quietly, "Thank God."

It had seemed to Katy a bewildering eternity between that morning and the hot sultry afternoon of the funeral. She realised that when her father had died she had been spared all the harrowing details which invariably accompanied such an event, for she had been that much younger and these had been dealt with by her mother and sisters; whereas when Neil had drowned she had simply not been there at all. But now, with Sarah's health so precarious and Edith getting near her time, the whole responsibility devolved, of necessity, on to her's and May's shoulders. True, on receiving their telegram, Henry had wired back to say that he would come for the funeral, but this had been quickly followed by a letter in which he stated that he would like to bring his wife and child with him. He added that Marianne would be quite happy to remain at the Mill House while the funeral was taking place, where she could possibly have the tea ready for everyone by the time they returned, besides taking care of Edith's children as well as little Frank. This had upset not only Sarah but—possibly owing to her delicate condition—Edith, who had said that she would not have a moment's peace leaving her offspring in the care of a Froggie. She had seemed to forget that some of her ancestors on her mother's side had come from across the Channel. Katy had been obliged to go up to the post-office and send Henry a second wire: 'Owing difficulties please come alone', disliking the slant-eyed look which Mabel Snoad, the postmistress, had given her as she paid the requisite elevenpence-halfpenny.

Yet it had been the flowers on the morning of the funeral which had bothered Katy most. Many of them were sent straight to the house, arriving with a kind of sinister, insistent regularity, heralded by heavy male footsteps. She hadn't known where to put them at first, because May had taken Sarah down to the workroom to make an adjustment to the collar of the new black foulard dress she had made for her. Soon, the Mill House seemed to be full of flowers, their scent sickly and overpowering in the hot, stuffy living-room. Wearily, according to May's instructions, she began making a list of their donors in order that they should subsequently be sent a letter of thanks, for the Lodge family did not believe in the impersonal, formal notice which others sometimes inserted in the *Westonbury Journal* on such occasions. Presently, because of the heat and the anguish they were causing her, Katy started taking all the wreaths outside, laying them down in the shadiest part of the garden to await, as Flo's coffin upstairs was awaiting, the arrival of the ancient hearse belonging to Arnold Parker, the local undertaker. Sadly, she knew that when the time came, the coffin would have to be lowered from a bedroom window, there being no other way of transporting it down the narrow, tortuous stairs.

She had just been putting out the last tribute of pinks and Michaelmas daisies, when she heard Sarah's voice behind her, enquiring whom it was from. On being told that Archie Perrick had just brought it, her mother simply held out her hand and said, "Give it to me, child." Horrified, Katy then watched her disappear with it in the direction of the mill-race, realising only too well what was to be its fate. She wondered whether, had she mentioned it, the red roses sent by Guy and Grace Armitage with In Remembrance attached to them would have been disposed of in the same way. When Sarah's memory was working properly, Katy thought miserably as she went back indoors, there was no forgetting old scores even in the midst of present grief.

Yet neither, it would seem, did Sarah forget her manners, especially in public places. As they left the graveside that afternoon, she held out her hand to the Reverend Donaldson, thanked him quietly and courteously and asked if he would like to join them for a cup of tea at the Mill House a little later on. Then, on Henry's arm, she allowed herself to be helped to Arnold Parker's old horse-drawn cab, which was waiting outside the cemetery gates.

May had arranged, despite Sarah's opposition, for one of the more sensible girls at the mill to come in to the house and have two kettles on the boil by the time the family came home, but Katy was both surprised and distressed at the number of other people who now quickly appeared, crowding into the small living-room or standing, a little uncertainly, just outside the front door. It had seemed bad enough having to bury poor Flo without it being deemed necessary to provide tea and currant cake afterwards. When she felt that she had done her duty as far as she was able, she slipped away to the bottom of the garden, and it was here that Henry came looking for her some three quarters of an hour later.

"I've come to say goodbye, kid. My train goes at five fifteen."

"Oh, I'm sorry. I . . . we all hoped you'd stay longer. Can't you catch a later one?"

"I'm afraid not. I had a devil of a time getting here as it was. It isn't all that long since I had to ask for leave to come to Neil's funeral. Besides, Marianne's expecting me."

"Yes." She hesitated. "Henry, how many people are still up at the house?"

"About nine or ten, I should say. Why?"

"It's just that I don't think I can face going back

for a bit. Would you like me to come to the station with you?"

"I'd like that very much. I'll slip up and say goodbye to Mother and May and tell them you'll be coming to see me off. We can take the meadow path."

As soon as they were on their way, Henry said, suddenly, "What are you going to do, Katy, now Flo's gone? Go back to London?"

"No," she answered, quietly, hurrying to keep up with his long strides, "I'm needed here. I've sent for my things. Even though Mother's better, May needs help with the sewing."

He looked at her with some concern. There was less of the happy-go-lucky manner about him now. Like Edith, he seemed to Katy to have aged considerably since she had last seen him.

"You won't regret it, will you, kid?"

"No." She paused and then, as if to reassure herself more than anyone else, repeated, "Oh no. Besides, I never particularly wanted to be a nursery-maid."

He nodded, apparently satisfied. Soon, they were obliged to walk single file, hemmed in by a high hedge on either side, the branches of elm and elder intermingling overhead. She was reminded, sharply, of the day, not so very long ago, when the sky had all but been blotted out by the same kind of tracery on Putney Heath. From over her brother's shoulder, she heard him say, "I suppose it's not the time to ask, really, but I wish you could put in a good word for Marianne with Mother now and then. I'd like to bring her and little Frank to the mill on my next leave. I might be sent to Germany this winter and it doesn't seem right his grandmother's never seen the boy."

"I'll do my best, Henry. I'd love to see little Frank myself, and I know May would, too."

He stopped, suddenly, and felt for his wallet, eventually extracting from it a somewhat crumpled photograph which he handed to her, proudly.

"Spitting image, isn't he?" he remarked, as she found herself looking at a woman holding a small boy who did, indeed, look astonishingly like a photograph of his dead uncle taken at about the same age.

"He's lovely, Henry," she said, wishing she could say the same for his mother, for she could hardly recognise her sister-in-law.

Possibly sensing this, Henry went on quickly, "Marianne's put on a bit of weight since his birth. She's not looking her best in the photo, I'm afraid. 'Course, it's not been easy for her, Katy, living over here, getting used to another country . . . and people haven't been all that kind. But she's not a bad sort, when you get to know her. She's been very hurt by Mother's attitude."

"Yes. Yes, I'm sure she has." She handed him back the photograph and he put it carefully away and walked on. They came to the first stile and he helped her over it. She did not like the thought of his going abroad again. It was good to know that he was in England, even if she rarely saw him. She wished sincerely that there had not been such a rift in family relationships.

On the slope up to the station, she said again, "I really will do all I can, Henry, about Mother. Although, of course, we can't push anything just now."

"Oh no. I realise that. But I thought, perhaps . . . you know . . . little Frank looking so like the other one . . . It might help, somehow."

"Yes. It ought to."

She stayed on the platform, waving until he was out of sight, her eyes filling with tears as she turned to make her way home. Why couldn't her mother open her heart just a little, instead of locking herself up in that proud, obstinate, private world of hers? She must have had warm, impulsive feelings once, surely? It was common knowledge in the family that she had eventually managed to get her own parents to consent to her marrying Sidney Lodge. But what exactly was it that had made her do so? Had she experienced something of the same kind of feelings which Katy had done earlier that summer on Putney Heath? What else could have made her cleave to the prospective, though impecunious, young manager of the Felt Mills and given birth to Frank nine months after the wedding? Had she ever, Katy wondered now, regretted it? Those six other confinements which followed? Especially the last two: Neil a simpleton, and she, herself, such a sickly child. And then all that had happened since: Frank killed in the war, an early widowhood, Neil drowning and now Flo's death from cancer at the age of only thirty-one.

A little way from home, she sat down for a while on the river-bank, watching the water flowing over the weeds, making them wave and undulate like dark green snakes. A family of swans came sedately into view, paddling upstream, the cygnets fussily bringing up the rear. In the distance she could hear the mill-race echoing, as the hymn which the congregation in St Mark's church had sung a few hours earlier, still echoed in her mind. Never before had the well-known lines seemed so poignant. She had first learnt them as a small child, standing by Sarah's side when her mother sometimes sang them as she did her washing in the mill. Later on, she had sung them herself at the National School, at the Thanksgiving service at the end of the war, at her father's funeral and today at Flo's—although, after the first verse, tears had forced her to stop.

Katy closed her eyes. Time, like the Willon, was an

'ever-rolling stream' all right, she thought sadly, as she rested her head on her knees, bearing, far too quickly, all its sons—and daughters—away.

20

"So perhaps you would like to come to nursery tea next Sunday," wrote Nanny Barlow. "John William and I and the new girl, Ettie, will be staying at the Hall all through September and maybe longer. The matinée jacket you knitted for his birthday fits just right. He can't have too many now, what with there being quite a nip in the air sometimes when we go into Hyde Park . . ."

There was not exactly a nip in the air as Katy walked up River Lane and across Wilhampton market-square on the afternoon in question, carrying the small suitcase which Nanny Barlow had lent her when she had come home at such short notice three months earlier. The sun was still hot enough for her to be thankful that she was wearing a black straw hat with a fair-sized brim, instead of being bareheaded as she had been on the last occasion when she had hurried to the Hall with Lady Fairfax's dress. But there was certainly just a hint of autumn in the yellowy tinge of the elm trees in the rector's garden and smoke could be seen spiralling up from one of the allotments on downside, which meant someone had committed the heinous crime of making a bonfire on a Sunday.

Just as before, Katy became aware of the inevitable half-hidden faces peering at her from behind front room curtains, of the suitcase attracting the interest of more than one passer-by and even prompting prim Miss Whatley, the midwife's sister, to murmur, "Not leaving us again, Katy, I hope," as she shepherded her charges to Sunday School. On arriving at the Hall, once again Ena Perrick answered the door, although this time in a much more civil fashion.

"Sorry about Flo, Katy. But I hear it was a happy release."

"Yes."

Ena's eyes strayed towards the suitcase and Katy explained to whom it belonged.

"Then I should just put it down inside here for the moment. Nanny Barlow and Master John are out in the rose garden. She said as how you were to go out there. Do you think you might come back for good now? I don't think Ettie's exactly giving satisfaction."

"No, Ena. I'll be staying home to help May with the dressmaking. It needs two and Mother still has to take things quietly."

"Yes. Yes, I suppose she does." Ena began to accompany her a little way down the flagged path. She obviously had something on her mind. Presently she said, "Forgive my asking, Katy, but what happened to the wreath our Archie brought down to the mill the morning of the funeral? Mum said that when she went up to the cemetery the next day to look at the flowers, she couldn't see it. She wondered whether Arnold Parker left it behind. But if he had, she thought one of you would have been sure to go back with it."

"I . . . I'm sorry, Ena. I really don't know."

For the second time that afternoon Katy had reason to be thankful that she was wearing a hat, hoping its brim was sufficiently broad to hide the colour which now flooded to her face. She did not like lying. Miss Whatley had always warned her of the terrible punishment which would result from such a sin, especially if committed on the Sabbath. She could remember being terrified as a child at Sunday School, listening to Miss Whatley warning them about all the things which would bring down hell-fire if indulged in on that day, her words supported by a curious reference to French shopkeepers who had tried to stay open seven days a week and had all suffered dire consequences. As everyone knew that Miss Whatley had scarcely ever set foot outside Wilhampton, Katy used to wonder how she could possibly have come by such unexpected information.

"Oh, well, never mind. Just as long as you let your Mum know one was sent," Ena went on.

"Yes." Katy could picture the pink and mauve wreath quite clearly in her mind's eye, much clearer than any other, in fact, including Lady Fairfax's arum lilies. She could even imagine it bobbing about in the mill-race, until it got broken up and carried away, along with so many other things which the Willon seemed to dispose of in its impassive omnipotence.

They were now in sight of the high box hedge which surrounded the rose garden and Ena turned to go. "See you again, then, Katy, before you go home, I expect. There's not all that much to do today, thank the Lord, none of the family being in residence."

"Isn't Mrs Moreton here?"

Ena stared at her. "No. Didn't you know? She's in a sanatorium. Her ladyship's gone to visit her."

"*Sanatorium*?" Immediately, Katy's mind went back to the previous winter and the hurried departure of Amy Robinson.

"You mean . . . she's got tuberculosis?"

"Lawks, no." Ena gave a quick glance towards the hedge in front of them, obviously anxious not to be caught gossiping by Nanny Barlow. Then, in a mysterious, almost conspiratorial manner, she tapped her forehead. "I overheard them saying in the servants' hall it's a nervous collapse. Seems as how she got in such a state no one could do anything with her. Perhaps I could pop down to the mill on my next half-day and tell you more . . ."

Ena turned back to the house. Slowly, Katy walked on to the rose garden, hardly knowing what to think, other than it wouldn't do to have Ena coming to the mill and that, whatever happened, their friendship could never be the same again.

"Why, Katy." She found Nanny Barlow sitting on a cushion on one of the old stone seats. Beside her was a pram in which John William's mother had once sat and where now her son, wearing a white cotton sun-bonnet and showing four new teeth, smiled broadly at the visitor.

"I do believe he remembers you, Katy." Nanny Barlow gazed fondly at the infant. "He's very forward for his age, aren't you, little man?"

Katy bent over the pram and held out a finger, which the child clutched firmly before becoming distracted by a bumblebee droning nearby.

"Perhaps you'd like to hold him for a while before we go indoors for tea. I told Ettie to have it ready by half past four." She undid the baby's harness and lifted him up. "There, John William. Who's a pretty boy, then?"

Katy sat down on the seat and took the child in her arms, astonished at how much larger and heavier he had become since she had last seen him.

"He's pulling himself up now," Nanny Barlow continued proudly. "But I'm not encouraging that. Children who walk too soon get bandy legs. Best keep them babies as long as you can. Now, how's your mother, my dear? And May?"

"As well as can be expected, Nanny." She was

surprised at the ease with which they seemed to have slipped into an altogether different relationship: no longer nanny and nursery-maid. Suddenly, it came to Katy that, for all its limitations, she was now a person in her own right. She might not be independent of her family, but she was no longer in domestic service, that state of life about which Sarah had always held such contemptuous views. Coming home had certain compensations, even if it did mean that she would never see Philip Mason again. Only the previous week she had written to tell him this and said that she thought it would be best if he did not write to her any more.

Katy was surprised that Nanny Barlow did not refer to Alicia Moreton's illness until the end of her visit, although she was aware that she was of a far more taciturn nature than Emily Harwood and, owing to her unique position in the household, much more likely to respect any confidences. Only as she got up to leave and a somewhat timorous Ettie had been sent to prepare the baby's bath, did the older woman say, "You must come again, Katy. I think we shall be staying here even longer than I first thought. I'm afraid John William's mother has been ordered a complete rest, so it seems best for us to stop with his grandmother for the time being."

"Thank you," she replied, "I'd like that very much," while realising that the only means of hearing more about what had happened to Alicia Moreton was through Ena Perrick, and that possibility was probably best avoided.

Fred Ashford's dogs set up barking as she neared the west gates and the man himself came out of his cottage and wished her a gruff, "Good-evening." She hurried on, not altogether liking the expression in his eyes, an expression which she could not help having noticed on many another man's face since she had come home. She was aware that all the Lodge girls were reputed to be good-lookers; what she did not know was that the youngest, for all her delicacy as a child, was turning out to be the best.

She became worried when she saw May standing by the mill gates, obviously watching out for her as she came down River Lane and, on drawing nearer, a look on her elder sister's face which she couldn't quite make out. For a moment she wondered whether Sarah had lost her memory again, yet somehow May seemed more excited than anxious.

"Oh chippatoo, Katy! You'd best get up there quickly."

"Up where, May?" She paused, and then said, incredulously, "You don't mean ... Edith's baby's arrived?"

"No, lovey. But someone else has. I've sent him up the meadows. It's your young man from London. It seems as how he's come to spend his holiday in Wilhampton. He's got lodgings at the Snoads'. He's on about doing temporary work, maybe helping with the harvest if we know of a farmer who wants some casual labour, so all I said was . . ."

But Katy did not stop to hear what May had said. She was gone, rushing up through the mill, pulling off her hat as she did so, face flushed, eyes dancing, her hair a little dishevelled as she almost threw herself over the first stile.

She saw him standing by the Black Arch, just where Maurice Fitzherbert had stood not so very long ago. When she came within hailing distance, she shouted, "Philip." He turned and began running towards her, so that when they at last met it was almost a collision. He swung her up in his arms. Then he put her down again.

"Fancy writing like that, Katy," he said, looking at

her in that strange compelling way she remembered so well, "as if you'd never see me again."

21

Much to Sarah's displeasure, Philip Mason lodged at the Snoads' for a week. Had it not been for May's intervention, Katy might well not have been allowed to see him at all during that time. Her mother accused her of having been brazen, deceitful and wicked in keeping his existence so secret. In consequence, he was offered no hospitality at the Mill House, but in the evenings, after he had knocked off work—having shown commendable initiative in obtaining some straight away at Bulbarrow Farm—he was allowed to take Katy for a short walk, "providing you're back before it gets dark, my girl", Sarah would say as she went out of the door.

Once alone, she and Philip would link arms and, on reaching that secluded corner of the meadows which Katy called Nomansland, he would stop to kiss her. But possibly because he realised how much he had scared her on Putney Heath, possibly because he himself was more than a little scared of Sarah, he was gentler with Katy now, exercising—albeit not without difficulty—a restraint which made her feel safer with him. She no longer resisted his advances. Although her acquisition of a young man was sadly frowned upon, it was at least now out in the open and much of her previous guilt about their relationship disappeared. In fact, sometimes as they started home in order to comply with her mother's curfew, she felt frustrated and disappointed with Philip for reminding her that the light was fading fast.

Only on the final day of his holiday were the two of them able to spend longer alone, both acutely aware of the impending parting. He had ceased his labours at Bulbarrow now, for the harvest was over and preparations were going on that very Saturday afternoon for the harvest supper which was to take place in the big tithe-barn later that night. They had therefore set out earlier and gone further afield, crossing the Willon by the Black Arch and then taking the steep short cut up the downs to Breconbury Woods. At the top, as if by mutual consent, they had stopped and turned round, gazing silently down on the whole of Wilhampton, spread out like some tiny toy town below them.

"It's a lovely place, where you live, Katy," Philip said, at length, with his arm still round her. "Shouldn't mind having a place in the country myself one of these days."

She looked at him shyly. He was very tanned now. His work on Bulbarrow, though but short, seemed to have suited him. She had been surprised at the way he had enjoyed—and apparently become quite skilful at—pitching sheaves.

"I know your mother's taken against me, Katy," he continued. "I wish she hadn't. I don't like to think of her and me not getting on, when we're married."

"*Married*!" She was astonished, exultant.

"Why, yes." It was he who now showed surprise that she should ever have doubted the fact. "Of course we're going to be married. I'd hoped to have been able to fix everything up this week. But I can see your mother's got to get used to the idea, not being well and all that. I'll come again, Katy, as soon as I can. Meanwhile, see if you and your sister can't put in a good word for me."

His arm tightened around her and she leant against him, inwardly almost laughing with joy, wondering whether any girl had ever had such a strange, self-assured proposal—if she could actually call it that. Even though it might take a little time to get Sarah's consent, even if she had to go on helping May for a year or so first and she and Philip could only be together sometimes, they could surely become unofficially, and then officially, *engaged.* She would be a young woman with a 'bottom drawer', waiting to marry the man she loved.

He began to kiss her. Without quite knowing how it had come about, she found herself lying stretched out beside him on the warm, springy turf. She was aware of different scents, the ones which belonged to down and woodland: gorse, bracken and wild thyme. Those of the meadow and mill seemed far away. She closed her eyes. His body felt very strong and hard against her own.

"Katy." The urgency which both had experienced on Putney Heath overcame them again but now, with her eager and willing participation, it reached a far greater intensity. "Katy," he kept murmuring and, whenever he gave her breathing-space, she heard her own voice replying, "Philip, oh Philip." Through her thin voile dress and petticoat, she felt his hand caress her breasts and then gradually move lower until it seemed as if it was half-hesitantly, yet half-purposely, pushing between her legs. She began to tremble, conscious of a very different sensation to any she had hitherto known. Then, all at once, he took his hand away and guided one of her own to the same place in his own body. "Please," she heard him say, "Please, Katy." Suddenly a deep shudder seemed to go through him and he called out. After that they both lay still and silent, while a lone plover circled overhead.

Presently, he touched her face very gently. "You didn't . . . mind, did you, my love?"

"No." Did she mind? She was confused, unsure.

"I mean . . . it's not as if . . . anything happened."

"No." She buried her head in his shoulder, anxious that he should not see that her eyes were bright with tears. Even if, as Philip had said, nothing had really taken place, yet, in her heart of hearts, she felt as if it had. If he had not 'come'—which she supposed, to use May's word, he must have done—when he had, would their love-making have progressed further? Would he have gone on to seduce her totally? Would she have allowed him to? To her shame, she was afraid that the answer would have been yes. Even though she still had no clear idea of what exactly happened, she knew that, just for a moment, she had wanted whatever it was desperately. She had been ready not only to give in to Philip's desires, but her own. Scared though she was, she had not been shocked or disgusted. A naturally passionate nature meant that there had been no lasting scars after her unfortunate experience when Neil had crept up to her attic bed. Neither, today, had she pushed Philip aside, as she had done on Putney Heath. She had been prepared to abandon common sense, propriety, a lifetime of the strictest moral indoctrination for the sake of a hitherto unknown but overwhelming urge which she could not explain. There, high on the downs above Wilhampton, on a sunny September evening in 1920, she had been willing to risk the near-certainty—as she now saw it—of pregnancy, her mother's wrath, the door of the Mill House being closed to her for ever.

To Katy, a miss had never been as good as a mile. Her guilt returned, this time to a far greater degree. An overactive imagination started making fact out of fantasy. She had turned into one of those members of society whom Sarah had always held up as a terrible example to all her daughters from the moment they were old enough to understand. She was 'no better than she should be', a 'fallen woman', someone who 'had to get married', like Nancy Shergold, Cissy Lawes and, so rumour had it, Lilian Perrick (except that Ena was reputedly such a tiny baby that she had been able to be more or less successfully passed off as premature, on arriving eight months after the wedding).

The sun had disappeared behind the woods when they got up to go and began walking home through the darkening evening. In the distance Katy could see a figure coming towards them which, as it drew closer, to her consternation she recognised as that of an even worse type of female than the ones who had recently come so swiftly and unhappily to her mind. Grace Armitage, her blonde hair Eton-cropped, a jersey coat slung carelessly over her shoulders and the hem of her short purple tunic dress riding high above her knees, gave Katy a sideways look as she passed and muttered a scarcely audible greeting.

"Who on earth was that?" asked Philip, half turning to stare after her.

"Oh, someone I hardly know. She got hold of the man my sister, Flo, was once hoping to marry," she answered, defensively.

"*Did* she, now." Philip raised his eyebrows, gave a soft whistle and said no more.

As they came down the lane by Bulbarrow Farm, old Mr Swayne's daughter-in-law crossed over to the barn carrying a huge piece of cold boiled gammon. "Why, if it isn't young Philip Mason," she said, smiling; for although he had only worked for them for so short a time, she had not been able to help noticing the strong, thick-set, dark-eyed 'young chap from Lunnon', as he was good-humouredly referred to, each time she had taken tea out to the harvesters. "I reckon we shouldn't have got that last field ricked but for you. And, of course, the weather, thank the Lord," she went on, cheerfully. "You should be a-joining in the fun tonight, but I daresay you've got better things to do, eh?" She darted a quick, mischievous, yet friendly, glance at an increasingly dismayed and embarrassed Katy.

"Do they always have this kind of celebration at this time of the year?" Philip asked, as they walked on.

"Oh, yes. I believe the Swaynes fixed it up for tonight thinking their harvest would have been finished much sooner, but we had a lot of rain the week before last. That's why they were anxious to get all the help they could the last few days. Otherwise, I suppose it would have had to be postponed."

"What happens? At this supper, I mean?"

"Well, I don't know much because women never go, of course," she answered, absently, her mind still preoccupied with what had taken place on Breconbury Down and Dorothy Swayne's innocent but unfortunate remark.

"But you must know a bit. I'm curious."

She wondered how he could possibly be—amazed and somewhat resentful at how quickly he could switch to other matters, even to showing interest in Grace Armitage.

"Well, I suppose it's . . . almost like a private harvest festival . . . everyone at Bulbarrow being glad that all's safely gathered in. And it's a way for Mr Swayne and his family to say thank you to all the men who have worked for them through the year. They have speeches and toasts. And songs," she added, as an afterthought.

"What sort of songs?"

"Oh, I don't know. You've probably never heard of them." She was still offhand, unwilling to engage in a conversation in which temporarily, at least, she felt so little concern. "*Buttercup Joe*," she threw out, curtly, "and *Dick Turpin*. I believe the head carter does an accompaniment on the accordion. And they sing *God Save the King* at the end."

Philip Mason was silent for a while, taking in all she had said. Presently, he asked, "Does anyone else go? Besides the farmer and the farm workers?"

"Oh, yes. A few visitors get asked. The rector and the schoolmaster. And Bill Lawes, the blacksmith. And of course, Fred Ashford, the Fairfaxes' head keeper."

"Nothing like that happens in London," he said wistfully, almost to himself.

"No, I don't suppose it does. But then . . . it's different in the country." Her simple words were, perhaps, more profound and of much more significance to their present situation than she could possibly have realised.

She wished him goodbye at the mill gates, holding out her hand almost formally.

"You'll come to the station to see me off tomorrow, won't you, Katy?" He looked at her anxiously. "My train goes at midday."

"I . . . I think perhaps it would be better if I didn't. Mother's been worried . . . that there must have been talk. Especially with you stopping at the Snoads'."

"Talk?" He frowned, scuffing one of his feet on a stone.

"Yes. I can't explain, Philip. But your coming from London . . . us being seen together . . ." She looked away, uncertainly.

"Then your mum should have been more reasonable. Asked me in. You told me how it was between her and her own parents. Katy, we needn't wait. I want to marry you. We could run away." He caught hold of her shoulders, forcing her to look at him, his dark eyes staring at her, willing her to agree. She was aware of footsteps in the lane and shook herself free.

"No, Philip. Please ... wait a little." She turned and made for the gates, her thoughts in confusion as she ran the short distance to the house.

May was sitting on the sofa sewing, as she came in. She glanced up quickly and put a finger to her lips. "Best be quiet, lovey. Mother's got a headache so I've sent her on up to bed. Did you have a nice walk?"

"Yes ... thank you. Oh, May ..." She went across the room and threw herself down at her elder sister's feet, burying her head in her lap, the tears which she had long been fighting back now spilling over, her shoulders shaking with a sobbing she could not control.

"Hush, lovey. We don't want Mother to hear. I know Philip's got to go tomorrow, but you mustn't take on so." May stroked Katy's head gently, somewhat perturbed and more than a little curious, waiting for her to become less distraught. Then, when it seemed as if no further information was likely to be forthcoming, she went on, quietly, "Lots of couples have to have partings—and sometimes quarrels. Perhaps that's what happened tonight? But never mind. Philip Mason may be your first young man, but that doesn't mean he'll be the last."

Even in her distress, Katy sat up and stared at her. "How d'you mean?"

"What I say, lovey. There's plenty of fish in the sea. After all, you've got another fine one already, right here in home waters."

Still Katy stared, in utter bewilderment, so that May was forced to say, at length, "Oh, come now, lovey. You must know. Maurice Fitzherbert's been sweet on you from the moment you first came back from London."

22

"You're very quiet, Katy."

It was a fortnight later. She and May were in the workroom, busy putting the finishing touches on, of all things, a tweed, heather-coloured coat-dress for Alicia Moreton.

"I want it to be a surprise, Miss Lodge," Lady Fairfax had said to May on a totally unannounced visit. "Now that the poor darling is having to stay longer in the nursing-home and so missing John William—and, of course, her husband," she added, hastily, "I felt she needed a little present. There's nothing like new clothes for cheering a woman up when she's depressed, is there? So I bought this length of material when I was last in London, knowing full well that you were the only person in the world who could do justice to it, and be able to make it up without needing a fitting. You have all my daughter's measurements in that little red book of yours. You know her figure to a 'T'."

Lady Fairfax had then gesticulated rather vaguely and turned to Katy, who was still standing hesitantly by the workroom door, having previously risen to answer their visitor's imperious knocking. "And how Nanny Barlow misses *you*, my dear," her ladyship went on, "poor Ettie being not quite . . ." But what poor Ettie was 'not quite' had somehow then been carefully lost in a flurry of goodbyes, possible delivery dates and the information that "Next Tuesday, my dear Miss Lodge, believe it or not, the Hall will be on the *telephone*," as if May might be going to ring up to confirm that the dress was ready.

Katy had not made any reply to May's observation about her quietness. She had simply persevered with the oversewing she was doing, trying not to worry about the fact that the period she had been expecting five days earlier had not yet arrived. She thought that May had probably guessed what was troubling her, for it was impossible, living at such close and inconvenient quarters, to keep their respective times of the month secret from one another, even though her elder sister was now sleeping in Flo's room and Katy herself was alone in the attic.

She wondered whether to confide in May, but dearly as she loved her, and however sure she was that that love was reciprocated, she did not quite know what to say. The logical, sensible side of her told her to stop being a fool. She knew that she had nothing really to worry about. She had not been seduced. She was still a virgin. Yet the wilder, passionate, imaginative side of her nature kept superimposing itself on the other, guilt lending it momentum, making her believe that, in some mysterious way, what she had feared could have easily happened had actually come about. Otherwise, why was she not 'so', as her older sisters always referred to it.

After tea that day it was May who decided to take Alicia Moreton's dress up to the Hall herself. The evenings were closing in fast and rumours of Sidney Lodge's ghost coming out of Hatch Alley had unfortunately started up again. She knew that Katy had heard some of them and she did not want the girl to become more distressed than she already seemed. Now that the dress was finished she was determined to have a long talk with her the following day about whatever it was she had on her mind.

Some time after she had gone, Katy took a candle and went up to the attic. Here, she knelt down by one of the old ottomans, lifted the chintz-covered lid and ran her hand down its sides until she came upon what she was looking for. Then, carefully hiding it beneath a bundle of dirty clothes, she went downstairs again. Fortunately, Sarah appeared to be busily occupied, crocheting an elaborate new shawl for Edith's baby, which was due any day now and, on the pretext that she wanted to do a little washing, Katy picked up a lantern and went into the mill, choosing the furthermost building for her proposed action. Here, behind the big hammer which, throughout the day, resounded with a dull regular thud as it beat the crude, half-made felt into hard, manageable strips, she began to skip, the familiar tune which she had sung at school coming swiftly back to mind: 'Here we go looby-loo, here we go looby-light, here we go looby-loo, all on a Saturday night.' Every so often she did a little twirl with the skipping-rope, first to the right, then to the left. Occasionally, she did some fast double-skipping. She had forgotten just how good she had once been at it. The exercise, if nothing else, relieved her tension. 'Here we go looby-loo,' she sang more loudly, oblivious for some time of the shadow cast up on the opposite whitewashed wall, the shadow of Sarah standing silently watching her.

"And what, my girl, do you think you're up to?" Her mother moved closer, her shadow looking larger and infinitely more menacing as she did so.

"I'm . . . skipping . . ." Katy's voice faltered.

"I can see that. Why?"

Before she had time to reply, Sarah came round by the big hammer and caught her arm. "I can tell you why, my girl. It's that young good-for-nothing from London, isn't it? He's got you in the family way, hasn't he? I always said to May that we should never have let you go out with him. Coming down here to stay as bold as brass and then making himself scarce as soon as he'd got what he wanted . . ."

"No." Katy pulled her arm free. Anguished, she managed to break into her mother's tirade. "No. It wasn't like that."

"No? Then what are you skipping for? I reckoned you were late some days back. I may have been ill and not known what was going on for a while, but there's not much gets by me now."

"Mother, I promise you. I'm not . . . pregnant. It's just that . . ." To her overwhelming relief, she heard footsteps and May appeared.

"Whatever's going on?" She was still in her outdoor clothes, breathless and anxious at having found the Mill House empty.

There was a kind of triumphant anger in the way Sarah now rounded on her elder daughter. "Well may you ask. I told you so, didn't I? But oh no. You with your fine romantic notions. You knew better. You've always given in to the child. And now look where it's landed us."

For a moment the three women stood motionless in the dim silent mill, for after the men knocked off work each night, no gas-lights could be lit until the following morning. Then, as the tears started to stream down Katy's face, May went across to her, put an arm round her shoulders and said, "Come, lovey. We'd all best get back to the warm now."

Once inside the living-room, Sarah sat stiffly upright by the range, her hands folded in her lap, her eyes fixed on the sofa where her two daughters also sat, the elder still with a protective arm around the younger.

"Are you . . .?" May began quietly, suddenly remembering with painful clarity the afternoon at the White Lion when Major Walter Perkins had taken her virginity. For a moment she found herself sending up a little prayer. Then, when Katy shook her head so vehemently, she felt it had been answered, for she did not believe that her youngest sister would lie to her. "You've been scared, perhaps, lovey?" she went on, gently.

A muffled "I suppose so" came out between the sobs.

May looked across at their mother and then back to the girl beside her. For all her own warm-hearted spontaneity, she was well aware that she did not possess Katy's vivid uncontrollable imagination. Yet she could remember many a previous love affair and knew that it was perfectly possible for an impressionable young woman to become fanciful, to succumb to irrational ideas which, in consequence, might act adversely on her physical well-being, even to delaying the onset of a period, or actually producing a phantom pregnancy. She seemed to remember something of the sort having happened to one of the Donaldson sisters, who had mysteriously left Wilhampton for a time, although how she had come across such private and personal information, she had no idea. She only knew that Katy's basic good sense and honesty was making her speak the truth.

"She's had a bit of an upset with her young man, Mother," May continued. "Katy's not quite herself. I think we should leave her be for a while."

Grim-faced and grudgingly, Sarah turned and stared into the fire. The very next day, Katy's period appeared.

It was, perhaps, fortunate at this juncture, that Edith's baby—another boy—was born. The event took Sarah's mind off her youngest daughter and, each day, she walked up to downside to see how mother and child were progressing. Katy herself, having spent a year under Nanny Barlow's tuition and therefore considered by her family to be highly trained in child care, found herself actually sleeping in her married sister's home for at least a fortnight. She did not particularly enjoy it, but it was preferable just then to remaining at the Mill House. She found her other nephew and nieces, together with the new baby, exhausting to deal with and wondered how Edith could possibly be pleased at the prospect of a non-stop round-the-clock working life for what looked like countless years to come. The constant crying of Norman Sidney Ernest—as his proud parents were intending to have him christened—got on her nerves and when May received a sudden order for several new outfits from the mayoress elect of Wilhampton, she was glad of the excuse to return home.

"I'd never have thought," her sister said, as they sat huddled over the workroom fire one raw November morning, tacking and stitching an unusual voluminous black cloak, "that Miss Fortescue would have wanted to be mayoress. I mean, not having a husband and all that, and being so busy with her writing."

"No." Katy rethreaded her needle. She could visualize Miss Fortescue clearly: a clever, beady-eyed lady who lived at the Moat House and who had both scared and fascinated her during her childhood. She was reputed to have had many a celebrity staying with her from time to time: authors and artists and poets. Many of them came, so Mabel Snoad said, from some place called Bloomsbury which had always made Katy want to laugh, as she couldn't help connecting it with bloomers. They were somehow strange-looking people, the men with beards and longish hair and the ladies often wearing cloaks like the one she and May were making now. Miss Fortescue could be seen taking them for walks on Sunday afternoons, although she herself always seemed to dance rather than walk, waving her little hands about in an airy-fairy way as she acknowledged the greetings of all and sundry. But despite her eccentricity, she was well-liked in the little town, even if her visitors would keep going into the post-office and pestering Mabel to send unintelligible telegrams back to London or sometimes even foreign parts. Next to the Hall, the Moat House, with its curious comings and goings, was a constant source of interest to the local residents.

Presently, Katy said quietly, "I think Miss Fortescue won't make a bad mayoress, when you come to think of it. She's fond of Wilhampton. Didn't she write that history of the place some time back?"

"Yes, I think so." Unlike Katy, May was not much interested in history or books. Her mind dwelt much more on the here and now, and the lighter reading matter which was to be obtained from the new women's monthly magazine, *Eve*. "Anyway, she's going to cut quite a dash in this, isn't she," she continued. "She's even sent down some of the buttons and facings from her father's old naval cloak for us to use on it. Now, where did I put that bit of buckram for the collar?" She got up to look for it glancing, as she did so, out of the window and exclaiming, "Why, there's Mabel's brother coming through the gates with the second post. D'you want to see if you've got a letter, lovey?" She knew that Katy was still eating her heart out because she had not heard from Philip Mason since he had left. Her natural compassion went out to her, even though privately she had come to the same conclusion about the young man as her mother. Somehow he was an alien, unused to Wilhampton ways, not good enough for her youngest sister. May wished the girl would cast her mind in other directions.

Katy needed no second bidding to go and see what Bill Snoad had brought. She put down her sewing and ran up to the house where her mother handed her a letter with obvious curiosity. "It's not from that there Philip, my girl, if that's what you're thinking. It's a Wilhampton postmark."

Acutely disappointed, Katy took the envelope and tore it open, pulling out a sheet of thick, heavily-embossed writing-paper. With growing astonishment and even apprehension, she read:

East Lodge
Wilhampton,
Nr. Westonbury,
November 4th, 1920

Dear Miss Katy,

There is a dance in aid of the Red Cross to be held at the Town Hall on Friday, November 26th. It would give me great pleasure if, by any chance, you could come to it with me. There will be others in the party, and my mother is arranging a small buffet supper at home beforehand. She will be attending the dance herself. If convenient, I could call for you at, say, six-thirty, and would escort you home at eleven p.m.

I do hope you may be able to manage it. I look forward to hearing.

Yours sincerely,
Maurice Fitzherbert

"It's an invitation, Mother," she said, at length, uncomfortably aware that Sarah's eyes were still watching her. "You'd best see for yourself." She passed the letter over, dismayed at the expression of satisfaction which seemed to creep over Sarah's face as she, too, read it.

There was even exultation in her mother's eyes when she finally looked up at Katy again. "Well, there, Miss.

The sooner you forget about that young varmint from London, the better," was all she said.

23

"Taffeta," May said. "Midnight-blue taffeta, Katy. You'd look lovely in that."

"Would I?" She was still confused and had yet to reply to Maurice Fitzherbert's invitation. The thought, not only of going to a dance with him but of having to have supper in his parents' home first, was tantalising but at the same time daunting. Mrs Fitzherbert was such a remote, forbidding kind of woman: tall and thin, with sparse grey hair scraped back from a vaguely disapproving face. If Katy had known how difficult it had been for Maurice to persuade his mother to include her in the party at all, and that she had finally left it to him to issue the invitation rather than write to Mrs Lodge herself, she would definitely have refused.

"Oh, chippatoo! Just think. Your first long dress, Katy." For once, her elder sister's enthusiasm somehow jarred.

"They're not wearing full-length dresses so much in the evening now, May."

"Not in London, maybe. But you'll find they'll all be in long ones at the town hall. I wonder what Mildred Fitzherbert will wear herself? She's never been a one for clothes. They say she buys them off the peg in Burts in Westonbury. Anyway, I bet you'll be the best-dressed girl in the room that night."

"That's if I go."

May stared at her. "Katy, love, you're surely not

going to throw dirt in that young man's face, are you? Why, there's a lot of girls round here who'd give their ears to be asked to a dance by Maurice Fitzherbert."

"Perhaps. But anyway, I expect they all know the latest steps."

May banged the iron down on one of her own skirts which she happened to be pressing. There followed an angry hiss of steam as it met the damp cloth which she had placed carefully over the hem. "That's easily remedied. You'd best have a couple of hours with Annie White."

"*Annie White*?" Katy seemed to remember that at the beginning of the war both Flo and May had gone into Westonbury for dancing lessons with a woman called Annie, who lived next to the asylum. "You can look out of her upstairs room and see the inmates running round in the courtyard below," Flo had said. "I recognised Arnold Parker's brother, the one with that funny grin and the streak of yellow in his hair. I suppose that's where poor Neil might have ended up if it hadn't been for Mother." Her words had made Katy feel quite frightened at the time.

"Yes, I'll drop Annie a line," May continued, putting the iron back on the trivet in the grate and draping her skirt over the back of a chair. "She's still going strong, as far as I know. I'll make you a present of a lesson or two. Annie would probably be only too glad of a little extra money, what with that old barracks of a house to keep up and having to look after her crippled mother. Proper old witch, Mrs White is. Poor Annie. I believe her fiancé was killed just before the armistice."

With so much pressure put upon her, Katy wrote a formal note of acceptance to Maurice Fitzherbert and found herself walking the three miles into Westonbury early one Saturday morning to visit Annie and buy material for her dress. "See you get the *best* taffeta,

Katy," May had said. "Nothing tawdry, mind. Give it a good feel. You want to find something that's going to stand out in the room, without it being too shiny or showy. And you could look around for some dancing slippers while you're about it. Silver, I think. I'd like to come with you, but I've simply got to get on with the Snoad girl's wedding dress."

Katy had set off apprehensively. She would have liked to take the old-fashioned lady's bicycle which was kept in the lean-to by the closet, but Sarah had never really approved of any of her daughters riding a bicycle, especially into Westonbury, and consequently, over the years, it had seldom been used.

She was lucky in straightaway finding in Burt and Burt exactly what she was looking for and, having purchased a pair of evening shoes for three shillings and ninepence and a length of deep blue taffeta at two and elevenpence-halfpenny a yard, she made her way to Annie's house. Here, in a long upstairs room which, as Flo had said, overlooked the grounds of Latimer's Folly—as the asylum was called—she was instructed for almost two hours in such dances as the waltz, the quick and slow fox-trot, the one-step, the Boston two-step, the veleta and the polka, while an old Sonora gramophone was constantly wound up to play the appropriate tunes. Even the scandalous and much-frowned-upon tango appeared not to be beyond Annie's expertise. "Although," she remarked, drily, "we'd best not waste any time on that kind of caper. I can't see the Wilhampton Conservative matrons allowing any cheek-to-cheek hanky-panky to go on in the town hall. Nor the ones in Westonbury, for that matter."

When it was nearing one o'clock, Annie said, "There. We'd best give over now. I've got Mother's dinner to see to. You've done very well, kid. I shouldn't think you'd need to come again, although you'd always be welcome. You're a natural, like your sisters. How are they, by the way?"

"Flo . . . died, Miss White."

"*Did* she now? I'm very sorry. Must have missed it in the *Journal*. Call me Annie, will you? Everyone else always does."

As Katy put on her coat and picked up her shopping-basket containing her purchases, her purse and the sandwiches she had brought to eat in the shelter in the war memorial gardens before starting home, Annie continued, "Funny thing. I somehow had a presentiment about Flo. I saw a halo round her head once. They say as how I've got second sight. She was a good young woman. Too good, for this wicked world."

Katy's eyes widened. She was glad that Annie thought her proficient enough not to come to her again. For all the pleasure the dancing had given her that morning, she felt there was something eerie about the place she was in. She did not know how much it had to do with the proximity of Latimer's Folly and the remembrance of Flo's words, the nearness of the unseen and supposedly witch-like Mrs White, the drabness of the decor in Annie's house or possibly, more than anything else, her final strange revelations combined with her unprepossessing manner and appearance. She was the last person whom Katy would have suspected of being a dancing teacher. For one thing, she was so large and muscular, and there had been a definite smell of sweat about her as their session had progressed. It was obvious that she did not go in for twice-daily washing and the use of Burow's solution under the arms, as the Lodge girls had always done. It was hard to believe that Annie had ever had a fiancé. But perhaps she had let herself go—as May would have said—since his unfortunate death. Katy paid her the two shillings and sixpence for which she asked, and hurried gratefully away.

As November 26th drew nearer and her dress was almost completed, despite having still heard nothing from Philip Mason, Katy found it hard not to feel a certain excitement, even if it was more often than not overshadowed by trepidation. Sometimes, of an evening, she and May would go into the deserted mill and, humming some of their favourite songs, do a little dancing together, May being careful to take the man's part.

"I wish you were coming, May," Katy said at the end of one such session. "You used to lead such a gay life once. Don't you miss all that?"

"Yes and no. I suppose you could say that I had my fling while the war was on. There's no one in Wilhampton I fancy now. Besides, there's not a lot of choice. So many of them were taken, poor things. You don't know how lucky you are, Katy, to have had this invitation from such a fine young man."

Katy was silent. She supposed that she was. There were, she knew, very few possible suitors in the locality, especially of Maurice's age and background. In fact, she could think of hardly any and wondered who the other young men in the Fitzherbert party would be. There was definitely no one around nowadays for May, as she had rightly said. Apart from Mr Fuller, who continued to cast sheep's eyes at her whenever he had the chance, her elder sister seemed to have no beaux now.

"Why didn't you marry, May, in the war?" Katy asked, at length, when they were back indoors again. "I mean, you must have had plenty of chances." She had never put quite such a direct question to her before, but Flo's death had thrown them closer together, even though both still held back from certain confidences

For a moment, May hesitated, wondering whether to tell Katy about what had happened to her at the White Lion, but then decided against it.

"I kept thinking there were plenty more fish in the sea, I suppose," she answered, slowly. "But Mr Right just didn't seem to come along." She had no wish to disillusion her youngest sister about men, particularly at this moment. She felt that it was a mercy that no permanent damage appeared to have been done to the girl after the Neil episode. It must have been God's will that she had gone up to the attic just when she had that night. Katy still evidently had a normal interest in the opposite sex. She wondered what exactly had taken place between her and the young man from London; but whatever it was she obviously hadn't been completely put off his advances. She couldn't have had quite the kind of experience that she herself had undergone with Walter Perkins. The girl, unfortunately, was still hankering after Philip Mason. It was a pity that since he had come into her life she no longer seemed to have the high matrimonial aspirations which May knew she had harboured a year or so ago.

They were alone in the living-room now, for Sarah had gone up to bed. She watched Katy covertly as they sat, one on either side of the fire, drinking a final mug of soup together. Her little sister had certainly grown up a lot lately, May thought. She had a sweet face, a beautiful one, but there was rather too much sadness in it now. True, she was still young, but to May she seemed to be cut out for marriage—as long as it was to the right man, of course. Maurice Fitzherbert was better than she or Sarah—or Katy, if she did but know it—could possibly have hoped for. He would look after her and she needed looking after. May couldn't quite explain it, even to herself, but she sensed that Katy was more passionate than she had ever been. Perhaps that was what was troubling the girl. Whereas she herself had enjoyed many a flirtation and had often played the coquette, she had never really wanted things to go further. She suspected that Katy was different. She was single-minded. She would only be interested in a deep and lasting relationship. She might want—even need—a physical union with some man, although her upbringing would surely see to it that she wore a wedding-ring first.

May continued her musings long after they had gone to bed. She supposed things had got a little out of hand with Philip Mason. But that would never happen with Maurice Fitzherbert. He would always behave impeccably. Nevertheless, he was obviously very smitten. Otherwise he wouldn't have stuck his neck out as much as he had already done. To be seen dancing with her youngest sister in public, even if it was in a party chaperoned by his mother, was bound to cause tittle-tattle. He must mean business. May wished she could get Katy to see it. Maurice would never let her down, not like some men she could think of—Walter Perkins and Guy Armitage springing instantly to mind. And even sober, old-fashioned Cyril Butt, the auctioneer, who lived in Mulberry Cottage at the corner of the market-square and who May had always thought was devoted to Flo—not that she had ever given him any encouragement—had never come near the Mill House once he heard that she had cancer.

The clock above the town hall struck midnight and still May was unable to sleep. If only Katy could forget Philip Mason. He was no good to her. Perhaps the dance would alter things. She hoped so. She would love to be a fly on the wall that night. Without realising it she had, for some time, been living vicariously through her little sister, transferring all her own half-wise, half-foolish, romantic ideals on to her slender young shoulders. Now that Flo was gone, she would, she knew, miss Katy sadly when she married, but if it was to Maurice Fitzherbert the girl would not be much more than a stone's throw away. As for help with the sewing, she would try to find some school-leaver whose mother might be only too pleased for her daughter to gain some experience in return for her services. Of course, it would mean having to do a lot more work herself. Her apprentice would have to be watched. Even Katy, despite a short period at Miss Maidment's, had taken quite a time to do a flawless button-hole. But it would be worth it, just to know her sister had made such a fine match and was happily settled. It somehow did not occur to May that Katy would be anything other than that, once the knot had been tied. Moreover, there would be no need to worry over Sarah quite so much. Their mother seemed almost to have taken on a new lease of life since Maurice's invitation.

On the evening of the 26th, May closed up the workroom early and prepared a hip-bath for Katy in front of the range in the living-room. "But I shall want to clear it well away by half past five," she warned her. "We must have everything nice and shipshape by the time Maurice calls for you, even if he doesn't stop to come in. I suppose you'd best dress in the attic." Thoughtfully, she had left a parraffin stove burning there throughout the day, for the weather was freezing. "But it's better than rain," May went on, cheerfully. "I wouldn't like to think of that blue taffeta getting wet round the bottom. Whatever happens, mind and pick it up when you're walking through the streets."

"Yes." In spite of herself, Katy's eyes were bright, her cheeks already more than a little flushed. Naked in the hip-bath, with her thick brown hair piled high on top of her head and wielding a back brush, she looked, in the lamplight, like some desirable nymph, half innocent, half beguiling—a combination of attributes which, had she known, had firstly tormented Philip Mason and was fast ensnaring Maurice Fitzherbert.

The scent of Floris's malmaison soap soon filled the living-room. By the time Katy had stepped out of the bath, dried herself in the big white towel which had been put to warm by the range, dabbed Burow's solution under her arms and applied a fine cloud of malmaison dusting powder, it was all-pervading. Back in the attic, May helped her to dress, her everyday warm woollen underwear being, for once, discarded in favour of Jap silk. "Though I hope you won't catch your death, love. It's shramming outside," she said, unconsciously lapsing into West Country dialect. She had lent Katy a blue fringed shawl, appliquéd with kingfishers of a deeper blue, as well as her old fox fur jacket. "I should keep the shawl on at supper," she continued. "They say the Fitzherbert house is on the cold side. Still, the town hall usually warms up quite quickly once the dancing starts, as long as Arnold Parker's boy gets the big stove going in time." It was somewhat of a joke in Wilhampton that the more Willy Parker neglected his duties, the better it was for his father's undertaking business.

There was no long mirror in the attic, so Katy went down to survey herself in the one on the front of the wardrobe in what was now May's bedroom. There was no doubt that her elder sister had done a wonderful job on her dress. She had reckoned that Katy was young and attractive enough not to have to follow the latest fashions completely which, in any case, May considered ugly; she had therefore decided to go in for more classical lines. "With an evening dress, that's always permissible, Miss Lodge," Lady Fairfax had once said to May, "just as long as it is *well-made*, from *good* material." So, having pored over various pattern books, May had opted for a simple V-shaped neckline, a definite waist and a full skirt. With Katy's hair now done up in a chignon, the minimum of Icilma cream and Tokalon powder on her cheeks, May's amethyst pendant hanging just above the contours of her small rounded breasts, her Dorothy bag containing comb, handkerchief and *papier poudre* slung over one slender white-gloved arm and her feet encased in her new silver slippers, there was something almost princess-like about the little figure—or so Maurice Fitzherbert thought—when she opened the door to him on the stroke of six-thirty. Rather as Philip Mason's heart had done when she had run to meet him at the London bus-stop, he found his own beginning to beat much more quickly.

He came inside the house just long enough to shake both Sarah's and May's hand; then, helping Katy on with the fur jacket, they left to walk—shyly and almost in silence—the short distance to East Lodge. On arrival, an elderly maid called Nellie Harwood—a cousin, Katy believed, of Emily's—came forward from the dim recesses of the hall and ushered her upstairs to a large spare bedroom. Now that she was actually in the Fitzherbert house, any previous anticipation immediately gave way to panic. For one awful moment, she wondered whether she would simply say that she was not feeling well and ask to go home. The sound of voices and laughter floating up from somewhere below was, indeed, making her feel slightly sick. She felt that Nellie's eyes were upon her, disapproving and resentful. She should never have accepted the invitation. She was out of place in such society; and she had forgotten to practise slipping her hand through the vent of her glove as May had told her she must do when she ate. Besides, no one would want to speak to her. She would be unable to make any conversation herself. Those notions which she had once entertained in Upper Brook Street about leading a grander life were as wrong as they were ridiculous. It had sometimes been bad enough having to talk to Maurice's father professionally, but it would be ten times worse at a party in his own home.

Miserably, she followed the dour parlourmaid along the passage and down the stairs to where Maurice was waiting for her at the bottom. As if sensing that she perhaps needed more than mere physical support, he held out his hand to her long before she came to the last few steps. Then, after Nellie had disappeared once more into the nether regions, he led her to the drawing-room door, pausing just long enough before he opened it, to say, quietly, "I've never seen a prettier dress."

She flushed. The compliment, coming as it did so unexpectedly but at just the right moment, sent her into the room looking suddenly radiant. Even Miss Fortescue's nephew, a sophisticated young solicitor from London, who was standing in the furthermost corner, found himself quite unable to remember what he had been saying to the eldest Donaldson girl after he had been introduced. Only Mrs Fitzherbert failed to seem impressed. "Well, now we are all here," she said, calmly, "perhaps we should go into the dining-room and have some refreshment."

It proved to be not quite the ordeal that Katy had feared. Maurice's father went out of his way to ply her with things to eat. Elizabeth Donaldson, though used to such company, nevertheless still appeared gauche and self-conscious, standing stiffly in an unsuitable dress of pink tulle and constantly dabbing a perspiring nose with her handkerchief. Her young brother, Benjamin, who had just left school, and a girl called Mary Tottenham from Westonbury whom Katy did not know were both extremely polite and friendly. Maurice and Gilbert Fortescue always seemed to be hovering close at hand. It was just the hostess who somehow appeared disconcertingly unaware of Katy's presence, as she passed vaguely by carrying a plate of sausage rolls or some rather thick ham sandwiches.

At the dance itself, to which her husband did not accompany her, she sat on a seat in the corner of the room in the same detached kind of fashion, a lonely shapeless figure in an ill-fitting dress of beetroot-coloured velvet. Katy could not help noticing that it had about it a combined whiff of mothballs and stale perspiration, which became ever more pungent as the evening progressed, and reminded her of poor Annie White. Having danced the first dance with her son—a slow fox-trot to the tune, somewhat inappropriately, of *If You Were The Only Girl In The World*—although some of the older generation came across the room to talk to her, she did not take to the floor again throughout the entire evening, an evening which Katy herself soon found she was enjoying tremendously. Both Maurice and Gilbert turned out to be surprisingly good dancers. She seemed to be dancing non-stop. Even young Ben Donaldson proved to be adept at the Tato polka. When *God Save The King* was suddenly struck up at eleven p.m., she felt that she could have gone on all night.

In contrast, Mrs Fitzherbert, with obvious relief, made a quick dart towards the cloakroom, marshalling her three young ladies behind her like some officious mother hen. On the steps of the town hall their little party broke up. The Donaldsons made for the Rectory, together with Gilbert Fortescue, who was staying the night at the Moat House with his aunt. A car and chauffeur were waiting for Mary Tottenham. Maurice and his mother both accompanied her home.

It was freezing very hard now and the moon, shining on the river by the mill gates, seemed to flood the whole of River Lane with ethereal white-bright light. As they passed Hatch Alley, Katy shivered slightly, but not altogether with cold. It was, she knew, ridiculous, and even wrong, to think that her father, of all people, would haunt the place; yet on a night like this it was impossible to forget the stories which she knew were going around. She was aware of Maurice glancing at her curiously. She supposed that none of the Fitzherberts would have heard the rumours, although one could never be sure. Dr Fitzherbert and the Reverend Donaldson had a disconcerting way of knowing a surprising amount about what was going on in Wilhampton.

At the end of the lane she held out her hand gravely to both her escorts and thanked them. Then, as Maurice bent to help her through the trap door in the big gates, she heard him say, quietly, "I'm so glad you could come, Katy. Let's hope there will be more occasions."

Once inside, she locked up quickly with the key which had been hidden in its usual place beneath a brick and ran the last few steps to the house. She was not altogether surprised to find that May was waiting up for her, a saucepan of milk keeping warm at the side of the range. Her elder sister did not need to ask whether she had enjoyed herself. As soon as she entered the living-room, eyes shining, a feathery paper squeaker sticking out of her Dorothy bag and carrying a small parcel which May suspected was probably a prize, it was all too obvious that the evening had been a success.

"Tell me who was there, lovey," she said, as she began pouring the milk into a glass.

"Oh, anyone and everyone. I do wish you'd been

there, May. And you were quite right. They were all in long frocks, except Grace Armitage."

"You don't mean she put in an appearance? Who-ever with?"

"Some man she said was a cousin, I believe. But they didn't *seem* like cousins, not the way they danced. And you should just have seen her dress. It was scarlet satin with one of those dipping hemlines. It was so short in front and the back was cut so low that Arnold Parker's eyes were nearly popping out of his head. And, oh May, just look . . ." She thrust the parcel she was carrying into her sister's hands. "This is for you. It's a box of chocolates Maurice and I won doing the veleta."

Only when she came to the end of her detailed account of the evening and mentioned that not only Maurice but also his mother had accompanied her home, did May purse her lips slightly. She hoped that there was not going to be trouble with 'Old Mother Mothballs', as she privately thought of the doctor's wife.

24

Shortly before Christmas, there occurred three things of more than a little interest to the Lodge family, particularly its youngest member. Katy heard from Philip Mason; Alicia Moreton, together with John William, Nanny Barlow and Ettie's replacement, was reported to be staying at the Hall for an indefinite period, while the most incredible rumours were going round Wilhampton about a *divorce* between her and her husband. Lastly, the cold weather at the end of November, after a brief respite, returned with greater intensity, so much so that Lord Fairfax asked his agent to ask the Swaynes who, in turn, immediately instructed Ted Shergold to 'flood Lower Croft', in order that it could become a skating-rink for all the local inhabitants.

Maurice Fitzherbert was one of the first to avail himself of this gratuitous amenity whenever he could safely spare the time; and soon he was knocking on the Mill House door asking if Katy would accompany him.

"But I can't," she said, flustered, "skate."

"That's no problem. I'll teach you."

"But I haven't any skates."

"You can borrow my sister's. Connie left a pair behind when she married. I'm sure they'd fit. They're screw-ons."

Flattered, tempted, yet still doubtful, Katy agreed to cycle the short distance to Lower Croft with him at two o'clock that Saturday afternoon. For once, Sarah made no objection to such a hitherto disapproved-of form of transport for one of her daughters.

The number of people already whirling and twirling and suddenly sitting down amongst shouts of laughter which she saw as soon as they arrived, both surprised and delighted her, even though the letter from Philip Mason was still uppermost in her mind. But soon she found it necessary to concentrate so completely on keeping her balance, even that took second place. Maurice had fastened on her skates while she perched on one of the wooden planks which Ted Shergold had thoughtfully placed near the edge of the ice. Then, helping her to stand, she had staggered forth beside her companion, floundering, falling and picking herself up again or, rather, being picked up.

Maurice proved to be an excellent teacher: good-humoured, patient and immensely strong and steady, qualities which she began to appreciate more and more as the afternoon wore on. With his arm constantly round her, his quiet voice giving her both instruction and encouragement, she became aware of a well-being and happiness which she rarely experienced. Once, when he left her to rest for a few moments on an old willow stump while he went off to do a few quick turns by himself before resuming their lesson, she was reminded of another Saturday afternoon, long ago, spent in these selfsame water-meadows when her father had taken her fishing. Just for a while she had known then a kind of peace which, despite all the excitement of the present setting, she knew today. If only, she thought suddenly, as she watched Maurice heading back towards her, Philip Mason had not written again.

They stayed on the ice until after three-thirty, by which time it seemed as if half Wilhampton—especially the older generation—had taken to skating. To her astonishment, at one point she caught sight of Lord Fairfax himself doing a very neat figure of eight. Occasionally, Arnold Parker flashed by, shouting, much to Maurice's amusement, "Watcher, Katy." Even Mabel Snoad (all fourteen stone of her) and retiring Miss Whatley, the Sunday-school teacher, had ventured forth; while towards the end of the afternoon Miss Fortescue appeared, dressed in a most fetching scarlet and black outfit and black velvet toque, in the company of a strange bearded gentleman with a cushion strapped firmly round his bottom. Katy began to wonder how she could have come to miss such occasions in previous cold winters, but supposed that her own delicate health as a child, followed by the war and her two brothers' disappearance into the army, had probably had a lot to do with it.

As a red ball of sun started to sink over Breconbury Woods, Maurice and Katy glided, with considerably more aplomb than when they had first started out, towards the planks at the side of the ice. Here, Maurice repeated his self-appointed task at her feet, this time removing her skates which he then tied together and slung, along with his own, over the handlebars of his bicycle.

"Tomorrow? Will you come again tomorrow, Katy?" he asked, shyly, as they neared River Lane. "I think my father and mother want to have an hour on the ice themselves, probably after church. Say we make it two o'clock, like today?"

"Yes. That would be lovely." She looked at him gratefully, albeit privately amazed that anyone as seemingly staid and sober as Mildred Fitzherbert could skate. Maurice seemed to be constantly surprising her now with little things he said or did, presenting her with vignettes of an entirely new world. It was not the world of the Moretons of Upper Brook Street which, in any case, she had only glimpsed from behind invisible but nevertheless impenetrable barriers; it was not the world of an unpredictable, headstrong son of a London bookseller, who fancied himself an embryo author; nor was it the world of two very different homes in the locality: the Hall, with its remote, timeless, well-ordered way of going about things, or the Mill House itself which, after all the vicissitudes which had recently overtaken the family who dwelt in it, was somehow, Katy felt, a sad place, especially since her mother, far from mellowing with age, had turned into such a querulous martinet. Maurice Fitzherbert had shown her, albeit briefly, a world in which, despite her previous misgivings, she thought she might nevertheless be at home. His free and easy manner, the way he was so obviously liked and respected by all and sundry, was very gratifying. She felt both proud of him and proud that he had made it so plain he wanted her as a companion.

As they cycled home the following Sunday afternoon, now much more at ease in each other's company, he suddenly said, "You know, Katy, there's something I've been wanting to tell you ever since that night of the dance when we came back down River Lane. Those rumours . . ." he hesitated and gave her a quick smile. "I think you should know," he went on, "that I am the so-called 'ghost' of River Lane."

"*You* . . .?" She was so startled that for a moment she took her eyes off the road, allowing the front wheel of her bicycle to wobble alarmingly.

"Steady," he said, waiting for her to right herself before continuing. "Yes, I've been feeling awfully guilty about it ever since I first heard the stories that were going round this winter. I thought back to the November of last year and realised that the incident must have coincided with a couple of nights I'd spent at home. On that particular Friday morning I'm afraid I'd been up to some of my old tricks. You know how our garden runs down to the Willon. Well, I've baited eel-hooks there for as long as I can remember. I don't suppose Ernest Fielding would have approved, what with his precious eel stage, but I don't think he ever knew. And it seemed a fairly harmless peccadillo. In fact, so far as I know I think our family has always had the riparian rights along the East Lodge bank, although I suppose eel-baiting might have been considered a bit over the odds."

"I *see*." She, too, was smiling now, even though she was a little disconcerted about his use of 'peccadillo' and 'riparian' and would have to look the words up in the little dictionary his father had given her as soon as she got back to the Mill House. "Thank you very much for telling me."

"Well, I felt I just had to. I was absolutely mortified when I saw you shiver as we passed Hatch Alley. You see, that was where I came out after baiting the hooks. I remember this figure on a bicycle suddenly swerving—a little as you did just now. I never thought much about it at the time. I'd decided to go straight on and pick up the gun Fred Ashford had promised to lend me. The Fairfaxes were having a tenants' shoot and because they had happened to learn that I was at home, they'd sent word to ask if I would join them. They were a gun short because old Mr Swayne up at Bulbarrow wasn't well enough to make it, and apparently his son doesn't shoot. Oddly enough, I never knew about your poor brother until Mother wrote to me about the tragedy after I got back to London. And naturally Father would never have said anything."

"I *see*," she said again.

"Anyway, I'm terribly sorry for all the distress I must have caused you and your family. You will let your mother and sister know, won't you?"

"Of course."

They were nearing the mill gates now. As they parted, he said, "I'm afraid, being a weekday, I shan't be able to spend quite so long at Lower Croft tomorrow, although Father and I aren't exactly overworked at the moment, thank goodness. It's healthy weather. Much better than the floods. Say, all being well, I call for you at about a quarter to three? We could put in perhaps half an hour?"

"Yes, that would be best for me, too," she replied, adding, a little hesitantly, "I have work to do also," although she knew perfectly well that May would be only too willing to let her off.

"Of course. I was forgetting." He smiled, helped her

through the small door with her bicycle—the big gates being closed for the weekend—lifted his cap and was gone.

They were quite the last to leave the ice that Monday afternoon. Katy had by now progressed so well that, rather like the night of the dance, she felt she could have gone on skating for ever. When, eventually, they finished their final round, Maurice seemed to take an extra long time to remove her skates, as if he, too, was unwilling for the afternoon to come to an end. She watched him as he knelt at her feet: noted the fine golden hair curling out from beneath his check tweed cap, the sweep of his long, equally golden eyelashes, the glowing cheeks and the firm jaw, the thin, delicate, yet capable fingers which were slowly and carefully dealing with her skates, as she supposed they must, at other times, deal with far more serious and complicated operations.

"Will 'ee shut the gate, zur?" Ted Shergold's voice suddenly called to them from the roadway and Maurice looked up quickly.

"Yes, Ted. I'll see to it."

"Thank 'ee. Good-night, then."

"Good-night, Ted."

The man rode away on his bicycle, confident that if there was one person who could safely be entrusted with such a task, it was Dr Maurice, who he had been quick to notice was in no particular hurry. But he was also well aware that he himself was in charge of Lower Croft and the temporary function it was fulfilling. There might not be any danger of escaping cattle, but it was necessary for him to see that all the skaters had left the ice and the place was properly closed up each evening. Now, well content, he reckoned he had done his duty, besides having given Dr Maurice and that pretty little Lodge filly a bit of a bonus into the bargain.

He was no spoil-sport and he thought the world of the Fitzherberts: father and son. The young doctor had done a good job when his wife, Nancy, had had a miscarriage back in the summer. Of course, he hadn't been able to save the baby, but that was probably just as well. There were already quite enough mouths to feed in the Shergold household.

It was very quiet in Lower Croft now. Over the still evening air Katy could even discern, quite plainly, the sound of the mill-race echoing in the distance. A homing pigeon swooped low overhead and once or twice there came the faint barking of a dog, belonging to the dairyman in one of the Bulbarrow farm cottages on the opposite side of the valley. Otherwise, there was only the crackle of footsteps on frosty grass as they walked slowly up to the roadway and Maurice carefully shut the gate.

She was surprised when, as she started to take hold of the handlebars of her bicycle, preparatory to turning it round for the homeward journey, Maurice suddenly restrained her and she found both her hands caught in his.

"Katy," he said, simply. "Will you marry me?"

She was dumbfounded. She stared at him, mutely, appealingly, as if he had presented her with too great a problem, much more difficult than a mere proposal of marriage.

"You don't," he went on, quickly, sensing her embarrassment, "have to say now. I know it must seem awfully precipitant. But just think about it. I wasn't, in any case, contemplating getting married until after Father retires, probably at the end of next summer, but . . ." and here he gave her a look of such adoration and trust that, for a moment, she turned away, "I think I've been in love with you, Katy, perhaps without knowing it, ever since we climbed up the Wilhampton church tower to see old Donaldson's bells."

He stooped to kiss her then. It was a very tender kiss, altogether different from the kind she had experienced with Philip. She could not quite explain it but when he let her go, as gently as when he had taken her in his arms, she felt in some way disappointed, as if the afternoon had suddenly been spoilt, that it was a pity for love-making to have to come into their particular relationship.

There was a certain constraint between them now, as they cycled home, even though Maurice was as charming as ever and asked her, in the same diffident but hopeful way, if she could bear to come with him again on the morrow. "Not that you really need any more *lessons*, Katy. Just practice. You're well able to take care of yourself now."

She laughed. "I'm glad you think so. But I don't believe I'd fancy going up to Lower Croft alone, somehow." Yet even as she accepted his invitation, she knew that, whatever happened, things could never be quite the same between them again and that, more than ever, it was necessary to do something which she had been putting off: answer Philip's letter.

As soon as she got indoors, she went straight up to the attic and took it out of the drawer in which she had hidden it. So far, she had kept its content to herself, although she knew that May had known of its arrival and was longing for Katy to confide in her. Now, seated on one of the old ottomans, she spread it out once more and, in the fading light from the window, aided by one of the gas-lamps which had just come on at the mill gates, she began to reread it, astonished that after so long a spell of silence, Philip was able to start off in such a cheerful, optimistic and self-confident manner:

Dearest Katy Mine,

I haven't written before because after you never came to see me off at the station, I thought maybe I should try to forget you. But I haven't been able to, Katy. I wonder if it has been like that with you? Something tells me that it has.

I want to come and see you again because I have some very good news, which I think will make a lot of difference to our situation, especially as far as your mother is concerned. I shall have to work late in the shop on Christmas Eve, it being one of our busiest times, but I shall catch a train from Waterloo on Christmas morning. I've booked to stay until Boxing night at the Holmwood Guesthouse in Westonbury. Oh Katy, I can't wait. I'm sure everything will come right for us now.

Ever your own,
Philip.

Still in her hat and coat, she remained seated by the window, outwardly calm and expressionless, inwardly distressed and confused. It was thus May found her some twenty minutes later.

"Katy, love. What is it?"

She turned to her silently and then, after a pause, said quietly, "He's asked to marry me."

"Who? Philip Mason?"

"No, well . . . not exactly. I mean, Maurice Fitzherbert."

"Oh, chippatoo! But you're not really surprised, are you, love? It's been sticking out a mile, although I must say I didn't think as how he would come round to it quite so quick." As always, when excited or under stress, May's grammar, as with other members of the family at such times, temporarily failed her. "What did you say?" she went on, eagerly.

"I didn't say anything. I mean, there's no hurry. He said so himself. He . . . won't be free to marry until after his father retires at the end of next summer."

"No. But naturally he wants to become engaged. Have it announced. I mean, in his position, Katy, he can't afford for there to be talk, not that there hasn't been some already. And the dear thing doesn't want to compromise *you*. My word, next summer will come round in no time. A lot of couples have a much longer engagement. Why, his sister Connie was engaged to that farmer for well over three years. Oh, lovey, I'll see you get a much better trousseau than either she or even Alicia Moreton ever had. September would be just the month for a cream satin wedding-dress and perhaps a pale gold shantung going-away outfit. I expect he wants to come and speak to Mother, doesn't he?"

"We didn't get that far, May."

"But you'll let him know, my dear, won't you? Poor young man. He's so in love. And just think: you'll be the doctor's wife, one day mistress of East Lodge. It's like a dream come . . ."

Katy cut her short. "Don't say that, May. Please. I don't know. That's the trouble. I'm in a muddle. I just don't know."

"Don't *know*?" May looked at her, uncomprehendingly.

For answer, Katy passed her Philip's letter. She was surprised at her elder sister's quick and uncharacteristically harsh reaction.

"You'd best write to that young jackanapes at once, my child. He spells trouble. You know that as well as I do. I thought at first that maybe he was a help to you, what with all the sadness over Flo dying, especially as he was so keen on books, like you. But then, I don't know. He was too cocky, somehow. We can't have him poking his nose in now. You'll get a bad name. You've been seen out and about this winter with one of the finest and straightest young men in the district. How d'you think Maurice Fitzherbert's going to feel if he catches sight of Philip Mason hanging around River Lane, out for what he can get?"

"But he says he has good news, May."

Her elder sister made a sound she had seldom heard her use before: a most derisory, unladylike snort.

"And what d'you suppose that might be? Has he written a book or something? You said he fancied himself as a writer. You must get a letter off to him first thing tomorrow. Come along down now. It's perishing up here. I'm shrammed. We've got the place to ourselves. Mother's gone up to mind Edith's kids while she has the rest of her teeth pulled. Herbie's going to fetch her when he knocks off work, because she felt a bit queer after the gas last time."

Katy did as she was bidden, sitting lost in thought while May made a pot of tea and toasted some bread on the end of a long fork before the open range. Sensing, perhaps, that she had said enough for the moment, she then got on with her sewing and remained quiet for the rest of the evening, merely reminding Katy before Sarah returned that, whatever happened, she must stop Philip Mason coming to Westonbury at Christmas and that she would have to tell her mother about Maurice's proposal. "Although it might be as well," she added, thoughtfully, "not to say anything until tomorrow. She's always tired when she's been up to Edith's. Those kids are a bit too much for her. But when you do speak, for the Lord's sake don't mention your other young man."

Katy slept fitfully that night, pondering on the strange sequence of events which had recently overtaken her. If it had not been for the cold weather, she would never have been out with Maurice three days running, for in their particular circumstances there were so few opportunities to get to know each other better. She knew that it was unlikely that Mildred Fitzherbert would welcome her as a casual visitor at East Lodge. It was unthinkable that she could ever entertain Maurice in the Mill House. Other than an occasional visit to the pictures in Westonbury—to which he had made a tentative suggestion the previous afternoon—she could think of no other eventuality which could have given them such a splendid chance of enjoying each other's company—and such *close* company—as skating on Lower Croft. She knew that if it had not been for that, she would never have listened to May for a moment about putting Philip Mason off, however much his visit would upset Sarah. As it was, she had yet to write the letter. She still badly wanted to see him. She wanted to hear about his good news. She wanted—and here she found herself going all hot and actually blushing under the bed-clothes—to feel his arms around her, his hands . . . This time, she made a conscious effort to think about something else.

Katy was startled when, having dozed off for an hour or so, she suddenly awoke to find her head and neck arched backwards, a fierce, rhythmical, semi-frightening yet strangely pleasurable throbbing taking place in the lower half of her body. She had no idea what was happening to her. She only knew that whatever it was it had something to do with Philip and that she had been dreaming of him just beforehand.

She did not sleep again that night. Miserably, she listened to the dull roar of the mill-race, punctuated at regular intervals by the town-hall clock as it struck the hours. The moonlight was still filtering through the thin curtains when, at six o'clock, she heard May's alarm go off and then her sister get up and go down into the mill to wash. For once, she did not join her. Presently, she heard her return and take the usual dipper of soapy water into Sarah's room. Just before six-thirty, there were footsteps in River Lane and the scraping noise of a key in a lock, as Tom Henstridge came through the gates and passed under her window. Gradually, as the day gathered momentum, other sounds became apparent: more footsteps trooping down River Lane, bicycles being leant against a wall, the coughing, spitting and clearing of throats in the raw December morning, snatches of conversation, a short burst of raucous laughter, as the men congregated outside, waiting for the shrill blast from the hooter which governed their lives to summon not only them, but countless other inhabitants of Wilhampton, to work.

25

When Maurice Fitzherbert failed to call for Katy at quarter to three that Tuesday, both she and May supposed that a patient must have detained him. It seemed unlikely that he would let her down without good reason.

"He's probably been called out to Arnold Parker's daughter," said May, somewhat uncharitably, Katy felt. "You know, Ethel, the one who had to get married to Percy Hooper's brother. I remember when I was fitting her for her wedding-dress last June, I reckoned she was about three months gone and her time would be around Christmas. She was already a twenty-seven-inch waist." (She kindly did not add that only the previous week Emily Harwood had mentioned that her cousin Nellie, at East Lodge, knew for a fact that Grace Armitage was forever sending for the doctor nowadays on one artful pretext or another, and it was "as plain as a pikestaff which one she hopes will call at The Warren".)

Katy merely nodded. She had been in the same class at school as Ethel Parker, a doe-eyed, loose-lipped girl about whom, on more than one occasion, she had heard the familiar defamatory remark: 'no better than she should be'. All the same, it hardly seemed fair or even reasonable immediately to pick on Ethel as the sole cause of Maurice's non-appearance at the mill gates. Although he had said it was healthy weather, there must surely be plenty of others in the district who might suddenly require the urgent attention of either Dr Fitzherbert or his son.

In many ways, Katy felt relieved that she would not be going skating today. For one thing, her bad night had made her feel heavy and listless. For another, having been late in rising she had, in consequence, only had time to make do with some sketchy ablutions at Sarah's washstand. Moreover, she had still said nothing to her mother about Maurice's proposal; nor had she written her letter to Philip.

Surprisingly, it was not until seven o'clock that evening before the news came to the inhabitants of the Mill House, explaining just why Maurice had not called for Katy earlier on. Even then, the information did not come through him but, of all unlikely people, Edith's husband. Herbie stood at the door, anxious and breathless, asking whether one of them could come up to downside because Edith had been taken bad again. After the previous evening's extraction, she had apparently had a lot of bleeding from her gums and as soon as he had got home he had hurried—so far as his heart would let him—back to the surgery to get something to stop it. Here, he told them, he had been confronted by a strange locum because Dr Fitzherbert, "the old one," as he went on, "had a fall on the ice at midday. He's in Westonbury Infirmary. A bad business, by all accounts. Straight over on the back of his head."

"Oh, *no*!" Sarah clapped a hand over her mouth. Katy simply stared at her brother-in-law. May, with admirable presence of mind, immediately started taking charge of the situation, electing this time to go up to Edith's home herself. "You'd best stop here with Mother, Katy. I expect Maurice will send word himself as soon as he can," she said, as she hurriedly packed a few night things and put on her hat and coat. Then, sensing that it might be as well to give her youngest sister plenty to do, she added, "I'd be glad if you'd get on with that oversewing on Mrs Donaldson's afternoon frock, and if I'm not back by tomorrow morning, there's all those sequins to be sewn on Miss Fortescue's velvet coatee."

It seemed to Katy a long, depressing evening after she had gone. Sarah, sitting by the range, upright in her high ladder-backed chair, was silent other than occasionally murmuring, with a shake of her head, "Poor man. I don't know. I don't know, I'm sure."

Hunched over Mrs Donaldson's dress, Katy kept blinking back tears, remembering how good Maurice's father had been to her as a child, his daily—sometimes twice-daily—visits when she had had diphtheria and meningitis, the little dictionary which he had given her, the courtesy he had shown her when she had come to his home as a guest but a few weeks ago.

When, at half past eight, there were footsteps and a gentle knock at the door, both women looked at each other apprehensively. Katy put down her sewing and went to answer it. As she expected, Maurice Fitzherbert was standing outside.

"Please . . . will you come in? I'm . . . so sorry. We have heard the news."

The young man accepted gratefully, stooping to enter the small, clean but cluttered living-room, where Sarah at once rose from her chair and held out her hand. "Good-evening, Dr Maurice," she said, quietly. "May I get you a cup of tea or . . ." and here, to her youngest daughter's astonishment, her mother added, "perhaps a little brandy?" So far as Katy knew, there was only a thimbleful left in the 'medicinal' bottle, which had last been brought out when Flo died. It was therefore somewhat of a relief to her when Maurice—albeit not altogether unexpectedly—chose to have tea.

"I thought," he said, slowly, as he sat drinking it, "you would have been bound to hear about the accident sooner, but I'm sorry I couldn't let you know myself. My father hadn't intended to skate at all today, but he was called out to see one of the dairyman's children in the cottages not far from Lower Croft. As he had his skates in the back of the car, he thought he would have a quick turn or two before coming home to lunch." There was a pause and Maurice passed a hand wearily over his face before continuing, "He just fell . . . backwards. He's still unconscious. My mother is spending the night at the hospital. I'm afraid I can't say . . . what the outcome will be."

Katy could not help but respect and admire the calm and dignified way her own mother now spoke, as if, however sad and distressing Maurice's words had been, she knew instinctively how to respond to them. "We shall all pray for your father, Dr Maurice. Not just myself and my family, but all Wilhampton. He is a good man. Everyone owes him so much."

She watched Maurice put down his cup and look at her mother very directly. "Thank you, Mrs Lodge," he answered, simply. "Thank you very much indeed." It was almost, Katy felt, as though, for the moment, she herself was excluded, that Sarah and Maurice had some strange, indefinable, silent rapport. Presently, he stood up. "There will be a bulletin posted outside East Lodge each day, but I will do my best to keep you informed personally. Thank you very much for the tea, Mrs Lodge."

"Thank you for coming, Doctor." Sarah rose also, reached up for the bundle of keys hanging by the mantelshelf and handed them to Katy. "My daughter will see you out and lock the gates." She held out her hand gravely and wished him good-night. When it came to a time like this, Katy thought, as she returned to the house, as long as her mother was well, one could hardly fault her behaviour.

In the days that followed, an undisguised gloom seemed to settle on Wilhampton. True, most of its inhabitants invariably took a morbid interest in tragedy, almost seeming to relish the misfortunes of others; but there was not a soul who did not wish Dr Fitzherbert a speedy recovery and truly grieve for him and his family, anxiously waiting on the bulletins pinned up on East Lodge gate and passing on any fresh information to others. Special prayers were said for him in St Mark's by the Reverend Donaldson. Small gifts were constantly being left with Abie Grant at the surgery. Even though Mildred Fitzherbert was not as popular as the rest of her family, people watched out for her, murmuring, "Poor woman, poor woman," as they saw her being driven to and from Westonbury by her son who, himself looking tired and drawn, carried on with the practice. No one, other than a few strangers, felt like going to Lower Croft to skate any more. In any case, the cold snap was showing signs of coming to an end.

Although the situation, distressing as it was, made it easier for Katy to reach a decision about putting Philip Mason off coming to Westonbury—for it was unthinkable now that she could possibly see him—nevertheless, the letter which she eventually sent to London took her several hours to compose. "Dear Philip," it began,

Thank you for writing as you did. I am very sorry but owing to unforeseen circumstances I'm afraid I would be unable to see you if you came here, so it would be best if you made other plans for Christmas. I trust you will understand. It is difficult for me to explain. I send you every good wish for the future and am glad about your good news, whatever it might be.

Yours sincerely,
Katy.

She was not at all satisfied with her final effort, even as she put it into the posting-box, and still had misgivings about the bald, matter-of-fact way she had phrased it. She only knew that it was imperative, not only to put Philip off coming anywhere near the district, but also to put him right out of her mind altogether. At the moment, the latter was not as difficult as it might have been, for all her time seemed to be taken up with concern for Maurice and his father, and most evenings the former either called or sent word to the Mill House so that, as he had promised, the Lodge family was kept informed of the very latest developments. For a few days, she still held back from telling her mother of Maurice's proposal, but soon his attentiveness, the way he seemed to derive a certain comfort from his brief visits, the look in his eyes as he wished her good-night, made it almost incumbent on her to say something.

"I am no fool, my child," said Sarah, soberly, in response to her halting statement, one evening when they happened to be alone, May having gone to pay a quick visit to Edith, who was still feeling shaky and depressed after the loss of all her teeth. "When this crisis has passed—and please God, it will be for the better—and Dr Maurice feels free to speak to me, I shall be pleased to give you both my blessing."

Katy bent lower over the stocking she was darning, experiencing, not for the first time, a sudden suppressed anger that her mother and May took so much for granted, and that she herself was trapped, a victim of events over which she seemed, perforce, powerless.

It was well after nine o'clock on Christmas Eve when Maurice arrived with some small packages for them all—"definitely not," he said, with a disarming smile, "to be opened until tomorrow"—and told them that there had been a slight improvement in his father's condition. "Although it is still only early days," he continued, as he sat down to drink his customary cup of tea. "But, at any rate, he opened his eyes this afternoon and my mother knew that he had recognised her. I'm driving straight into Westonbury to fetch her home when I leave here. She's hoping to attend midnight mass at St Mark's as usual."

Sarah inclined her head. "We shall all be going, too, Dr Maurice. I'm sure your father will be uppermost in everyone's prayers."

At that moment—no carol-singing having preceded it—some swift footsteps, followed by a loud banging on the door, startled them all. It was loud and positive, as if the caller was determined to brook no denial and that whatever he or she had to say was unquestionably urgent. It was May who rose, pushed back the tapestry curtain and answered it. Philip Mason, where all could see him, was standing on the threshold.

There was a short electrified silence and then, striding into the living-room, he went straight towards Sarah and held out his hand.

She did not rise. An expression of undisguised hostility came over her face. Yet, conscious that it was important to maintain some semblance of manners in front of her other and infinitely preferred visitor, she allowed him to shake her hand and said, coolly, "Good-evening, Mr Mason."

"Good-evening, ma'am." He smiled, pleasantly. There was something more mature, even more likeable, May felt, about the young man to whom, in the late summer, her mother had practically shown the door. Eager-eyed, fresh-faced and dressed in a smart, velvet-collared, navy overcoat, he had about him a quieter, less brash self-confidence, an air of success which was not altogether unattractive. She felt that he had his feet firmly on the ground now, knew exactly what he wanted and how to go about it.

He turned next to Katy and, diving into the pocket of his coat, produced, as Maurice Fitzherbert had also produced shortly before, three parcels, gaily wrapped, which she guessed, instinctively, must be books. Completely betraying her supposed ignorance of the slightest possibility of such a meeting, she said, "I thought you couldn't get away until Christmas morning."

"That's right. When I wrote, I didn't think I could. But I've just taken on a good new salesman. Three days ago I reckoned I could leave him to it tonight." The reference to 'I' and the fact that Philip himself seemed to be so very much in charge escaped no one.

Quietly, Maurice Fitzherbert rose. "I must go, I'm

afraid, Mrs Lodge. Thank you for the tea. A very happy Christmas to you all."

Sarah had by now also risen. "Good-night, Dr Maurice," she said, this time making a point of very courteously holding out her hand. "Let us hope that tomorrow you will have even better news for us."

After he had gone, she turned and looked Philip Mason straight in the face. "And I would thank you to leave also, Mr Mason. There is no reason for you to come to this house again. My daughter, with whom you appear to have communicated lately, is otherwise committed."

Philip frowned. "Committed? What do you mean, ma'am. How? Who to?"

"To the gentleman who has just left."

"What? The *doctor*?"

"Yes, Mr Mason. If it were not for his father's serious accident, their engagement would have been announced by now."

For the first time, Philip's confidence seemed to desert him. He rounded on Katy, a desperate, almost haunted look in his eyes. "It's not true. You can't tell me it's true."

Miserably, she stayed silent, while hearing her mother reply, levelly, "It's quite true, Mr Mason."

He turned back to Sarah. "But it's me, Mrs Lodge, she's going to marry. I can give her a good home now. My father has left the shop and passed all the running over to me. He's just married again himself. Married *well*, you understand, ma'am. He's gone away to live in Wales. There is nothing to stand in the way of Katy and me . . ."

She cut him short. "I am sorry, Mr Mason. It is too late. I must ask you to leave."

Helplessly, hopelessly, Katy watched him fling himself out of the house. For a moment, she remained quite motionless, as if no longer in command of her own fate or fortunes. Then, before either Sarah or May could stop her, she dashed out of the door after him, coatless, feet flying, her voice calling, "Philip, Philip," as she caught sight of his figure fast disappearing into the night.

Halfway up River Lane, he stopped and turned. In the light of the gas-lamp, she saw a look of incredulous joy come over his face as she drew closer. He opened his arms and she ran into them, the sound of the mill-race not even the faintest echo in her ears.

26

On Friday, February 18th, 1921, there appeared in the *Westonbury Journal* three items of news which May Lodge carefully cut out and took up to her bedroom that night. Here, she placed them in her rosewood box with its pretty mother-of-pearl inlay on the lid, which always stood on her dressing-table and where, over the years, she had safely tucked away many a keepsake.

The first of these items, printed on the front page of the paper, was headed SON TO CARRY ON, and read:

We are happy to report that Dr Claud Fitzherbert, of East Lodge, Wilhampton, who suffered a serious accident while skating on the ice at Lower Croft, Bulbarrow, last December, has now returned home from hospital. While still confined to a wheel-chair, Dr Fitzherbert is nevertheless making a slow but steady recovery. Though originally not due to retire until the end of the summer, he has now completely passed over the practice to his son, Dr Maurice Fitzherbert, who interrupted his medical training to serve in HM Forces during the latter part of the war.

Later this year, the mayoress, Miss Fortescue, is hoping to arrange a presentation party for Dr Fitzherbert in the town hall, in gratitude for his long, selfless and devoted service to all those countless patients whom he has attended in Wilhampton and its surrounding district since 1889.

The second item, which appeared on one of the centre pages of the *Journal*, could almost have had the same caption as the first, but was instead entitled, somewhat baldly, DEATH OF BARONET, after which came the words:

The death occurred on Friday last of Sir Harry Moreton, Bt., of Bishopsdown House, Suffolk. Sir Harry, who was seventy-five, is succeeded by his son, Captain Sir Charles Moreton, M.C., who, with his wife, the former Honourable Alicia Fairfax, of the Hall, Wilhampton, will be taking over his late father's country estate. Sir Charles and Lady Moreton have one son, John William Harry, now heir to the baronetcy.

The last item, though the shortest, was the one May looked at longest before closing up her little treasure chest. It consisted of four lines only, halfway down the MARRIAGES column on the back page:

MASON—LODGE. On February 12th, 1921, at St. Mark's Church, Wilhampton, by the Reverend Donaldson, PHILIP GORDON, only son of Mr FRANCIS MASON and the late Mrs MASON, of 51 Davies St., London, W.1., to KATHERINE VERA EVELYN, youngest daughter of Mrs SARAH

LODGE and the late Mr SIDNEY LODGE, of the Mill House, Wilhampton.

It had not been at all the kind of wedding May had envisaged. There had been no cream satin dress or pale gold shantung going-away outfit. Yet, when she took into consideration everything that had happened to the Lodge family during recent years, it had seemed entirely appropriate for Katy now to be married very simply and very quietly, wearing a sober, beige alpaca coat and a small feather-trimmed velvet toque of the same colour. Moreover, she had still been married in St Mark's, once May had finally managed to overcome her mother's opposition to the match and persuade her to bow to the inevitable. It had been either that or having the girl run away, and she knew that the last thing Sarah wanted was the remotest possibility of anyone in Wilhampton suggesting that her youngest daughter had had to get married.

Even though the wedding had been hastily arranged, so far as she knew, May reflected, as she took the pins out of her hair, there had not been any gossip of that kind—only great astonishment and regret that the groom was not Dr Fitzherbert's son. Since those few tense traumatic moments on Christmas Eve, when May had run up River Lane after Katy, somehow decorum had been re-established, convention upheld. The door of the Mill House was opened to Philip Mason—however grudgingly at first—but the more May saw of him the more she had come to like him. Naturally, her tender heart grieved deeply for poor Dr Maurice; and she and Katy had sat down and had a good cry the night after he had called with a wedding present: a painting of Wilhampton done from the top of Breconbury Downs by a most distinguished artist, a friend of Miss Fortescue, who often stayed at the

Moat House. May hoped that it would not be too long before the young man married someone else, for she had always believed that a doctor needed a wife. She prayed that he would find some nice girl who would make him a good one; although she felt that it would have to be someone placid and forbearing. It certainly wouldn't be easy being a daughter-in-law in the Fitzherbert household now, she mused, not the way it was; for it did not look as if the older couple would be moving to a smaller home, as had originally been expected. Katy, with her passionate, imaginative nature, might have found it more than a little frustrating and circumscribed.

After brushing her hair, May knelt down to say her prayers before she undressed, as the room was cold and so were her feet, which she was looking forward to warming on the stone hot water bottle which Sarah had earlier placed in her bed. Then, methodically folding up each garment as she took it off, she put on her long-sleeved flannelette nightgown and climbed into bed, her thoughts quickly returning to her youngest sister, as she blew out her candle.

She found it impossible not to wonder how Katy was getting on. Soon she would be back from her brief honeymoon in Brighton. Somehow May felt sure that it would have been a success. It was a love-match, all right. Although, sadly, she seemed to recall having once said that about Alicia Moreton's betrothal. Still, one could never tell. All those scandalous rumours about a divorce had evidently been untrue. Of course, there was never smoke without fire and—although it seemed wicked even to think it—May supposed that it was always possible . . .

She tried to remember how much time the Moretons had spent in Wilhampton since Katy had first referred to her employer's indisposition. Not a lot, on the whole.

Certainly, apart from the Christmas before last, when they had stayed at the Hall for quite a while, she had not caught sight of Sir Charles—as she must remember to call him—in church, looking, as she invariably thought, rather bored. On the other hand, Emily Harwood had told her that during the last year Grace Armitage—for whom she appeared to have an especial loathing—had often left her husband in the care of Cissy Lawes' mother and gone waltzing off to London to do goodness knows what. But surely . . . no, it was inconceivable . . . Besides, the Captain had saved Guy Armitage's life, hadn't he? It was amazing how long it had taken for that to become known. Charles Moreton had been commendably modest about winning an M.C. She would say that for him. He was a most courageous, well-bred young man, not at all the sort to carry on with Guy's wife. Particularly when he had such a beautiful one of his own. It was good to know that she was now Lady Moreton and would soon be settled in Suffolk. Dear Miss Alicia . . . Somehow it would always be difficult to think of her as anything other than that. And a little while ago she had really looked quite bonny, thank goodness, when she had summoned May to the Hall to discuss three crêpe de Chine rest-gowns for summer wear, which she wanted her to make up. The particular choice of garment, for use some months ahead, had made May wonder whether perhaps she was going to have another child. As she was showing her out, Nanny Barlow had somehow hinted that it never did to have all one's eggs in one basket and that it would be nice if a brother or sister came along to stop John William from becoming spoilt. It was funny to think that, but for a few strange twists of fate, Katy might still have been a nursery-maid helping to look after him in Suffolk, instead of the wife of a young, go-ahead, London bookseller.

May closed her eyes, trying to switch her mind on to all the things she must remember to do in the morning. It was a pity, she felt, that she had to spend so much time supervising her new apprentice. She couldn't yet trust Arnold Parker's youngest daughter with even the simplest hemming, but she supposed that would come. The girl was cheerful and willing. She would say that for her. Fortunately, she appeared to have inherited her father's optimistic attitude to life, despite his lugubrious profession.

The clock above the town hall struck eleven and still May lay awake, acutely conscious of the familiar sounds of the night in the overall stillness. She could hear Sarah snoring rhythmically in the next room; occasionally, a small breeze rattled the catch of her window. From somewhere over Bulbarrow way an owl hooted. Once or twice there were halting footsteps in River Lane—probably Lilian Perrick's husband returning from The Punchbowl. And in the background, as always, came the relentless, insistent roar of the mill-race. Somehow, May felt, it seemed louder than usual tonight. Of course she realised that there had been a lot of rain lately and the Willon was running high. Duck and Collar, silly man, had remarked on this all-too-obvious fact when he had waylaid her at teatime as she came up from the workroom. She knew that it wouldn't take many more downpours before she might hear those other sinister sounds, the ones they had all come to dread each winter: the slapping, gurgling and rising of water beneath the downstair floorboards. After all, it was February. February filldike. The floods could still come . . .

May pulled the bedclothes up a little higher and pushed her feet further down the feather mattress, searching for the hot water bottle. She told herself that it was no good worrying. It was always best, like

Arnold Parker, to look on the bright side of life. And if the floods did come, she thought, as she drifted off to sleep, at least Katy, her youngest sister, would now be spared them.

Zoe Fairbairns

Stand We At Last £2.50

'Quite splendid a thoroughly intelligent and entertaining sage which follows five generations of women through the history of their emancipation' COMPANY

'Travels a long way in time and space gives a resume of the last hundred years of the women's struggle for emancipation while telling a rattling good tale' THE TIMES LITERARY SUPPLEMENT

Gail Godwin

A Mother and Two Daughters £1.95

A novel about the richest of all subjects, families funny, sad, provocative, ironic, compassionate, knowing, *true* everything that a novel should be' WASHINGTON POST

'A major novel from a talented writer really hitting her stride' KIRKUS REVIEWS

A novel to live with and live in' NEWSDAY

Lewis Grassic Gibbon

A Scots Quair £2.95

From the years of the Great War to the hungry thirties, Lewis Grassic Gibbon's magnificent trilogy spans the life of a woman and the story of a people This powerful saga of Scottish life through three decades is now published in one volume.

'His three great novels have the impetus and music of mountain burns in full spate' OBSERVER

G. J. Scrimgeour

A Woman of Her Times £2.50

A woman's story that every woman will live as if it were her own. Through three continents, two world wars, through marriage and motherhood, love and pain and betrayal, Elizabeth Wingate is a woman of her times: a dutiful wife in Ceylon, a socialite in 1920s London, penniless and alone in 1930s Hollywood – journeying through decades in search of a destiny only time can reveal.

'A remarkable book ... great style, scope, masses of colour ... Elizabeth Wingate's story touches the heart' BOOKSELLER

Susan Howatch

Cashelmara £3.50

A glorious, full-blooded novel which centres on Cashelmara, a coldly beautiful Georgian house in Galway, ancestral home of Edward de Salis.

The fast-moving plot follows the turbulent fortunes of an aristocratic Victorian family through half a century of furious encounters, ill-advised liaisons and bitter-sweet interludes of love.

'Another blockbuster from Susan Howatch' SUNDAY TIMES

Penmarric £3.50

'I was ten years old when I first saw the inheritance and twenty years older when I saw Janna Roslyn, but my reaction to both was identical. I wanted them.' The inheritance is Penmarric, a huge, gaunt house in Cornwall belonging to the tempestuous, hot-blooded Castallacks, Janna Roslyn is a beautiful village girl who becomes mistress of Laurence Castallack, wife to his son.

'A fascinating sage ... has all the right dramatic and romantic ingredients' WOMAN'S JOURNAL

Pamela Belle

The Moon in the Water £2.50

Thomazine was born heiress to the lands and fortune of the Heron dynasty, and she was bon under a dark and troublesome star. Orphaned at ten years old, growing to womanhood among cousins, she met the headstrong Francis and they both dreamed of the mystic unicorn. The sweep of the times was against them. Francis was banished and imprisoned, Thomazine forced into loveless wedlock, and the onrush of beating drums and naked steel heralded England's Civil War

'Masterly . . . vivid tapestry of a family sage, richly crowded with flesh-and-blood people' ROSEMARY SUTCLIFFE

The Chains of Fate £2.95

The blood-red tide of civil war ran deep over the land, and Thomazine became the wife of a man she would learn to hate, believing her Francis to be dead. When she learned the truth – that Francis lived – Thomazine rode north on a mission hung with the chains of fate. Those chains weighed down her journey as she moved through land occupied by enemy soldiers, found the man she loved at the price of deserting her own child, and lost Francis again to the cause of Montrose . . . Time and again Thomazine and Francis would be torn apart, yet one day, the chains of love must prove stronger . . .

Annabel Carothers

Kilcaraig £2.50

A turbulent saga of three generations set against the grandeur of the Scottish isles . . . The Lamonts of Kilcaraig belonged to the Isle of Mull as surely as the proud birds of prey belonged to the mountains of Glen More. Through six decades their chronicle unfolds – Catriona, the grandmother whose dark secret shadowed the family's future; Grania, the daughter who finds love only after she has chosen a husband; Niall and Rorie, twin grandsons of contrasting destinies, and Catriona the granddaughter, as beautiful as her namesake . . .

Laura Black

Strathgallant £1.75

The indomitable old Lady Strathgallant had decided. Her ward Perdita was to be married and to inherit the Strathgallant estate. Rupert would have been the perfect match, but Rupert had fallen in the damned Indian Mutiny. The four Ramsay boys, the great-nephews Harry, Colin, James and John would be summoned to attend Perdita's eighteenth birthday ball. As each arrived, Perdita fell in love with each in turn. Then came Jules Delibes, connected to the family by a French marriage and keen to be the fifth suitor . . .

Castle Raven £1.75

Katie was ill-suited to the elegant world of Ravenburn Castle. Her stepmother and uncle were trying to turn a tomboy into a Cinderella. But with their neglect she was free to roam the Highland wilds, coming across the ruined castle buried amid the heather of Eilean Fitheach island. On this enchanted island, shunned by the locals, she would meet dramatic and terrifying events, the truth about her parents, and a sudden deadly peril . . .

Susanna Moore

My Old Sweetheart £1.75

'Susanna Moore is an original, and this flower-stream, jasmine-scented study of childhood, love and betrayal is a remarkable debut' BOOKS AND BOOKMEN

'Fine fluent prose her absence-of-love story lingers long after you've turned the last page' NEWSWEEK

Published by Pan under the Pavanne imprint.